MEN GIVING MONEY, WOMEN YELLING

MEN GIVING MONEY, WOMEN YELLING

INTERSECTING STORIES

ALICE MATTISON

WILLIAM MORROW AND COMPANY, INC. NEW YORK

It is the policy of William Morrow and Company, Inc., and its imprints and affiliates, recognizing the importance of preserving what has been written, to print the books we publish on acid-free paper, and we exert our best efforts to that end.

Library of Congress Cataloging-in-Publication Data

Mattison, Alice.
    Men giving money, women yelling : intersecting stories / Alice Mattison.— 1st ed.
        p.   cm.
    ISBN 0-688-15109-4
    I. Title.
PS3563.A8598M46   1997
813'.54—dc21
                                                                96-47658
                                                                CIP

Printed in the United States of America

First Edition

1 2 3 4 5 6 7 8 9 10

BOOK DESIGN BY LEAH S. CARLSON

THIS BOOK IS FOR

Jacob, Ben, Andrew, and Lara,
my dear and clever companions and children.
And it is also for Janie.

ACKNOWLEDGMENTS

I'D LIKE TO THANK James (J. J.) Jones, who told me Kent's story in "Broken." Additional thanks go to the Corporation of Yaddo, to the Community Soup Kitchen, and to Edward, Sandi, Joyce, Don, Lloyd, Bridget, Jude, Claire, the other Alice, and all my Susans.

Some of these stories appeared first in journals: "We Two Grown-ups" and "Selfishness" in *The New Yorker*, "River-tossing" (with the title "Confusion City") in *Boston Review*, "Pekko's Boat" in *North American Review*, "Home Home" in *New England Review*, "The Dance Teacher" in *Southern Humanities Review*, "Last Wash" in *Boulevard*, "Sebastian Squirrel" in *Glimmer Train*.

CONTENTS

MEN GIVING MONEY, WOMEN YELLING

WE TWO GROWN-UPS

TODAY WAS THE happiest day of my life so far, even though it didn't include actual sex or the World Series, and even though as usual people are suffering in places famous for trouble and also of course in every other place. I live with my parents—to save money—although as my mother puts it I am a grown man. I just filled my parents' dishwasher after dinner, wondering as I turned it on whether it really was the happiest day—because other days had more potential—but it was. I think that until today the happiest day was the day I went camping with my first girlfriend and we saw two deer and swam nude and made love on top of the sleeping bag, near the fire. Earlier happy days mostly included home runs. Dinner tonight was only meat loaf. Lunch was pizza. The happy part was in between.

I went to Wilbur Cross High School, in New Haven, where Ida Feldman, who had an old lady's name but was young and blond, though fat, was my English teacher junior year. One day, an administrator was talking on the public-address system, and he said, "Any seniors wishing to take the SATs should make an appointment with their penis." Ms. Feldman flopped forward on her desk and laughed, her arms wide, her hair spread out, as if she'd fallen off a dock with surprise and lay helpless in the water. Her face pressed into her grade book, so when she picked up her head there was a groove on her cheek from the spiral binding.

I loved her from then on. I majored in English at Southern Connecticut, almost in her honor, even though everyone was majoring in business. Two different deans asked me, "What are you going to do with *that?*" Whenever I visited Ms. Feldman she remembered me, but I wasn't as important to her as what she was doing right then. One time, she was trying to get a pregnant girl to stay in school and at least think about an abortion. "I wouldn't say it to her, Tom," she said quickly. "But I have to think of a way to let it cross her mind."

I hadn't thought much about abortion. "But it's her *baby,*" I said.

"If I wanted her to abort her after-school job at Wendy's," she said, "I wouldn't be crying about it." I could see then that she did look blotchy. When I remember that day now, I know she was letting me right in, but then I was uncomfortable. I didn't stay and talk.

Ms. Feldman didn't look sexy, at least the way we think sexy women are supposed to look—she looked bouncy and dreamy at once, with her weight and her waist-length blond hair, and I'll argue now that this is precisely what we mean by sexy, but then I wouldn't have. But she always had to do with sex one way or another. Talking about literature in her class, we found sex everywhere, even the Gettysburg Address. But it was more than that. If spiders made love on a window at Cross, they'd pick Ms. Feldman's window.

When I got out of college I went to work for my brother-in-law. He's a contractor who builds additions to houses and does renovations. He's a noisy man. When he started going out with my sister, who was living at home, he always sat back too fast in the lounge chair at our house, late at night, so it crashed open. We'd sit up in bed and know Barbara had brought John home. At work he doesn't listen to the radio, but he drops things and sets boxes down hard, or lets go of an armful of two-by-fours half a foot off the floor. And he talks in a loud voice. From the first, if we were working on an addition to a house and the people were home, they heard me get instructed, because I knew nothing—John took me on out of kindness, or maybe he knew that English majors were meant to build additions. The first day, a woman was sitting in a rocker breast-feeding her baby next to the open window, and as I looked over John's shoulder into the window, I could see the interest in her face when he explained loudly to me that he always cut outside the line and I must do the same, so our pieces of wood would be inter-changeable.

"What line?" I said.

"The line you draw." He was using a temporary sawhorse he'd set up in this woman's backyard, and now he drew a fine pencil line where he needed to cut, and sure enough, he cut on the outside of the line, so it was just visible on the edge of the board. I could hardly pay attention. I wanted to look at the woman, maybe to go in and show her the line. Her baby was looking over his shoulder at me, too.

I did everything wrong the first few months with John, but he liked having me around anyway. "A college graduate like your-self . . ." he'd begin, while we were hammering together. I learned to get nervous when he said that. "Tell me why a woman's nipples get brown if she nurses a baby," he said recently. So he'd been watching that woman, too—watching more closely than I'd been. I wouldn't talk about her. We'd finished that house long since, of course.

"I was an English major," I said.

"So you know about England?"

"I read a lot of American literature," I said. "Did you ever hear of Ezra Pound?"

He wasn't sure. I told him Pound was a good poet who made anti-Semitic broadcasts during the Second World War. "Now, do we forget the poetry because the man was wrong—or crazy; I guess people think he was crazy—or do we read the poems anyway?"

John talked about that one for days, dropping into a room where I was working alone to ask, "Are the poems against the Jews?" and "How good are they, anyway?" On the whole he thought we should not read Pound, but he could see arguments either way. Finally, he said I should show him a poem by Pound. I didn't know what had made me think of Pound. I hadn't read much of his work. I said I'd find my Norton anthology and have something copied.

John and I also talked about sex.

"There's a year in everybody's life when all you think about is sex," he said, implying that I was in it. "Then you remember it's not the only thing."

"When you're young," he said to me more than once, "sex comes by itself, but as you get older, it sneaks into things and things sneak into it." Barbara is having a baby. I knew that had something to do with what he meant. But I also thought he was noticing what I kept noticing—the way people were near us and yet far away when we worked on their houses. That first, breast-feeding lady—she'd pass by, usually carrying the baby, wearing a bathrobe. She didn't look sloppy but mysterious, like a woman in a misty dress in a damp meadow on the box of some feminine hygiene product.

IT INTERESTS ME to work in someone's house, but it's easier when the house is empty. Sometimes John gets contracts to renovate houses that are being made into residences for retarded people or some other group. There are special requirements—extra fire exits, wheelchair accessibility. Just now John and I are renovating a house where psychiatric patients will live. We have to put in two complete bathrooms. Today John said we could quit early because he had to go to the dentist. An old filling had been bothering him. "What do you think?" he's been asking me. "Will he drill again?"

We quit installing plumbing at three. John has a plumber he uses for tapping into the sewer pipe, but we install sinks and toilets and bathtubs ourselves, and of course we also do wiring and put in heating ducts and so forth. John had taught me to set the wax ring that seals a toilet in place, and this was the first one I did entirely on my own. I'd ruined a few wax rings before.

John had to send some contracts to the state, and before he left he asked me to take them to the Federal Express office when I was done cleaning up. I have my own key to the house—we each have one, so it doesn't matter who arrives first in the morning. After locking up, I decided to stop at home on my way downtown and pick up the Norton anthology so I could have some Ezra Pound copied. There's a copy place right near the FedEx office on Whitney Avenue.

I come and go, and my mother tries not to be nosy. She was home when I came in. "Did you ever send anything Federal Express?" I asked her.

"Of course. My boss sends things all the time."

"How do you do it?"

"They don't take cash," she said. "You fill out a form."

"Did you ever read Ezra Pound?" I said. I didn't know which poem to copy.

"I don't think so."

When I walked into the FedEx office the woman behind the counter saw me looking around and pointed to a table at the side, and when I looked over there, the first thing I saw was a big, worn-out, turquoise-colored bag—one of those Danish schoolbags—and my stomach lurched, because it looked so familiar and yet as if it came from far away. Ms. Feldman had carried that bag, or carried one just like it, always with straps and buckles dangling, and there she was, in a green raincoat, her blond hair spread out over her shoulders. When I approached, she put the bag on the floor without turning around. She was filling out a form.

"Ms. Feldman," I said. That is, we weren't on a first-name basis yet—except that she'd always called me Tom. She was going to be Ida within seconds, but right then she was still Ms. Feldman.

"What are you doing here, Tom?" she said. I explained about the contracts and the state and carpentry, and we stood there, leaning on the table and talking. She seemed the same age as she did when I was in high school and she was a new teacher. She reached her arm in front of my face to point out where I should write what on the form. The sleeve of her sweater, sticking out from her coat, was a soft, dark pink, and I wanted to touch it. As slowly as possible, I copied the address John had given me. Several things had happened, and I was trying to round them up, like marbles rolling in different directions. "Ida," I said, to get used to calling her Ida, for a start.

"What?" She'd gone back to her own form.

"What are you sending?"

She put the turquoise bag on the table between us again, and looked at me with a spark in her eyes, and then she took a long, thin loaf of French bread out of her bag. "I'm sending it to my mother," she said.

"Why?"

"I baked it." The loaf didn't fit in the envelope, and she broke off six inches. Then it fit at a slant.

"Won't it be stale?" I said.

"Of course." She laughed. She put the rest of the bread on the table and we sealed our envelopes. "Or maybe not," she said then.

The next thing to get used to was that I wanted her just as much as I did when I was seventeen. Wanting Ida unfolded again like an umbrella that had been in my closet all that time—a big golf umbrella in six colors. And what seemed even better, as we carried our envelopes to the unsmiling woman who'd been there all along but didn't seem to be listening, was that we were now the same age. When we met I was seventeen and I suppose she was twenty-three— a woman and a boy. But six years don't count, once you're grown up.

Ida broke the remaining bread in half as we left the FedEx office, and we ate it. Even without butter, it was excellent. She paused as we reached the sidewalk, wiping her mouth, then brushing crumbs off her front. Instead of saying good-bye, I asked her about Ezra Pound, and we thumbed through the anthology. "The first Canto, I guess," she said. "What made you think of Pound?"

"I don't know," I said. "We were nailing up molding and he just came to mind."

"*Pounding* those nails, I suppose," she said.

I groaned and said, "Come with me to get it copied"—and though it seems simple, this was the hardest thing, but once it was said, everything was different. I was trying out the new way we were going to be—we two grown-ups.

"Does it bother you that he was anti-Semitic?" I asked, as we went into the copy shop. Feldman was a Jewish name, I realized.

"You think I *like* it that he was anti-Semitic?"

"But you read him anyway?"

"Now and then." And she read aloud—dramatically, while people turned and watched—from the Canto:

And then went down to the ship,
Set keel to breakers, forth on the godly sea, and
We set up mast and sail on that swart ship,
Bore sheep aboard her, and our bodies also
Heavy with weeping, and winds from sternward

Bore us out onward with bellying canvas,
Circe's this craft, the trim-coifed goddess.

At "trim-coifed goddess," she stuck out one hip and touched her hair, shaking it back with a funny gesture. "It's so good to see you!" she said.

But I don't think she knew yet. She didn't know we were going to be lovers. "Want to see the toilet I just installed?" I said.

"Bread, plumbing," she said. "Very able people."

"I'd like to talk," I said and shrugged.

"I have to be someplace," she said, "but not for two hours."

With a copy of Pound's first Canto in my pocket, we walked to my car. She had come on foot. I'd parked legally, I hadn't been towed or ticketed, the contracts were on their way to Hartford, and Ida Feldman was sitting in my car while I wanted her just as much as I did at seventeen, when I pressed my face into the pillow at night, as if she were waiting under it and I could gnaw through and reach her.

The house we're working on is a big, frame one-family with a porch, owned by a nonprofit group. I guess the state chipped in, or maybe they just sent the rules over: a rail near the tub and a ramp in case there's a wheelchair user, sprinklers in the kitchen, and so forth. I felt proud of the house, fitting my key in the lock while Ida peered in the porch window.

I turned on the lights. The electricity is on, so we can use power tools and see what we're doing, but there's no heat yet. We kept our coats on. I took her through the first floor, letting myself touch her elbow to guide her. She did a little dance in the living room to say it was big—you know how people signal that a room is almost a ballroom.

"But I haven't seen your toilet." She loved the bathrooms, she said. She was impressed that John and I could make bathrooms where none had been before. "Are you going to keep doing this kind of work?" she asked.

"Should I?"

"How should I know?"

"You're right," I said. "I guess I thought you'd say I should become an English teacher."

"Is it better to be a teacher or a carpenter?" said Ida. "We need both."

"The people who are going to live here need more than carpentry," I said.

"I don't know," said Ida, patting the basin. "If I were a psychiatric patient, I know my problems wouldn't go away if I had a nicely installed toilet. But it wouldn't hurt!"

I explained how I'd set the toilet in place. "A rather mundane piece of life," she said, "but I never knew before how it was done."

"May I kiss you?" I said.

She nodded slowly, looking surprised but not surprised. My lips had barely touched hers—I had just got the first hint of the feel of her mouth, which is dry and soft—when the doorbell rang, a double chime that seemed to announce the arrival of a whole tea party.

We jumped apart. "I should warn people about kissing me," said Ida. "This invariably happens." She resigned herself. "Nothing is simple," she said as she started down the stairs. We clumped noisily to the front hall.

"I hope we're not interrupting," said the woman on the porch, and we shook our heads stupidly. "I'm Pamela Shepherd—"

"And we're the flock," said the man behind her. He was a young man with dark hair and a quick, mocking look, and behind him was a short, thin, middle-aged woman. Pamela Shepherd was a social worker, and these were going to be residents of the house.

"We planned just to drive by and look at it," said Pamela, "but we saw the light."

I explained who I was, and in came Pamela and the flock. The man immediately asked when we'd be finished so they could move in. "I've been at the hospital for five years," he said. "Never should have been there in the first place. Long series of mix-ups. Lost medicine. Doctor died. He was going to spring me."

"I'd hate it if my doctor died," said Ida.

"Woodchucks all over the grounds," said the man. "White squirrels. I bet you never even saw a white squirrel."

The little woman looked up at him through thick glasses. She looked as if she were going to ask a question, but she didn't. Pamela began to ask about the renovations.

When they went into the kitchen, Ida and I stayed behind in the hall to kiss. It was easier this time—it was as if it were our tenth kiss, except that the feel and the taste of her were new. I'd thought about it many times, but I hadn't imagined the slight coolness of her skin or the way her hair would get in my mouth. We heard the flock coming toward us. They were about to leave, and then the doorbell rang again.

It was a woman carrying a bag of groceries. "I saw a light," she said. "I live on the block. I was making sure nobody broke in."

She looked all of us over. I couldn't tell whether she was a nice person who was curious or somebody out to make trouble. Our two future residents happened to be standing on either side of me, and I had a silly impulse to spread my arms wide as if to guard them. The silent lady in the thick glasses, who stood to my left, looked a little like this woman who had just come in. They both had gray coats with gold buttons. "Is everyone from the state hospital?" said the woman. I didn't know whether she was asking if we were all mental patients or whether everyone who was going to live in the house was from the state hospital.

"No," said Pamela. "A mixed group."

"My husband," said the woman. "He keeps talking about who's

10

moving in here. He's been talking to the neighbors. After all, there are old people on the block."

I got upset. It was the only time all day I was really upset.

"Old people?" said the young man. "An old man killed someone for starting a fire—for burning leaves, which you know is against the law. But your husband doesn't burn leaves, does he?"

"Burton," said Pamela firmly. Ida began to laugh, and so did the silent lady, but the woman with the groceries didn't laugh.

"I'd like to grow tulips," said the quiet woman.

"Oh, tulips, well," said the woman with the groceries. She shook her head doubtfully, as if tulips grew only in certain rare conditions that you didn't find much around here. And then she left, and so did Pamela Shepherd and the flock, and Ida and I went back to kissing.

Ida said, "I should have *known,*" and we moved awkwardly from room to room while kissing. After a while I stopped and said, "That lady's going to make trouble."

"She might," said Ida.

"What will we do then?"

"We'll decide when the time comes," she said firmly, and I was comforted, or almost comforted. I don't know yet what kind of trouble the lady is going to make, if any. I don't know how her trouble could get into the happiest day, but it did. And still it was the happiest day. We kissed some more. Ida left her bag on the living-room floor and we kissed our way from room to room, looking for a place to lie down—but there were only hardwood floors. Then I heard a key in the lock and then clattering. It was John, who'd gone from the dentist to the lumberyard and come back with a load of lumber. "Get an early start tomorrow," he greeted me when we came to the door. He looked across the living room at the turquoise bag, flopped there with its buckles open, and then he looked at Ida.

"We have a Canto of Pound's for you," said Ida.

I handed it to John and he read it. "Nothing about Jews," he said, "one way or another." He looked at Ida again and then he looked at me, and I could tell that he saw how happy I was, that he saw Ida just the way I did, as if he, too, had loved her for years, as if he'd turned into me for a moment, just to see how it felt. Which seemed remarkable—that someone should care to know. Ida and I didn't say anything. We stood there like fools, our hands at our sides, like people being measured for something. We were looking at John as if he were the future, while he looked at us as if he wondered what we were working up to. We all stood there longer than you'd think, and after a while I began to enumerate tomorrow's tasks in my mind: we're going to build a doorway with the new lumber, and then we'll put in a kitchen floor. Soon, when Ida and I have been lovers for a week or two, and the shape of her naked breasts is already familiar and dear to me, heat will come through the clanking metal ducts John and I have been fastening into place day after day. And if we put in the plumbing right—if nothing goes wrong—then water will flow through pipes.

RIVER-TOSSING

KITTY DECARLO TAUGHT Western Civilization and U.S. History at Wilbur Cross High School in New Haven, Connecticut, and for two years she had lived with a roommate in a rented house in the neighborhood. The house had a narrow front yard where a previous occupant had planted red and yellow tulips. In the fall, a single maple turned scarlet, then abruptly bare. A few times a week, Kitty went running after work: it calmed her. One day in November she started late, and by the time she turned toward home, it was dusk. As she ran, Kitty's eyes took in tree after tree on her route. She studied the bare branches intertwined against the gray sky.

It grew dark. Listening to her own footfalls as she made her way up Orange Street, Kitty imagined being mugged—jumped from behind—and suffering just enough injuries to miss a couple of weeks of school and be cared for by friends bringing pans of lasagna. Kitty was conscientious; her mind moved on to the instructions she'd give the substitute teacher. Whatever she said, some of her students, for whom everything was already hard, would suffer.

In the dark—and in reality, not her fantasy—a passing car made a swift U-turn, but then recrossed the street and angled toward the sidewalk near her, facing the wrong way. A man got out, leaving the door open, and stepped quickly toward Kitty, and what came to her was advice she'd once read in a newspaper article on crime prevention. She was passing a house with a light in a downstairs window, and Kitty ran straight up the porch steps, punched the three doorbells she saw there, and shouted, "Mom, I'm home!" in a phony voice that sounded to her own ears— even then, when she was still frightened—like something out of bad children's television. The man got into the car and drove away, while the door in front of Kitty opened. There stood a young man with reddish, fluffy hair and a reddish-brown tweed sports coat. His hands were large, sticking out of the jacket sleeves as if he were outgrowing it as he stood there. He looked sleepy, and Kitty blurted out, "Did I wake you up?"—although he'd opened the door so quickly, she could have awakened him only if he had been leaning on it, asleep standing up.

"Oh, no," he said.

Kitty told him why she had rung his doorbell.

"Do you want to call the police?" said the man.

She was sweaty and beginning to feel chilled. She could see into the man's living room: bookshelves and more bookshelves, lamplit. "No, thanks," she said. "Maybe he just wanted to ask directions."

"I guess you'll never know."

"He was driving strangely," Kitty said.

"Maybe you'd better come in," said the man. "He could be waiting for you."

"I suppose so," Kitty said, and followed him inside.

The man said his name was Martin Corman. Kitty was shaky, and Martin brought her a glass of water, motioning her to sit. Library books and papers were lined up on his couch, and when Kitty sat down she started a small landslide. Martin knelt to pick up his books, and Kitty noticed one title: *Technology and American Economic Growth*. She drank the water. Her heart was beating hard.

"Are you all right?" said Martin.

"Yes," Kitty said. "I'll go in a minute. I have piles of quizzes to correct at home." She felt foolish for saying that.

"Are you a teacher?" said Martin, and within moments they learned that they knew someone in common. Martin was a graduate student at Yale, a social historian finishing his dissertation and working as a teaching assistant in a big course taught by a visiting professor from Georgetown, where Kitty had gone to school—taught by Henry Gradstein, of all people, her undergraduate adviser and graduate thesis director, and—for a few giddy, tempestuous weeks, toward the end of her time at the university—her lover.

"We're both just talking ourselves into this," Henry had said to her, five years ago, the last time they'd slept together.

"I'm not," said Kitty, before she thought.

"Of course you are."

Now, to Martin, she said, "He was my thesis adviser."

"Did you know he was here this year?"

Kitty hadn't known.

"Gradstein's a great teacher," Martin said.

"The best," said Kitty. "May I use your phone after all? I think I want my roommate to come for me with the car."

KITTY'S ROOMMATE, IDA, showed up in five minutes. "Did he have a weapon?" she said, as Kitty got into the car, shoving out of the way the big, floppy turquoise bag that accompanied Ida everywhere, even on five-minute errands.

"I hardly saw him," Kitty said. "I was stupid to panic. For all I know, it was one of my own students."

"Checking on an assignment, I suppose."

"I ran up on a stranger's porch and shouted, 'Mom.' I don't even call my actual mother 'Mom.' "

Ida glanced at Kitty. "He wanted to steal your money," she said.

"Or rape you." Ida was fat and dramatic, with blond hair that fell to her waist. She taught English at Wilbur Cross.

"Not every man who stops a woman wants to rob her or rape her," said Kitty.

"Of course not," said Ida. "But still."

"The man who let me in knows Henry Gradstein," Kitty said. Ida had reached their street and was parking the car. Kitty had told Ida about Henry long ago. "He's at Yale this year."

"You mean he's in New Haven and he didn't get in touch?" said Ida.

"I suppose he's busy."

"He was always thoughtless, from what you said."

"He's complicated," Kitty said.

"He should have called you," said Ida.

KITTY HELD AN essay contest in her history classes, offering the winners a trip to the movies at her own expense. Her students had complained that they'd been writing essays about Christopher Columbus and Martin Luther King for contests since they learned to spell, and surely there must be someone else to write about. Kitty had made some suggestions, and in the end fifteen essays were submitted and she selected three winners, one on W.E.B. Du Bois, one on Gandhi, and one on Simone Weil. The York Square Cinema was showing *Au Revoir, Les Enfants,* about the Second World War, and one night Kitty drove around town picking up her three winners, Josh, Tyrone, and Lakeesha. She stood behind them in the line at the movies, shooing them along when it moved—they were so busy talking they didn't notice—and guiding them back when they strayed. They were all taller and wider than she was, and they talked with such animation, Kitty couldn't keep up. "No, no," Josh was saying. "Not just one of them—all of them!"

"All of them," Tyrone chimed in, nodding rapidly. "*All* of them, man."

"All of what?" said Kitty gamely, but they didn't hear her.

Just then she realized that the older man in a bomber jacket standing alone in front of them was Henry Gradstein. "Henry," she said, and then, louder, "Henry!"

"Who's *Henry*, Ms. DeCarlo?" said Lakeesha, in a voice loud enough that finally Henry turned around, looking perplexedly into all four of their faces.

"Henry," said Kitty. "Kitty DeCarlo."

"Katherine!" He'd always called her Katherine. Henry's hair was grayer than Kitty remembered, and under the lights of the theater lobby his face seemed slightly unfamiliar. He stepped forward, grasped her shoulders, and kissed her cheek. Henry, too, was smaller than any of Kitty's students, and in contrast to their smoothness and youth and air of being about to slide off or up or out, he seemed a little battered yet firmly planted on the floor, his feet in neat brown shoes held somewhat apart as if to steady him. "I'm at Yale this year," he said with some excitement.

"I know." She was terribly glad to see him.

He beamed at her. "I have five TAs who follow me into the lecture hall, one step behind me."

"I met one of them," said Kitty, and then stopped to introduce her students. Henry shook their hands and repeated their names. "She's a good teacher, yes? I taught her everything she knows. If she gets anything wrong, you call me." He stabbed his chest with his finger. Lakeesha giggled.

"You met one of them?" he said then, turning to Kitty once more. "Which one? I don't have them all straight."

"Martin Corman."

"Oh, I know which one he is. The sleepy one."

"I thought he looked sleepy, too!" Kitty said.

"Where did you meet him?"

She had to tell the story. "I was running one night," she said, "and suddenly a man got out of a car and came toward me, and I panicked."

"My TA?"

"No—just a man. I ran up on the nearest porch, and the person who opened the door was Martin." She was not required, she decided, to put in "Mom, I'm home."

Her students listened attentively. "This guy have a gun?" said Tyrone.

"I don't know—I don't know if anything was really going to happen."

"Any man messes with me, I don't wait around to find out," said Lakeesha.

"A black guy?" said Henry, and Kitty thought she saw Lakeesha's face grow tense. She and Tyrone were black; Josh was white.

"It was dark," she said. "I couldn't see him."

"My cousin," Lakeesha was saying in a low voice. "He got shot. He was killed." Kitty drew in her breath. It was time to go into the movie.

"Wait—give me your phone number," Henry said.

After Kitty and the students sat down, she thought of popcorn and soda, and sent Tyrone out with money. She had lost Henry in the dark. The film began. It was harrowing, and somehow it kept reminding Kitty of Lakeesha's dead cousin; Kitty had to work hard so her students would not see her cry.

MARTIN CORMAN CALLED Kitty some weeks later. "I live on Orange Street," he said.

"I remember you."

"Henry wants to know the name of your dentist," he said.

"My dentist? Why didn't he call me himself?"

"Do you mind?" said Martin. "He seems to think we're friends."

Kitty didn't mind recommending her dentist.

"We *could* be friends," said Martin.

It was a Saturday in January and it had snowed—the first significant snowfall of the season. "Do you want to go for a walk and see the snow?" he said. Kitty and Martin walked to Edgerton Park, almost a mile away, and then tramped around its great curved paths. Children were sledding on the hill, while parents watched and scooped them out of snowbanks. The sun was out and the snow was dazzling. It was warm, and Kitty untied her muffler and pulled off her gloves. They talked about Martin's dissertation. "I read census reports and tax reports," he said. "Not very interesting." Kitty protested that she loved reading old documents. Her master's thesis had been on American schooling in the mid-nineteenth century, and she had read ancient rollbooks and budgets, fascinated even when they told her nothing.

"I know what you mean," said Martin, who was working on the demographics of the early American shoe industry. "But it's not like Henry's work." She understood. Henry had begun his career studying early factory life, but his most recent book had been on race relations in the automotive industry after the Second World War, and he'd been turning up as an expert, quoted here and there, on race relations anywhere, anytime.

"I'm having a similar experience, in a small way," said Martin, when Kitty told him about seeing Henry's name recently. "My landlady thinks I know everything. She's talked me into speaking to her senior citizens' group—I'm afraid they'll be expecting something more up-to-date than they get." Martin now taught a section of Henry's course on labor history—a different course; it was already the spring term.

Kitty didn't let herself talk about Henry anymore. "Do you like teaching?" she asked.

"I'm not good at it," said Martin. "But I like the students. I think I like them more than if I knew the same people for a different reason. I go in there and look at them—I don't know—my little *chickens.*" He blushed.

Kitty laughed. "I have chickens, too," she said.

They went back to Kitty and Ida's house. Ida wasn't home. Kitty made coffee because Martin looked sleepy now. It was getting dark. Carrying the coffeepot, Kitty glanced out the kitchen window. The snow was dusky and purple in the twilight, and she stared, then slipped the look of the purple snow into a sort of mental pocket.

Martin looked a little silly. He was wearing the same tweed sports coat he'd worn the day they'd met, but his feet were bare, with his stretched-out fuzzy tan socks steaming on a radiator behind him. His feet were big and pale like his hands. His wavy hair was mussed. What had Kitty expected—that he would lead her to Henry, tell her secrets about Henry, or tell her Henry spoke only of her? He put lots of milk and sugar into his coffee. Suddenly Kitty thought she might like Martin to be her lover.

IT TOOK THREE more walks, followed by three more visits, before he was. On the intervening occasions Ida was home, and they all drank coffee and talked. Once they had beer. Ida owned a collection of jazz records, and the day they drank the beer, Ida played a Miles Davis album for Martin, who stretched out, listening, sprawled over a chair in their living room, his hands and feet in four separate parts of the room. Kitty had to step over Martin's right leg to hand a bottle to Ida. He'd been talking about a troubled student, and now Ida was talking and Martin was listening to her as well as to the music. He listened like someone with room inside for what he heard.

Martin and Kitty became lovers not on a Saturday but on a Thursday, the day of Martin's talk to his landlady's senior citizens' group. He'd asked Kitty to come along for courage. As a public speaker, Martin was not quite lively, but he wasn't boring. People lingered to comment, and a woman borrowed a book from which he'd quoted, about blacks in New England in the nineteenth century.

Kitty had left two messages on Henry's answering machine in the last weeks, but she hadn't heard from him. He didn't come to Martin's talk; she'd let herself imagine he might. She was angry with herself for thinking about him and she wanted to be left alone with her dissatisfaction, but there was Martin; they had come together. At her house it was not quite dark, and the early evening had a touch of warmth to it. Spring was coming, but Kitty resisted it. She almost didn't ask Martin in; then she did. Her house was cold and dark. Martin followed her as she turned on lights and nudged the thermostat up a degree or two. In the kitchen she found a note from Ida, who had gone to dinner with friends. After Kitty read it, Martin suddenly began to kiss her, giving comforting kisses, as if to console her for the dark house and Ida's absence, or even for Henry's shortcomings or her own.

"Do you want to stay?" she said.

"May I?" He kissed her harder. "You're . . . lovely," he said in a choked voice, then blushed and shook his head, tossing away the inadequate, sentimental word.

Then they went to bed ("Maybe this *is* what I want," she almost said out loud) and after that day, there he was—around their house all the time.

WHEN IT WAS time for him to go home, he leaned on the wall, talking. Kitty would stand opposite him, glancing at the door, his coat in her arms.

"But he's *kind,*" said Ida, one night after he left. Martin had come for dinner and it had taken hours to get rid of him. It was a school night and Kitty had work to do.

"He sits there," Kitty said, "as if he's growing roots into the furniture. He likes me too much. I did get robbed that night. Martin robbed me."

Ida was cleaning the counter in a long apron, almost to the floor. She flicked her hair back. "You look glorious," Kitty said. What did Ida look like—the Statue of Liberty? No, a portrait by Rembrandt Kitty remembered: Saskia as Bellona, a grand woman with a shield, a helmet, and Ida's long hair and double chin.

"Pardon the question," said Ida, "but what's he like in bed?"

Kitty didn't mind the question. She'd heard about Ida's lovers. "He's kind of serious in bed, but that's fine," she said. "But every time he put down his fork at dinner, I didn't know if he'd pick it up again. Then, at last, he did. Well, I'd think, *that* much has been accomplished."

Kitty often visited Martin in the afternoons, and after a while she learned to dress in sweat clothes and running shoes. He cleared papers, welcoming her, and they perched in rare bookless spots in his apartment like hikers resting on stones in a tangle of underbrush. When she was tired of him—after they made love and had coffee and talked—she tightened the laces on her shoes and took off. Martin would be making some observation or other as she walked out the door. She'd step off his porch, already running, running as if she had something to run from, or something to run past, a damp fog that had a boundary, with cool sunshine behind it.

WHEN HENRY CALLED Kitty—because for God's sake it was the end of April already and he was leaving in May—she was so pleased that she invited him to dinner. If the weather was good, they could have a barbecue on the little front lawn. There might be tulips. "I'm a city boy," said Henry. "I don't need tulips."

She decided to serve barbecued chicken. She and Ida had bought a small grill the summer before. She invited Martin. The day of the dinner, a Saturday, Kitty was nervous, but there really wasn't much to do, and when Martin called she agreed to run an errand with him. "You'll calm me down," she said. It was a warm, sunny day.

"Remember the woman who borrowed the book?" he said. Martin needed it, but the woman, whose name was Rebecca, had hurt her knee and couldn't drive. "She lives in the woods in Guilford," he said. "Twenty-five minutes away."

Kitty just needed to buy strawberries on the way. She already had biscuits and cream for strawberry shortcake.

He drove over for her. "I wouldn't expect someone interested in race relations to live in the woods," said Kitty.

"I know. She seems urban," said Martin. "She told me she was active in the civil rights movement."

Martin drove on Route 1, which was slower than the turnpike, but there was plenty of time. He stopped for Kitty to buy strawberries and she put the boxes between them. Martin was a deliberate driver, and at times Kitty couldn't help pressing her foot into the floor, as if to add force to the gas pedal. He gave everyone the right of way, and at four-way stop signs he all but took a nap. Kitty tried to pay attention to the faint smell of the strawberries and to Martin's woolly smell—even without the sports coat—and to the sprays of white blossoms they passed, stippling the new bright green of the woods.

They missed the turn. Martin made a cautious U-turn. Rebecca's house was on a private dirt road deep in the woods. It was a modern, weathered wooden structure under the trees. Rebecca was a small, white-haired woman in jeans, who insisted on showing them through the house. Kitty explained about the dinner she had to prepare, but followed her. A wide window faced the woods, and when they came to it, all three of them fell silent, and Rebecca slipped backward into a chair, just watching what she saw out the window, the play of light on green. "I grew up in tenements," she said. "I didn't know what a woods was. When I read fairy tales about children lost in the forest, I pictured evenly spaced trees with grass underneath. When I saw my first forest, I didn't recognize it."

"What did you think it was?" said Kitty. Rebecca's voice was quiet, and Kitty spoke quietly herself, in turn. She, too, stepped backward and sat down, and so did Martin.

"I guess I thought it was an accident—a bunch of trees." Rebecca spoke as if to herself. "Now I love the undergrowth and moss. I love to look at the scraggly stuff under the trees."

Martin and Kitty looked at the scraggly stuff. Where sunlight broke in, the leaves on shrubs and maple weeds turned in a breeze and caught the light. At last Kitty shook herself and stood up.

"Did you like the book you borrowed from Martin?" she said— and finally Rebecca went for the book.

"I learned a lot from it," she said. "I wish I'd read more in my civil rights days. Did you know that in the 1830s blacks in Connecticut weren't allowed to vote?"

"What did you do in the civil rights movement?" said Kitty, though she knew they should hurry now.

"Walked my feet off with a lot of other ladies, black ladies and white ladies. We were not at the center of power. Mostly we talked about kids. . . ." Her eyes brightened. "I'm a teacher," she said. She offered to make coffee, then remembered they had guests coming.

"I'm a teacher, too!" said Kitty, but they really had to leave.

"I'll tell you a shortcut," Rebecca was saying. For a second, it seemed to Kitty that making dinner for Henry didn't count. She wanted to drink coffee with Rebecca and Martin in the room facing the woods. They could all talk about teaching.

Kitty didn't pay attention to the directions Rebecca was giving Martin. But now she was impatient. Her mood had shifted again in a moment. She wanted to be home slicing the strawberries' tops off, cutting up radishes, and planning the evening—what she would say, what Henry might say.

After two turns on the narrow woods roads, Martin got lost. Neither of them knew the way back to Rebecca's house. And then, after a sputter, a false recovery, and another sputter, the car stopped. Martin eased it to the side of the road, but it would go no farther, and he sat there, looking as if he were listening hard for it to tell him what was wrong. But he knew what was wrong. "It's out of gas, I suppose," he said. The sounds of the woods—birds, the wind—suddenly seemed ugly to Kitty. She began to cry, as if she thought they might lose their lives out there, like the lost children in fairy tales of whom Rebecca had spoken.

Then Martin started moving and talking. He was not apologetic; he ignored her tears. He seemed pleased, on the whole. He walked briskly around the car, then tried to start it again, as if he thought it might have been joking.

"We'll have to find a phone," he said. They didn't remember passing a house, so they walked in the direction they'd been driving. Kitty had stopped crying but she was furious. She walked beside him, not speaking.

At last they came to a mailbox and a driveway, but no one was home. The same thing happened a second time. It took a long time to walk down the driveways. At the third mailbox, Kitty waited while Martin walked in. This time Martin returned in a car with a man who had offered to drive him to a gas station. Kitty walked back to Martin's car and waited there for a long time, reading about

New England blacks in the nineteenth century. She took off her watch and put it into her pocket. Her wrist ached with a sort of consciousness.

WHEN MARTIN CAME back, he was elated. He shook hands with the friendly man who had helped him and waved as the man drove away. Martin had a can of gasoline, which he poured carefully into the tank.

"Such a decent person!" he said, starting the car at last.

He reached across the strawberries—which were becoming a little soft—to take Kitty's hand, but she pulled it away. Martin talked about the woods, about Rebecca. When he paused, she said, "You're selfish."

There was silence for half a mile. "You mean because of Henry," he said. "Dinner." Again there was silence. "You're right," he said finally. "I don't like him. I'd rather stay here and make love under the trees."

"Well, we're not," said Kitty.

At the house, Ida and Henry were sitting in the yard on kitchen chairs, drinking beer. Ida jumped up. She took the boxes of strawberries from Kitty's hands. Martin walked past them, smiling at Henry, who remained seated, tipping his chair back like a man in a general store telling a yarn.

"I was worried," said Ida.

"How long has he been here?"

"Forever. He came early."

"We got lost and we ran out of gas." Telling the story, Kitty looked past Ida, who was holding the strawberries to her breasts like a goddess of spring, and watched the men in the yard. Their shadows were long. Martin had stopped to greet Henry and was still standing.

Henry was speaking and Martin listened placidly, while three yellow tulips waved behind him.

"That was some dentist you sent me to," Henry said in greeting to Kitty, when she came toward him. "I'm still suffering."

Kitty had forgotten he'd asked for the name of her dentist. "Didn't you like him? How are you, Henry? I'm sorry . . ." She waved at the car, Ida, and the strawberries.

"No problem. Ida has been looking after me."

The dentist, it turned out, had sent Henry on to a gum specialist. "A gum *fanatic*. He's still working on me, when I give him a chance."

"Do you want another beer, Henry?"

"Not yet," he said. Kitty excused herself and went into the house.

Ida followed her. "Shall I start the fire?" she said. "I brought the grill up from the basement and washed it."

"You've been good to me," said Kitty.

She hoped Henry would come inside and talk to her while she got the food ready, but he kept on talking to Martin. Kitty went back to the kitchen, took out the salad bowl, and washed the lettuce leaves. She could hear her three friends outside. Ida laughed once.

Then she heard Henry say, "I'm going in search of another beer." She grew fluttery, and became conscious in an exaggerated way of her hands tearing lettuce. She was afraid that Ida or Martin would offer to come inside for the beer, but they didn't, and in a moment Henry came marching down the hall into her kitchen. He put his empty bottle on the table and stood tapping his elbow with his middle finger, a gesture Kitty remembered. Kitty opened the refrigerator, took out two beers, and gave one to Henry, who raised it in a rudimentary toast but said only, "Ran out of gas, did he?"

"I'm sorry," said Kitty.

Henry rubbed his forearm thoughtfully, and Kitty thought that the moment—they were alone for the first time in years—might be difficult for him, too. "So how are you doing these days?" he said. "In general?"

"Fine," said Kitty. "I really like teaching." She started to peel a cucumber. Now that she had him to herself, she didn't know what to do with him. "Did you like meeting my students that night?" she ventured.

"Your students? Oh, at the movies," said Henry. "Nice kids. Of course, they had a little con game going—the usual student con game."

"A con game?" said Kitty.

"I'm afraid they weren't interested in teacher's serious little film," he said. "They were there for the popcorn." He took a drink and put the bottle down.

"Of course they were interested!" said Kitty. "They're good people, my students." Henry must have seen them eat popcorn. He'd watched them when they couldn't see him. He was probably lonely that night.

"Good people, bad people," he said, pulling out a chair and sitting down. "I guess you haven't changed, Katherine. I seem to recall that you had a rather idealized view of me, too, at one time."

She looked at him, vegetable peeler in hand. "I don't think so," she said.

"Don't look so shocked," said Henry. "Your students wouldn't be. Kids in a city like this—they know life isn't perfect. Look, you were angry with me that night for asking if the mugger was black, but the kids weren't angry. They already knew he was black—or they knew I'd *think* he was black." He laughed shortly.

"But I didn't see the mugger," said Kitty once more. "And the kids—some of them are babies—" She broke off. "Chickens . . ."

Henry was hungry and it was making him difficult. "Go wait on the lawn," she said at last. "I'll cook faster if I'm alone." He obeyed, taking his beer with him. "But I loved you," she said as the door closed behind him.

When they ate the chicken and salad, it was almost dark and getting chilly. Ida had brought out two more chairs. Kitty balanced her plate on her lap, shivering a little, relieved that the chicken tasted good. She remembered she'd just spoken of her students as chickens, and she smiled. Well, there were days when cannibalism seemed too good for them.

"What are you laughing at?" said Henry.

"Just my students."

"I'm glad you find them funny," he said. His voice was gentle now.

"Oh, I do," said Kitty, suddenly eager to talk. "Or the whole situation can be funny—the administration . . ."

Ida had gone into the house and now she came out, pulling her arms through the sleeves of a sweatshirt. "Speaking of funny," she said, "we should tell him about the latest infraction."

"What's that?" said Henry.

"Some kids pick up another kid and take him down to the river and throw him in."

"What river?" said Henry.

"It really *isn't* funny," Kitty interrupted.

"There's a small river behind the high school," said Ida. "Anyway, this particular brand of deviltry hadn't been tried before, so the authorities didn't know what to do about it. Finally the principal came on the PA system and said, 'All right. Ten days' suspension for river-tossing.' I love that. River-tossing. What a way to put it."

"At least they don't do that at Yale," said Martin. "They'd probably throw *me* in."

"They don't do it because there's no river," Henry said. "You have a river, sooner or later someone gets thrown in. It's human nature. They'd think of it at Yale—they're pretty smart."

"They certainly are," said Martin. He leaned over and took another piece of chicken from the plate Kitty had placed on a tablecloth spread on the ground. "Smarter than I am. Most of the time, I don't know what I'm doing, teaching them."

"Well," said Henry, "there's a lot you don't seem to know. How to read a gas gauge." His voice was a little rough. "Of course, it does take ability to teach."

"I guess that's so," said Martin calmly, but Ida, who had just stood up, whirled around to face Henry and stood there in the growing dark, a sturdy, bulky figure, certain of herself and angry. "How can you *say* such a thing?" she said. "Martin is a splendid teacher!"

"How do you know?" said Martin, as Henry shrugged, looking embarrassed.

"I don't know how I know, but I know," said Ida, unfazed. "The way you talk about your students—the one whose father died, and you listened to him for hours?" She looked straight at Henry now. "Some people—some teachers—don't know students have feelings. They don't know students are real." She stood before him in her sweatshirt, arms at her sides, scolding Kitty's old teacher, Kitty saw, for his misdeeds and malefactions toward her. But Henry—uncomfortable because Ida was angry—would not guess what she meant.

THEY HAD STRAWBERRY shortcake late at night, inside. They'd all drunk a lot and laughed, and Henry had talked. Ida calmed down and talked about jazz with him. She knew Beatles songs, too, and she and Martin sang songs from *The White Album*. She told more stories about the school.

It was good strawberry shortcake. Kitty sat on the floor with hers. She was tired. The others were done with their cake, and she considered offering seconds. Then Henry stood up. He was leaving, and suddenly Kitty thought—in words joined to her head by a line of imaginary dots, as if she were a cartoon woman—"I will never see him again."

"Well, good luck, all of you," Henry was saying. Apparently he'd had the impulse to make a short speech. "Good luck with your teaching," he said to Ida, with a nod. "What was that you get ten days for?"

"River-tossing," said Ida.

"River-tossing," Henry repeated. "And you, Katherine . . ." he said, and then he didn't seem to know what to say. "Well, Katherine," he said again. He looked at her hard and shook his head and turned to Martin, and Kitty turned, too. "Geez, you're a sleepy son of a gun," Henry said—and at last, Kitty got over him.

PEKKO'S BOAT

WHEN I TURNED sixteen, I got a job at a frozen-yogurt place owned by a big white man with a curly white beard. His name was Pekko Roberts. The first week I thought he was old, but then I studied him and realized that he was only about fifty. "The staff here has always been diverse," he said when he hired me, which turned out to mean that a Korean girl had worked there the summer before, and that he was glad I'm black. "I want the black community to feel welcome here," he said, and I pictured a marching block of black people led by ladies in church hats, maybe twenty rows, twenty across, arms linked, all coming at once to buy frozen yogurt. "My dad is white," I said, but he had turned toward a customer and didn't hear me. The first time my father picked me up after work, I saw a string of feelings cross Pekko's face, though not much of it shows above the beard. He was disappointed that I wasn't quite as diverse as he had in mind—but then pleased, I thought, because my father, who also has a beard, looked something like him. "Are you adopted?" he said the next time I came to work.

"My mom is black," I said. I was annoyed. I look like my dad except for color.

When I'd been working in the store a few weeks, I was alone there one afternoon when a man in his twenties came in and ordered a cup of Dutch Chocolate Low Fat and sat down at a table to eat it. He had brown hair like a flat cap and it came down in spikes on his forehead. He had a sharp nose, and the nose sticking out from under the hair made him look a little like a dog. "What's your name?" he said after a while, speaking to me from the table, which happens when there's only one customer in the store.

"Tabitha."

"Do me a favor, Tabitha," he said.

"What's that?"

"Keep some money for me until tomorrow or the next day."

"Why?" I thought of bank robbers with marked money.

"So I don't spend it."

"How do you know I'll give it back?" I said.

"Oh, you'll give it back."

"How much money?"

"Ten."

"Ten dollars?"

"Right—what did you think, ten thousand?" We both laughed and I liked the way he laughed. Before I could decide what to do about him, he took a ten-dollar bill out of his pocket. Then he took a napkin and wrote something on it with a pen. Then he put the bill and the napkin on the counter and walked out. I looked at the napkin. It said, "UOMe $10 Denny."

I thought of telling my parents. I was afraid they'd laugh: "You fell for *that* scam?" Though I couldn't figure out how it was going to turn out to be a scam. All the scams I'd heard about—the person who tells you his car has been towed, the person stranded in New Haven who needs bus fare—involved being asked for money, not being given it.

When I put my jeans into the laundry, I transferred the money and the napkin to the left pocket of the clean pair. The next day Pekko and I were working together. We had lulls and then crowds, lulls and then crowds all day. It was a Saturday. Pekko said I could take the next Saturday off because the man who worked weekdays while I was at school wanted to work Saturday the following week. He had to miss a day and he wanted to make it up.

"Of course, I see that I'm depriving *you* of a day," he said.

"I don't mind." I wasn't sure if I minded. Saturday was my only full day, so I'd lose a lot of money—but it would be good to have a Saturday off.

"Well, if you do mind," Pekko said, "I need someone to paint my boat and clean my garage. It would take just a few hours. Would your parents object?"

"What kind of boat?" I said.

"Just a motorboat."

"Where do you live that you have a boat?"

"Guilford—a summer place, but I rent it year-round. It's sup-posedly winterized."

"On the water?"

"Right on the water."

Just then Denny came in. I was startled to see him. He ordered Dutch Chocolate again and said, "Thanks, Tabitha," and Pekko looked up from where he was making a pot of coffee, but lots of the customers had learned my name.

Denny sat down and gave me a funny, friendly look, as if we were playing a practical joke on Pekko. The look made me feel better about him. I'd been picturing him sullen. I took a cloth and wiped the tables. "Didn't you just do that, Tabby?" said Pekko over his shoulder. Another customer had come in.

As I passed Denny's table I gave him the bill and the napkin, which had been folded together in my pocket. He nodded and took them. I wiped the last table and went back to serve the customer, a black woman with heels and a briefcase who reminded me of my mother. She ordered a cone and left, carrying it with her. "Spring," said Pekko. "Warm enough to eat it in the street—but cool enough that it doesn't drip on her dress-for-success suit." I thought he'd say something about economic opportunities for blacks, but he didn't.

I decided not to work at Pekko's house on Saturday, but when I told my parents he'd asked me about it, my father said, "He doesn't try anything funny with you, does he?" and I said of course not.

"He sings Weavers songs," I said, as if that took care of everything. "You probably went on peace marches with him." Pekko was a *just* man, I was saying.

"He does look familiar," said my dad. Pekko had said the same thing. "What's your father's name?" he'd asked me.

"Parker Stillman."

"He's a lawyer?"

"An architect."

"Same difference—one of those people who came here for Yale and stayed on."

I nodded.

"I know him," he said. "I know *all* of them."

After that, if my father picked me up, he and Pekko would stand around for a while trying to decide how they knew each other. "Ever been to Quaker meeting?" Pekko would ask. Et cetera.

A WEEK LATER Denny came in again when I was alone, and again asked me to keep his money. "You're weird," I said.

"What's weird about me?" He wasn't weird. He seemed like someone who'd taken courses in auto mechanics in high school and who might work in a garage now, except that he didn't wear a uniform with "Denny" embroidered on the pocket. I wished he did. I kept thinking maybe his name wasn't really Denny.

"It's weird to ask someone to keep money for you," I said.

"But everyone does that," said Denny. "They ask banks."

I laughed. "Why don't you go to a bank, then?"

"No way," he said. This time he didn't bother with the napkin, and he stood at the counter until I put the money into my left pants pocket again. "What school do you go to?" he said then, but nodded and left as soon as I told him.

When he came back for the money the next day, I was alone, but he still didn't stay and talk. "What are you going to buy with it?" I said.

"Groceries."

The third time, he asked me to keep a twenty. It was a couple of weeks later, and spring was really coming. I took the twenty and then I didn't see him for a week. Now that it was spring I sometimes wore a skirt instead of pants. The skirt had no pockets, so when I wore it I put the money in my bag, not in my wallet but in an envelope at the bottom labeled "Denny." I was meticulous about it.

One day I got out of school early because of a teachers' meeting, and when my father heard that was going to happen, he said he'd take me out to lunch. He picked me up at school and we went to an Indian restaurant. My father and mother love Indian food and my brother and I grew up with it. My brother eats only one dish, chicken biryani, but I like everything. This time I had matar paneer, which is peas and Indian cheese. I don't eat much meat.

"I really want to make paneer," Dad said. He cooks Indian food. "It's essentially just boiled milk. You put in lemon juice to make it curdle." Then when the bill came, after he'd talked recipes with the waiters and everything, he didn't have enough money to pay it, and he thought they took credit cards but they didn't, and he didn't have his checkbook. "Do you have any money, Tab?" he said to me with the light in his eyes that he gets when he's done something foolish. I think he *likes* it: screwing up, being forgiven.

"I have a twenty," I finally said, "but it isn't mine."

"Whose is it?"

"A friend of mine."

I thought he might ask questions but I guess he was too nervous about the check. "Oh, that's all right," he said. "We'll stop at the money machine and I'll give you another twenty."

"I think it might matter that it's this particular twenty," I said, although I didn't know why that should be so.

"What—Jackson's picture is upside down?" my father said quickly. He sounded impatient.

So I gave him Denny's twenty, and then the automatic teller wasn't working and I was already late for work. I figured Denny wouldn't come in, but of course he did. Again I was alone, and it occurred to me that he waited around outside, peeking in, until he could see that I was alone. As soon as he came in, I looked right at him and said, "Listen, I don't have it." I told him what had happened. "I'll have it tomorrow," I said.

"It doesn't matter," he said.

"Does this mean you can't buy your groceries?" I said. I thought maybe I ought to invite him to dinner. What if he had no food?

"Oh, no," he said. Then, after a silence, he said, "Would you come for a walk with me when you get off work?"

"All right." I felt sorry for him. "I'll be done at five." The days were getting warmer and it was light into the evening, so I always walked home now.

Denny went away and came back at five. He was waiting for me at a little distance from the store when I came out. I thought I should introduce him to Pekko, but I didn't. Pekko would say I shouldn't go for a walk with him, I knew—that I didn't have to, just because of the twenty. He'd hand me a twenty.

We walked miles—all the way to the grassy park at the harbor. "So, do you consider yourself black?" he asked, first thing.

"Of course," I said.

"Well, logically you could be either one, with one black parent and one white parent," he said.

"What do you know about my parents?" I said, but he just shrugged. We talked about school. He asked me questions about my classes and teachers, and was interested in figuring out their hang-ups and why some of them annoyed me. When the wind got colder at the harbor, he pulled me close like a sweater or a blanket, and then he gave me a short kiss on the lips.

"Do you mind that?" he said. I didn't mind. I was excited that he was older, with a different feel and smell from the boys my age I'd kissed, and more interesting than he had seemed. I decided he hadn't just taken auto mechanics. "Do you have a job?" I said.

"I take courses at Gateway Community College," said Denny, "and I work for a cleaning service."

"Cleaning houses?"

"Right. Three of us at a time. We go in and blitz a place."

"Is it fun?" I said.

"Sometimes."

"When isn't it?"

"Bathrooms. And when the owners are assholes."

He was taking an English course for which he had to write his autobiography. "Maybe I'll show it to you," he said.

"You don't seem old enough to have an autobiography to write," I said.

"Plenty old enough," he said. "Did you ever do drugs?"

"No. Did you?"

"I used to."

"Not anymore?"

"Not anymore."

"So you're not dealing drugs or anything? I mean, the money."

"If I were dealing drugs," said Denny, "I'd have a lot more money than that."

"Well, I know," I said, not wanting to seem naive.

He knew about the gulls we saw fly over the water: how old they were, whether they were males or females. He pointed out one-year-old gulls and three-year-old gulls. I had no idea whether he was making it up or not. He moved toward me again, and this time when he kissed me I could feel his erection. "I like you," I said, but I backed away.

"I *really* like you," he said quietly, pushing the hair off his forehead so his eyes suddenly looked bigger and very clear. They were blue, I saw. Indoors, I'd thought they might be brown. We were in a lonely place, but the highway was nearby. I wondered if we could be seen from the highway.

"Are you thinking I'm going to rape you?" he said.

"It crossed my mind," I said.

"I'm not," said Denny, "but I'd like to talk you into it."

I didn't say anything because I wanted to have sex with him, but I knew I wasn't going to, even though officially I hadn't decided yet.

"I've got condoms," he said.

"It isn't very private here," I said.

"You don't *have* to," he said.

"Of *course* not!" I said, my voice sharp.

"Oh, that's not what I mean, Tabby," he said. He sounded sad now, and he steered me around and we started walking back toward my neighborhood. I felt bad. I didn't know what he could mean, if he wasn't talking about the twenty.

"What *did* you mean?" I said after a long time.

"Never mind," he said.

"That makes me furious," I said, stopping. "I don't put up with people saying 'never mind.'"

He said then, after a pause, "I mean, just because I'm a house cleaner and you feel sorry for me."

"Oh," I said. "I wasn't thinking about that." We kept walking without touching. Now that it was no longer possible, while we walked through the streets, I was sure I wanted to have sex with him. "Tell me about cleaning," I said.

"Fumes," he said. "Yuck. And vacuuming up dog hair. But I turn off here." He turned left and walked away from me. We were near the yogurt place and I walked home alone from there.

WHEN I GOT home my father was making Indian stuffed bread— aloo paratha, bread stuffed with potatoes. My mother was taking off her panty hose at the kitchen table—her money-makers, she calls them, because she wears them only to work. She wiggled her toes and sat back at the kitchen table watching my father. Her shoes were under the table. "The Indian lunch whetted my appetite," my father said. He was rolling out circles of dough all over the kitchen. "I have a twenty-dollar bill for your friend."

"He showed up," I said.

"Oh, I'm sorry!" said my father, and stopped what he was doing—enclosing a blob of potatoes in one of his dough circles. "Was it embarrassing?"

"He was cool."

But my father forgot to give me the twenty-dollar bill, and I forgot to ask for it, and I didn't think of it until halfway through the next day. Then, of course, Denny came into the store again. This time someone else was there, a woman drinking coffee at a table in the corner. Pekko had gone to the bank. I thought maybe Denny had looked in the window but didn't see the woman and thought we'd be alone. I looked up at him. I hadn't been embarrassed the day before, but this time I was. I was afraid he'd think I'd done it on purpose so we could take another walk, and I *had* been thinking about him. But that day it was raining.

I looked at Denny and said, "Hi," and acted as if he was just a customer, and he ordered a cup of frozen yogurt. When he paid I opened the cash register, took out a twenty-dollar bill, and gave it to him along with the coins he was getting for change. "Thanks," he said. He took his yogurt and left. I wanted him to stay, but I didn't know what to say and so I just said, "You're welcome." I knew he'd seen me take the money from the register, not from my pocket.

Pekko didn't say anything to me the next day, and I wondered what he was thinking. I thought he might go out of his way not to accuse me. The day I took the money, my father finally gave me the twenty-dollar bill, and the next day I put it into the till. But every time Pekko spoke to me, I was sure he knew, and that he was thinking of a way to bring it up. He'd be shocked that I'd done it. He might talk first about it to his old friend my father. They had never figured out how they knew each other, but they were still sure they did.

"That fellow Denny . . ." said Pekko one afternoon.

"How do you know Denny?" I said.

"He comes in here all the time," he said. "You know him."

"I didn't know *you* knew him."

"I wanted to ask him to do some work around my place," he said. "He hasn't been in today, has he?"

"No." I thought he was trying to get me to say something specific about Denny. Maybe he wanted to see if I'd confess. But it was true about his house—a few days later when I came in, Denny was there, and Pekko was telling him about painting the boat. But the next thing I knew, Denny had been fired. Pekko was angry with him—he'd left paint cans open and one had spilled; he hadn't cleaned up properly. Pekko grumbled all afternoon.

That night my father got a phone call, and from the way he looked at me, his eyes playing lightly with the image of me, I knew

42

that the person on the other end of the line was talking about me. I left the room, but when I came back, my father said that Pekko wanted to hire me to work around his house. My father had said it was all right with him, and that if I wanted to do it, he'd drop me off there on Sunday.

Sure enough, Pekko asked me about it the next day. "I just need someone who's neat," he said. He said he'd pay me what I earned in the store. He wanted me to help him clean the garage and finish painting the boat.

The next Sunday, my father dropped me off at Pekko's house in Guilford. He lived right near the water. There wasn't a swimming beach but a long, swampy piece of land behind his house, with a muddy trail going through it, and at the end of it, water. A green rowboat was on the shore near the water. It was a chilly spring day, but I took off my shoes to walk to the boat through the cold mud. The boat was already painted. Denny had finished it and I thought he'd done a fine job. Pekko and I examined it, but there was nothing more to do, so we went to work in the garage, which wasn't an impossible mess but was daunting. I started winding spools of rope and sweeping and sorting out trash. Pekko found a can of gasoline and the motor for the boat and took them down to the water. "Is the boat yours or the owner's?" I said when he came back.

"Mine," he said. "Maybe I'll take it out this afternoon."

"It's a nice way to live," I said. We had gone into the house when I arrived, and it was simple, like a summer cabin. I liked the thought of living like that.

"Nice for a kid," he said. "I never grew up." He was squatting to arrange things on the shelves while I swept. His thighs were big in his tan pants.

"I think you're pretty grown up," I said. He turned around and looked at me, and then he straightened up and stretched his arms out while doing knee bends—getting the kinks out, I guess. With his white beard and his arms spread wide, he looked like someone in a play, a priest or a king who might say something weighty in poetry. I swept the dirt from the corners and picked up the broom to sweep the cobwebs from the walls.

After a while Pekko and I had a huge pile of trash outside the garage, and Pekko said he'd drive it to the dump. I kept working. I went back to the rope, which I couldn't resist. There were five or six kinds of rope and they were completely tangled up. I happen to be the sort of person who can't help untying knots. Pekko had said maybe we should give up and throw the rope out, but I didn't think he meant it. It was good rope. I loved working out the knots. These were thick ropes—clothesline, bright yellow nylon rope, a very thick, rough, braided tan rope, and so on. I sat down on the floor of the garage with an enormous knot in my lap. Pekko drove away and I worked alone for a long time. It was quiet. Then I felt someone behind me. I turned and it was Denny, coming toward me across the weedy area near the road.

"What are you doing here?" I said.

"I've worked for Pekko before," he said.

"I didn't hear a car."

"I hitched."

"Why did you come here?"

"I left something."

"Did you know I'd be here?"

"Of course not," he said. "What do you think, I'm shadowing you?"

I thought I'd like that. He could have followed us out there. He could be shadowing my house. It would have been easy to find out where I lived. He could have followed me home from the yogurt place one night.

"I thought nobody was here," he said. "I didn't see a car."

"Pekko's gone to the dump," I said.

He said, "Is the house locked?"

"I don't know," I said. "Why? Do you need to go to the john?"

"I just wondered," said Denny.

He leaned back against the garage wall and watched me reaching my hands into the tangle and loosening it. I'd find an end and try to work it out. Some of the ropes had been cut, and sometimes when I worked and worked at a length of rope, it would turn out that the whole piece was just a yard or two long. But I had disentangled the bright yellow rope and rolled it into a coil, and the knot in my lap was smaller.

"I haven't seen you in the yogurt place lately," I said. I had thought about Denny every day. I kept waiting for him to come in.

"I've been there," he said.

"Not when I was there."

"I guess not." Then he said, "What do your parents think about me?"

"My parents?" I said. "They don't know anything."

"They know about the money, don't they?"

"Only sort of," I said.

"Look," said Denny. "He knows you took it."

"My father?"

"Pekko."

"How do you know?" I said. He had gestured in the direction a car would come, if Pekko came back, and I had the strange idea that Denny had told him, that this was a trap, that Pekko hadn't gone to the dump at all but was waiting somewhere, listening, while Denny got me to confess.

Denny shook his head. "Let's take the boat out," he said then.

"I don't think we'd better."

"Come on," he said, and he pulled at my hand. "I have something to tell you."

He pulled me down the path to the water. Pekko had set the

motor in place, and before I could get my shoes and socks off again, Denny had pushed the boat into the water, getting his pants wet, and climbed into it. He'd kicked off his shoes and he wasn't wearing socks. There was an oar in the bottom of the boat, and Denny used it to push away from the shore. When my feet were bare, I walked into the cold water and climbed into the bow of the boat. Denny yanked on the cord several times, and the motor caught. He headed the boat straight out into the sound. The water was gray, but the sun was trying to break through clouds, and it made the water glint. We bumped on the top of the water—each wave was a light blow underneath us—out toward the open sound. Denny was steering the boat straight away from the land, as if he planned to carry me directly across the sound to Long Island to start a new life. Then I looked back and saw a figure with a white beard running on the shore and waving its arms.

"We better go back," I said.

"I want to talk to you," said Denny. He shouted something over the sound of the motor and the wind. I couldn't hear him and he had to say it again. "I'm on Home Release," he said.

"What's that?"

"I'm in jail."

He leaned toward me, looking very slim and young, his hair over his eyes, and I moved closer, to the middle seat of the boat. "What do you mean, jail?" For a second I thought he meant something that would happen in a game.

"They let me out of jail."

"What were you in jail for?"

"Robbery," said Denny. "I figured you knew."

"No," I said. Pekko was getting smaller, and now I could hardly see him. "I'm cold," I said. It was much colder out on the water.

"Me, too," said Denny. He touched my arm with one finger, then his own. "I held up a store like Pekko's. He knows."

"He does?" I said.

"He knows everything about everyone," said Denny. "You don't want to go back there—you want to go where nobody knows you." He smiled so intelligently, leaning toward me and touching my arm again, that it seemed easy. It seemed that he could stop the boat where we were, or a little farther along, that we could be quiet, and think what to do next, and maybe even stay there, but soon Denny turned the boat in a wide curve and pointed it toward shore. As we slowed down, near the beach, it was easier to hear him. When I could see the ground under us, Denny jumped out and then I did. We dragged the boat out of the cold water while Pekko screamed at us, and then we all drove back to New Haven. In the back seat of Pekko's car, I was chilled and my face felt tight, as if we'd spent a long time, not just a few minutes, on that gray, bumpy Long Island Sound. The sun was almost out, but not quite, so the sky and the water glittered and it hurt to look around.

"I never said you kids could take that boat out," said Pekko, after a mile of silence.

"Denny's twenty-three," I said. I rubbed my bare arms to warm them.

After Pekko dropped Denny off, he took me to Clark's for a sandwich. I wanted just the right thing and I couldn't decide what to order. It was as if I were going to prison, as if it were the last time I'd be allowed to choose what I wanted. I kept thinking of something Denny had said in the boat, the last thing he said. "Would you tell lies for me, young black woman?" he said. "Would you do *that* if I wanted?"

I'D JUST COME to Rochester, the town where I grew up, to spend a week with my mother, and she was explaining why we had to bake the next day. It had to do with a play. A carpenter bakes his first loaf of bread. The other characters—his girlfriend, a social worker, two residents of a psychiatric hospital, and a neighborhood woman—eat it.

"Is that symbolic?" I said.

"I don't know about things like that, Ida," she said. Like the carpenter, she'd never baked bread before. My father's sister, Aunt Freddie, was the stage manager of the play and was supposed to provide the props. For rehearsals, she had bought bread from a bakery, but the director said it looked too professional.

"It has to be misshapen and lumpy," Aunt Freddie had said. She'd asked my mother to produce five long loaves, like French bread, one for each performance.

"I don't have to bake five times," said my mother. "I can freeze them."

Aunt Freddie is a large, practical old woman. At first I was surprised that she had become a stage manager, even for a small community theater, but she has always pushed people and things around. When she was young, I've heard, she and her sisters used to rearrange the furniture in their parents' parlor as an after-dinner entertainment. Their brother, my father, was middle-sized and not happy moving furniture, but I took after my aunts, not after my father—and certainly not after my mother, who is so small she sees only her conscientious brow in bathroom mirrors. At eight I had longer, more unruly hair than my mother; at eleven I was taller; at thirteen I weighed more.

I hadn't been in Rochester for more than a year. I'm a New Haven high school English teacher, the kind whose friends tell her she's an idealist. Three girls in my homeroom got pregnant this year; one also won a poetry contest. The visit was during my February vacation. "I'm going home," I had said to my lover, Parker, a few days earlier.

"Before you eat?" he said. He was cooking spicy eggplant and cauliflower according to an Indian recipe. "Or right after? Right after might not be a bad idea."

"Home home," I said. "On Friday." Parker is married. His wife, who travels for her job, was away that week, and his kids weren't home either, which was why he could have me to dinner (and, as it worked out, sex), but soon they'd be back. That night, on the phone, I finally told my mother Parker is married. I put the news into the same sentence as the eggplant and cauliflower.

"Does he have a dishwasher?" my mother asked. "Fancy cooking is easier with a dishwasher."

When I sleep with a lover, sometimes I wake in the night and think the person beside me is my mother. It isn't a memory. I assume it's my mother, the way a child who has fallen asleep on the floor assumes it's her mother when she awakens in the air. I walk in my sleep. As a teenager, I once walked down a never-used staircase in our two-family house, falling down the last steps, where mops and pails were stored, and bursting into the kitchen of the apartment below, where I woke up on the floor. The people called my mother and she came down for me. She was angry that they'd stored things on the staircase so I had tripped in my sleep.

My mother still lives in that house, but alone. She and my father bought it a few years before he died, and when the downstairs tenants moved away, my parents spread out into their apartment. Now she has two kitchens—one upstairs, one down—two living rooms, and many bedrooms. She seems even smaller in all this space. I picture the top of her head only halfway up a chair back, though that's an exaggeration.

My mother had tried baking bread the day I arrived, but the loaves never rose and she threw them out. "They were like thick matzoh," she said. In the morning we read the recipe and took out the ingredients. The yeast had to be soaked in a little bowl of warm water with a pinch of sugar. I liked the smell.

"The play opens tonight," said my mother.

"*Tonight!*" We were standing side by side watching the yeast bubble.

She nodded. "So," she said, "you're still seeing Parker?" I'd been sleeping with Parker for only a month and it was three days since I'd last mentioned him to her.

"Of course," I said. "It takes me at least a week to break up with people."

"Are you breaking up with Parker?" she said.

"No, I'm not breaking up with Parker."

Parker is considerably older than I am. I met him in the grocery store. I'm his third lover. The others were Karen and Simma. Karen has two golden retrievers and Simma is studying podiatry. Parker talked to me about them as if they were my cousins. He and his wife are now friends with both of them, and they know each other. The night we ate the Indian food, I told Parker about Aunt Freddie and about falling downstairs in my sleep.

"The time you slept over here, you walked in your sleep," he said.

"Why didn't you tell me?" I said. "Where did I go?"

"I don't know," he said. "I woke up and you were coming into the room. You said, 'Do you want me to water the plants?' I said, 'No, thank you, Ida; come back to bed,' and you did."

I was afraid of what I might have done in my sleep at Parker's house. "Does Sherry know you've had lovers?" I once asked him.

"Yes and no," he said. Who's to say I wouldn't write a note to his wife in my sleep, confessing, or alter something he wouldn't notice and she would? I might have harmed her, I thought. I might have put her box of Tampax out when she prefers to keep it discreetly hidden in the bathroom closet. I might have overwatered Sherry's plants.

My mother said some of the baking things were in the upstairs kitchen. There was a big board we would use to knead the dough. The day before, she'd used one she had downstairs, but it wasn't big enough. I went up and found the board and brought it down, using the front stairs, the ones we'd always used when I was a child. The rooms up there still seem more like home to me. I always sleep in my own old room upstairs, even though my mother sleeps downstairs.

"Do you remember when you fell down the back stairs in your sleep?" my mother said when I got back down.

"No," I lied. I didn't want her to know I remembered, because it's not something you could remember without pain.

"I was afraid you'd broken your back," said my mother.

"I can't remember," I said.

"What I worry about, with a married man," she said, "is that you'll get hurt."

"So I'll get hurt," I said, though I worried, too.

"He probably won't leave his wife," she said.

"No, I don't think he will."

She was stirring flour into the dough. "Do you think that's enough?"

"What does 'enough' mean?" Then she handed me the bowl and I understood she meant flour. When I stirred the dough, I could tell it needed more, but with a little more, it was enough. I had no trouble kneading.

"I didn't whack it like that yesterday," she said. "It was a worried day. I was worried about you on the plane, you with this man."

I slammed the dough on the board.

The cookbook said the dough had to rise in a warm place. She had tried the oven the day before, turning it on, then off. But she'd left the dough for hours and it didn't change. Now I searched the cookbooks until I found another suggestion. I put the bowl of dough, covered with a towel, in a pan of hot water. When we checked after a while, the ball was definitely bigger.

While the dough was rising, the phone rang and my mother answered. I knew from the way her voice tightened up that it was Parker. "She's right here," she said.

"I'll take it in the other room," I said.

"You might not want to do this," Parker said to me, and from the way he said "you" I had a feeling his wife was in the house—even in the room. He wanted to know if I'd stay in their house when he and his family went on vacation to an island somewhere. "You could water the plants," he said, "and take in the mail. But don't do it unless you want to—I thought you might like it." I said I'd think about it.

"He wants me to house-sit," I said to my mother.

"Are you going to do it?"

"I don't know."

"Is the neighborhood safe?"

I will never get used to the questions she asks and the ones she doesn't ask. "No neighborhood in a city is safe nowadays," I said. I checked again and the bread had risen.

*   *   *

PARKER AND I first met on the line at the corner grocery. He was ahead of me, hugging his milk and bananas, a gray-headed, haphazard bearded man with light, laughing eyes under big eyebrows, who searched the place with the gleam of someone facing his mistakes but not making too much of them, knowing they'll be forgiven. I fell for him immediately. He asked me, "Do you think I could slip out of the line and slip back? I forgot cookies."

"I'll hold your place," I said, meaning—I guess—"I will let you back in and throw my body on yours to protect you from those who may be angry." There were five or six people behind us.

Parker returned with Pepperidge Farm cookies and we talked about temptation. When we left the store we kept talking, then shook hands and said our names: "Ida Feldman." "Parker Stillman."

"Our names sound nice together," he said, touching my elbow as we went in different directions. "Nice funky bag." I always carry an old turquoise bag with lots of buckles.

But the first time we went to bed—after running into each other twice more and having a drink when his wife was away, followed by lovely kisses—while we were still naked he said to me, with that same shruggy look, a look that renounced all claims for himself, all presumption, "It's a measure of my insecurity that when I sleep with someone, it's someone like you."

"Like me?" I said, still feeling good.

"Well, you know," he said. I didn't answer. "You aren't exactly glamorous," he said. "I mean, of course, you don't *want* to be. . . . This is a *compliment*."

I'd been lying on my stomach on top of the blanket, my arms folded under my head. We were on a foldaway bed in his study. I rolled quickly onto my side, though he had not precisely said, "Your ass is too big." I said, "May I take a shower?"

"Oh, I said the wrong thing," he said. "This has to do with me—my hang-ups—not you."

"You remind me of someone I once slept with," I said, "but he was worse"—which made no sense, but I had to say something. In the shower, I wanted him to come into the bathroom and kiss me as the spray washed down my face. So I didn't give him up; it was as if I'd left something in his keeping. Picking it up at his house, I dropped something else that mattered.

MY MOTHER HAD never baked French bread before, but when I was twelve she baked a banana bread, which was easier. My father said it was excellent, and I should take a piece to his sister Freddie. Aunt Freddie has always lived alone, and when I was a child, her solitude sometimes made her seem powerful—she was the only one in the family who could leave a gathering without persuading some-body to come along—and sometimes it made her weak: when she went, it made a small dent in the group. On the issue of food, she was considered a little helpless.

My mother wrapped up a piece of banana bread and I set out. Aunt Freddie lived six blocks away. On the way, I came to a corner and wondered what it would be like to walk around it instead of continuing on my route, and then I did walk around it. Around the corner, things seemed glittery, as if someone had strewn a few se-quins.

I walked for block after block in increasing astonishment, as excited as if I were lost, though I knew where I was. Eventually I threw the banana bread into a garbage can and turned around and went home.

My mother said, "Did she like it?" and I said yes. A week later, my mother mentioned the banana bread to Aunt Freddie on the phone. She probably didn't ask about it directly; she probably said something like "I needed eggs because I used the last one in that banana bread," timidly encouraging Aunt Freddie to thank her for it—and then Aunt Freddie must have said, "What banana bread?"

When I came home from school, my mother looked frightened. "Ida," she said, "Aunt Freddie says she never got the banana bread."

"Is that so?"

"Did you eat it yourself? I'd have given you more."

"I didn't eat it, I threw it away."

My mother flinched. "Wasn't it good?" she said.

"It was good."

"I can't imagine why you did that," she said.

"I don't know why," I said, and went to my room. Later I came out and screamed at her, "Doesn't it *bother* you that I threw away the banana bread?"

"I think you must have had a good reason," my mother said, "but I don't know what it was."

THE FRENCH BREAD—two loaves—was baked with a pan of water in the oven. We weren't sure how long it should bake. It smelled great. When we took it out, I thought it might be overdone but we couldn't tell. Forty minutes before the performance, we handed a loaf over to Aunt Freddie at the theater, a little auditorium in a school. Aunt Freddie was counting props, counting arriving actors, counting chairs and tickets. Her big head, covered with white curls, kept popping up on all sides of us. She was wearing billowing black pants and a smock. She took time to give me a kiss. We're just the same size, and when I hug Aunt Freddie I feel like the other side of a yin-yang puzzle. "Ida," she said then, pulling me by the elbow down the aisle, leaving my mother behind, "I understand you're seeing a married man."

"Yes."

"How *interesting,*" she said. "I never thought you'd do something so interesting." Then she stopped and stood up straight. "But wrong," she said, and took my hand in one of hers to position it, then slapped it with her other hand.

IN THE PLAY, a carpenter is showing his girlfriend a house he and his boss are renovating. We see the living room, with some lumber and tools on the floor. One wall has been plastered and taped but not painted. The house is being made into apartments where former residents of a psychiatric hospital will live, and as the carpenter and his girlfriend are touring and kissing, a social worker and two of her clients—future residents of the apartments—arrive to see it. The doorbell rings again, and it is a woman from the neighborhood, a NIMBY type who is afraid the mental patients (a grumpy but obviously harmless man and a sad, quiet woman) will be dangerous. The neighborhood woman is carrying a bag of groceries. She's on her way home from the store and has rung the bell because she saw a light in the house. As they all talk, there are shouts and the sounds of sirens—all of which, I'd been told in advance, were the responsibility of Aunt Freddie. I thought I recognized Aunt Freddie's voice as one of the shouters. A loud voice says to the group on stage, "This is the police." An escaping bank robber has taken them all hostage. He is camped on the front steps of the house and is threatening to shoot into the windows if the police come any closer.

The rest of the play is what happens to the people trapped inside. They get hungry. The neighborhood woman, believe it or not, has in her bag flour, yeast, salt, and sugar, and the carpenter sets out to bake bread, aided by the grumpy man from the hospital. Together, the group figures out what to do, though nobody has done it before. Each person seems to know one step. "I think you have to moisten the yeast," says the woman psychiatric patient, coming out of her silence. (My mother nodded vigorously.) A baking pan turns up in a cabinet. The carpenter goes through steps that seemed startlingly familiar (but much in this play seemed like something I'd experienced in another life), mixing and kneading the dough. Sometimes he runs offstage, to a kitchen we don't see. In the carpenter's case, warming the dough in the oven works—but of course, he wasn't really doing it.

Meanwhile, the social worker tells the girlfriend her troubles, the NIMBY lady makes friends with the woman patient, and so forth. After an intermission, the carpenter hands around the pieces of bread—and that was even odder, because of course it was our bread. My mother, next to me in the second row, squeezed my hand and I squeezed back, then patted her enthusiastically on the shoulder, then squeezed again. I thought she was the most remarkable mother, to have gotten us into this situation. Onstage, everyone was eating our bread—the carpenter, the social worker, the residents-to-be, the NIMBY lady, and the girlfriend. We'd baked it too long after all. It was hard to chew—you could see them working their jaws up and down. There were crumbs all over the stage.

At the end of the play, the NIMBY lady (who has changed her mind about psychiatric patients) and the girlfriend give the bank robber the last piece of bread through the window. He gets into a conversation with them and turns out to be the son of the woman patient. In fact, his life of crime was what drove her crazy. He is deeply moved at the sight of his mother and gives himself up. She already shows signs of improvement as the curtain calls begin.

AUNT FREDDIE WAS worn out after the play was over, and we helped her straighten up. We promised to bake more bread. "I feel like baking right now," said my mother, when we got home. She was that excited.

"Would the gas and water be on in an empty house?" I said.

"The water would be on, and they could have had an electric stove," said my mother. "The electricity was on. Those were power tools."

"My kids could write a less sappy play than that," I said. "The coincidence was ridiculous."

"Amazing coincidences happen to me all the time," said my mother. "Maybe they don't happen to your students."

I walked in my sleep that night, but not down the back staircase. I was dreaming I had to do something, I don't remember what, and when I woke up I was half dressed in the clothes I'd left on a chair. I undressed and went back to bed, where I began to think about all I could do in Parker's big, comfortable house, asleep or awake. Then I thought how bad I'd feel in his house without him, while he was away. I imagined myself crying in the daybed, and I felt so sorry for myself that I cried there in Rochester, in my own old room, too. Simma and Karen had probably also house-sat. That was how everybody got to be friends, and now it was already my turn. I wondered if Simma and Karen had lasted longer as lovers. Parker would tell Sherry I was an interesting woman he'd met at the grocery store, a teacher. He'd introduce us. The affair would become a three-way friendship, though Sherry would always wonder. "Friendship," Parker would say to me, when I'd protest, "is harder and rarer than a sexual connection. And my wife is a much better person than I am." Which was surely true.

I could hear my mother walking around in the downstairs kitchen. It was two A.M., but she had said when she couldn't sleep, she fixed herself a snack. "Hot cereal is nice," she'd said.

"I might break up with him," I could say to her. "Not because he's married," I'd probably say. "I might find someone else who's married." I didn't want to say that if Parker wasn't going to hurt me anymore, someone else would; if I couldn't hurt Parker, I'd hurt someone else. I climbed out of bed, opened the door that had been closed all through my girlhood (except for the night when I walked in my sleep), and walked down the back stairs toward her.

CHARLOTTE LOPRESTI ONCE fell out of her life, at twenty-four. Charlotte had been born in New York, but she was living in California at that time, working as a community organizer in a youth program in Fresno. It was the sixties and there was poverty money, as some people called it—government funding for social agencies. The director of the youth program was a red-haired, difficult man named Lionel, and the only other employee was Luis Talamante, a young Mexican-American man; the Youth of the Youth Program, Lionel called him.

One day Charlotte and Luis drove the agency's old VW microbus down an obscure road into the country. The program ran a training course for baby-sitters, and Charlotte and Luis were engaged in what was called Outreach. ("Reach out! Reach out!" Lionel had called, as Charlotte backed the van out of its parking place behind their storefront office.) They drove to a migrant labor camp, where they hoped to pick up three girls who had attended the earlier classes. Two more lived in Fresno and would meet them at the office, where a nurse was going to discuss infant care.

"They've been baby-sitting since they were two," said Charlotte. "This is perfectly ridiculous."

"They are good girls," said Luis.

When they arrived at the camp, only one of the regular

participants, a girl of ten, was waiting for them, but as if to prove Charlotte's point, she had brought along her two little brothers, a toddler and an infant.

"The nurse was *planning* to demonstrate on a *doll*," said Charlotte, hearing what she was coming to think of as New York intensity in her own voice, its pitch rising and falling rapidly. She was amused, but Luis probably thought she was spoiled and impatient. Later she was asked why she had simply loaded all the children into the van as if they really were three novice baby-sitters. It was hard to explain. The excursion into the country, the baby-sitting course, even the youth program itself struck Charlotte as slightly silly but harmless. She thought they did help the children of Mexican-American farm workers, but mostly by mistake. That afternoon, for example, the nurse might bathe the baby. It was hot: a bath would refresh him.

Charlotte couldn't quite make out the baby's name. It was either Martín or Esteban, and Charlotte, who knew only a little Spanish, couldn't understand his sister's explanation of why she called him first one name, then the other.

"It's not important," said Luis. His proper job would be disarming youthful bandits.

Whatever his name, the baby began to cry bitterly—frighteningly, Charlotte said later. "Children cry," Luis said, but Charlotte insisted that this crying was different, something was wrong, it was a medical emergency. Then the baby threw up, and Charlotte drove to the hospital, where, after a two-hour wait, Martín or Esteban stopped crying and a doctor said nothing was the matter.

Meanwhile, though, Lionel had locked up the office and gone to a meeting he would later claim Charlotte knew about. One nine-year-old girl showed up for the baby-sitting class. When she found the door locked she ran home in tears, but was hit by a car, which broke her leg. The nurse who was supposed to discuss baby care arrived just after the police and the ambulance, and told the whole story to a newspaper reporter. She had opposed the youth program from the start, it turned out. Now the project was investigated, Charlotte was accused of irresponsible behavior, and a citizens' committee demanded that the program's budget be withdrawn. Newspaper articles appeared; angry board meetings were held. The little girl had a permanent limp.

"Why didn't I send Luis to the office?" Charlotte asked herself and Lionel over and over again.

"You were afraid he'd wreck the van," Lionel would say. "And you weren't thinking."

When the nurse attacked the program before the town board of supervisors, the local Mexican-American leaders didn't defend it. Not only had Charlotte been careless with their children, but she'd registered the baby at the hospital under the wrong name, Martín, because she was too ignorant or uninterested to learn that his name was Esteban, and she had invited the nurse to speak. Everyone knew that the nurse was unfriendly to Mexican Americans.

Lionel slapped his forehead and glared at her with each new attack, but he insisted the trouble would die down. When a hostile newspaper story came out, he invariably said, "Line the parakeet's cage with it!" though they had no parakeet. But he called the incident "Charlotte's Mess."

To her astonishment, Charlotte fell in love with him. By the end of the first year, the trouble was over, Luis had gone off to college in San Francisco, and Charlotte was sleeping with Lionel. She had made one woman friend in Fresno, and this woman was skeptical. "We have the same sense of humor," Charlotte kept telling her friend. "And the same values, at some level."

"No, you don't," said the friend, who had handed Charlotte tissues for weeks while Charlotte wept over the attacks on the program and over the girl with the broken leg.

One weekend Lionel and Charlotte went camping in Yosemite, driving north through Modesto to get to a high wilderness lake Lionel knew about. They backpacked a mile from their car to a campsite on the lake and slept there. In the morning, Charlotte awoke first, started a fire, and made coffee, but when she had drunk it, Lionel was still sleeping. A visible trail to a nearby peak began, invitingly, right near their campsite. Lionel had warned her that mountains in California weren't like those in the East. "They're not little bumps next to a parking lot," he had said. But Charlotte left him a note and set off alone up the trail.

It didn't look steep, but soon she was sweaty, fighting mosquitoes. The rocks grew larger and rougher. She had to scramble. She'd been hiking for over an hour when she came to an open place from which she could see down to their lake. She could even see Lionel—a dark figure—and she waved hard, but he didn't raise his arm.

She knew she should turn around, but she didn't. The peak looked close. The climb took another hour, but reaching the peak she was elated. There was a field of snow, though it was July. Charlotte ate snow. The sweat on her body dried and the wind chilled her. When she started down again, singing out loud in what she identified as *joy,* she began to trot, hurrying back to Lionel. But the going was difficult, even dangerous. She returned to the campsite exhausted.

Lionel was grim. Climbing alone, she had risked falling, hypothermia, dehydration. She hadn't even brought water. "I ate snow!" said Charlotte, but he kept talking.

She saw that he was right. She would never again climb a steep hill alone. But the disdain in his voice, entering ears that still ached with the thrilling cold of the mountaintop, changed her. She knelt near the lake to wet her face, and the cold water felt like another self bringing news to her cheeks and lips.

They packed and left Yosemite a few hours before they'd planned to. They drove down from the Sierras through land that was less and less mountainous, on a road with looser and looser curves—like string falling off a ball—until they reached the flat valley. The straight road into Modesto glittered with heat. Just outside of town, they stopped at a traffic light. Charlotte studied the face of a hitchhiker, a dark-haired man with a pack and a blanket roll who stood just beyond the intersection with his thumb extended. While traffic was stopped and no cars passed him, he began to walk—first backward, keeping an eye on the road, then, turning, facing in the direction he was going. Now Charlotte looked at the back of his head: medium-length, thick, wavy hair; a white T-shirt.

"I know that man," she said.

"What man?"

"The hitchhiker. He's a friend of my brother's. My brother's been worried about him."

"He's from New York?"

"Yes. He's running from his draft board, I guess. I don't know what he's doing here. Listen," she said. "Let me out. I'm going to talk to him."

"We don't have time," he said.

"No, I don't mean that," she said. "You keep going."

"How will you get home?"

"I'll hitch with him into Modesto. He's shy. He'd clam up if you were there. I'll take the bus home."

The light changed, and before Lionel could protest she reached into the back seat for her pack and got out of the car.

The hitchhiker, who had turned again, saw the opened car door and began to lope toward them, his blanket roll bouncing. Charlotte shook her head at him, smiling and shrugging, and banged the door closed. Lionel had driven into the intersection and stopped, but she waved him on. Cars behind him were honking, and Lionel drove away. The hitchhiker reached Charlotte and smiled inquiringly.

It wasn't true that she knew him. She'd never seen him before. She never returned to Fresno or to Lionel. Eventually she married the hitchhiker, a former seminary student, now an English teacher at the junior college in Sacramento. His name was Philip LoPresti, and he was a plain, big-nosed man with wide hands. He loved to tell their friends, later, that she'd decided to marry him before she got out of the car. "I was that attractive in those days," he'd say, shaking his head bemusedly. "It's true."

He had seemed attractive the way the mountain peak was attractive: scary—but Charlotte saw that error quickly. When he looked at her in the street, he seemed amused even though he didn't yet know what was funny. He was ready to tell her his secrets and to listen to hers. They walked most of the way into Modesto and then got a short ride with a woman bringing home her groceries. They had supper in a tidy park, sharing leftovers from their backpacks. Philip had some grass to smoke. Mildly stoned, they both took the bus to Sacramento.

Charlotte slept on Philip's sofa. He had a cat and she discovered that it had fleas. For days her work was pinching out the cat's fleas and drowning them in a glass of water. Then she found a babysitting job so she could help with the rent. After a week she called her friend in Fresno. "I figured you went to New York—or Canada—with this friend of your brother's," she said, and it took Charlotte a moment to remember who that might be. Philip wouldn't hear of her simply walking out of her life. "You expect your landlord to deal with dirty dishes in the sink and spoiled food in the refrigerator? And you own a car."

They borrowed a pickup truck, drove to Fresno, and emptied the apartment. Philip apologized to the landlord. Charlotte picked up her car. They did not see Lionel before driving back, and she never resigned from her job.

*   *   *

BUT CHARLOTTE AND Philip have lived out their lives on the east coast. After their first daughter, Amy, was born, they moved to New Haven, where Philip teaches at Gateway Community College. Charlotte first went back to school at Yale, thinking she'd become a professor, but dropped out because she was pregnant again, with another daughter, Olivia. Also, she wanted to work directly with clients. She got a job in a clinic for the elderly at Yale–New Haven Hospital. By now Amy is in college, Olivia in high school, and Charlotte has worked at the clinic for years.

Charlotte and Philip have the same best friend, a single woman named Daisy, who also teaches at the community college, and seems to live just to the side of Philip's mind. "We could give some to Daisy," he says of any bounty that comes to him and Charlotte— bushels of apples they pick themselves at an orchard, extra cookies or political pamphlets or poems. Charlotte discusses Philip with Daisy and Daisy with Philip, and yet nobody gets angry. She assumes Philip and Daisy also discuss her, but what do they say? "She does get carried away!"—would that be it?

"I almost cried," she said to Philip one night, about something that had happened at work.

"Probably it didn't matter," said Philip.

It was bedtime. He was fixing himself a peanut butter and jelly sandwich. The peanut butter jar was on the counter, the jelly on the stove top, both open. He stood in the middle of the room, the uncut sandwich looking small in his big hands. His hair was still dark. He laughed at her.

"Listen to me!" said Charlotte, annoyed. "I could do something stupid."

"You're not like Daisy," he said. "I overhear her at work, and she says the damnedest things to students. I love her, but I worry about her judgment."

He said it as if Daisy just happened to be the example that came to his mind, though she was always his example. While he talked about Daisy, though he was criticizing her, he was looking at the phone, and sure enough, it rang. Daisy often called just about now, at a quarter to eleven, because she knew Charlotte and Philip went to bed at eleven. Fifteen minutes was supposed to be enough, but it never was. When the phone rang with what Charlotte had come to think of as Daisy's ring, Philip tried to look irritated, hurrying to chew, but he looked eager instead. Charlotte felt less annoyed because she could see through him, which she liked. She could go to bed as soon as she made sure he wasn't going to leave the peanut butter open on the counter all night. He greeted Daisy.

"I know, I know," he said after a while. "But I thought you were moving in with Pekko." Pekko was Daisy's boyfriend. Then, "No, I don't want to hear the whole story. I'm having an argument with Charlotte, and I'm on the way to bed."

Charlotte leaned in the doorway. "Oh, she claims she blew it with a client," Philip was saying, but meanwhile he was clutching the phone between his head and shoulder while he put the lid on the peanut butter. Charlotte went to bed.

An old man had been brought into her office by a crowd of sons. The room was small, and they could barely squeeze in: a seething mob of young to middle-aged men, all losing reddish hair, some dressed like laborers, some in jackets and ties. When she stopped and counted the sons, there were only three. The father was forgetful. "He left the stove on!" accused the oldest brother, the one in a tie. "He burned a pan!"

"Eventually he realized," said the youngest brother, a quiet fellow in a work shirt who told Charlotte he worked for the dog warden.

The old man looked apologetically at Charlotte. His hair was white; his hairline curved like his sons' hairlines, but more deeply.

"We need a coherent plan!" said the oldest brother impatiently. His voice turned sarcastic. "Perhaps, ma'am, you don't realize . . ."

The middle brother turned to him. Charlotte had the impression of an honest fellow who worked with his hands, which he pounded on his own thighs and on her desk. "You!" he said to his older brother, and his chair knocked back against the wall. "You hit him! You went in there and hit Dad!"

"Nonsense," said the oldest brother calmly. "I'm the one who checks up on him. I found him choking. He'd have died—"

"Wait," whispered the youngest brother.

"Half of what my father says doesn't make sense," said the oldest brother, but Charlotte had already—unprofessionally—sided with the youngest one, who reminded her of the youngest brother in a fairy tale, someone who might take advice from talking animals. The oldest brother glared and looked away. Charlotte began talking hesitantly about Meals on Wheels, adult day care. When the oldest brother cleared his throat, she felt an agreement to hate flow between them.

"IT MADE PHILIP happy when you called last night," Charlotte told Daisy the next day. "Even though it was late."

"Good," said Daisy. "I needed him." They were driving to look at an apartment Daisy might move to. "I couldn't bear it if you were jealous," she said.

"Jealous?" said Charlotte, instantly picturing Philip and Daisy naked in bed together. It wasn't likely, she decided, almost disappointed, for the thought had given her a faint thrill.

At the apartment, which had a fireplace but was too expensive, Charlotte felt nostalgic. She loved looking at apartments with friends, and imagined moving into them herself and living alone in them. She and Philip and the children had lived in the same house for years, a fine house.

From the apartment she and Daisy went to a bar, where they sat at a small table. The bar was crowded with people watching a hockey game on television.

"Pekko thinks I've been fooling around with a student," Daisy said.

"He's not jealous of your students!" Pekko had a big white beard—he might be doing anything behind that beard. He owned a frozen-yogurt store.

"One particular student," Daisy said. "He's in his twenties, and we're friends. We *are* friends. And he works cleaning houses, so I had him over to my house to do one or two things."

"And Pekko is jealous of this?" said Charlotte. "What does he think, this guy will be vacuuming under your bed and you'll jump him?"

"I don't know what he thinks."

"That kind of jealousy baffles me," Charlotte said.

"That's because you're married to someone who doesn't fool around."

"Are you defending Pekko, then?" she said.

"No, I'm not defending him," said Daisy. "But I understand jealousy."

Charlotte had been aware for a while of a loud voice at the bar, dominating the room. A man was shouting. It had been bothering her before she thought about it. Now everyone in the place was speaking loudly, and the air had sharpened. "Infantile!" the man was saying. "That kind of thinking is infantile!"

Then he left his seat. Charlotte thought he was coming over to them—in fact, he looked at her and looked away, and she had the sensation of being kept from something she ought to know. The man was moving toward a woman just behind her—apparently he wanted to extend the argument to include the woman. "I can't *stand* this shouting!" said Charlotte as he passed, her own voice surprising her: it was loud itself, pouring out of her the way a trained actor's must, an actor who wants to be heard at the back of the balcony sounding conversational. She wanted the man to fight with her, she thought, one second too late to stop herself—and then she recognized him. It was the old man's oldest son. The man who had hit his father.

It was too late. "Do you have some *complaint* about me, Ms. Social Worker?" he was saying, his voice scornful. "Because I have a few about you."

"Fuck you," she screamed, and then repeated it standing up. All she could think, hearing herself, was that Philip should have listened when she was worried. Now she had done something serious. She let Daisy hustle her outside. She cried in the car. "He just seemed like an ordinary drunk to me," Daisy said.

"He's probably a murderer," said Charlotte, and all but wished he were. At home, where Daisy dropped her off, she found Philip and Olivia watching the hockey game. "Don't you have homework?" she said to Olivia with leftover anger. "What about your paper?"

"I'm taking a break," said Olivia.

"You have a paper to write?" said Philip. Only two pages, but it had to be in French. Olivia dragged herself upstairs and Charlotte had a fight with Philip, first because he hadn't asked Olivia about homework, then about the old man's oldest son.

"It's embarrassing that you shouted in the bar, but it doesn't *matter*," Philip said.

"I just couldn't handle his turning up there."

"Maybe he's the devil," said Philip. "If you meet the devil, you just say 'God.' The devil can't hang around if he hears the name of God."

"I should have been able to deal with him."

"With the *devil?*"

"Will you shut up about the devil?" said Charlotte, shouting again. "You can't take anything seriously—not me, not Olivia. And Daisy's in trouble and you aren't helping her either." She was surprised that she said that; she didn't know she had thought Daisy was in trouble.

"What do you mean, in trouble?"

"Pekko thinks she's sleeping with a student."

"Oh, *that* fellow," he said.

"She isn't sleeping with him," said Charlotte.

"I didn't say she was. She needs to be more careful. The way things are now—the very idea of teachers fooling around with students. You're not even allowed to *think* of it."

"Oh, you sound so pompous and superior," Charlotte said. "You assume Daisy has no judgment. You're just jealous. You wish Daisy would sleep with *you.*"

"With me?" said Philip, and he looked so surprised that she almost laughed. "Where would we do it? In our cubicles? Hers or mine?"

"Fuck you," said Charlotte, even though Olivia was coming down the stairs, even though it was what she'd said to the man in the bar who might have been the devil. She went crying to bed, leaving him to deal with Olivia, who had now panicked about the paper in French. How could she write a paper in French? Her father didn't understand her. He didn't understand how hard things were for her. Cheering her daughter for abusing her father until it was too late to write the paper, too late to get up on time in the morning, Charlotte fell asleep.

* * *

IN A COPY of the Yale Calendar lying on a colleague's desk, Charlotte spotted a notice. Professor Luis Talamante, chair of the Chicano Studies Department at the California State University at Chico, was to lecture. For a moment she thought it had to be an older man with the same name as the boy she'd worked with in Fresno, but then she realized that Luis would now be forty-three. Of course, it *still* might just be someone else with the same name. His topic was "The Politics of Irrigation in the American Southwest." She made a note of the date and place. She tried to remember the silent boy she'd worked with.

The old man's oldest son complained about Charlotte to the director of the clinic. He asked to have his father assigned to a different social worker. That hadn't happened to Charlotte before. The director spoke earnestly to her about it. "I made some mistakes," said Charlotte.

"He's a difficult person. But he said you were abusive."

"I was abusive?"

"I doubt it."

Charlotte had just finished work for the day and she drove to Daisy's apartment. Daisy was packing pots and pans; she had found an apartment and signed a lease, and she was moving in just a few days. "Was I drunk that night?" said Charlotte.

"On one glass of wine?"

"Why did that happen?"

"You were attracted," said Daisy. "Or threatened. Or both."

"Now I'll never prove he's hitting the old man."

"Won't someone else prove it?"

"But I'm the best," said Charlotte. She had failed.

"What does Philip think?"

"Philip?" said Charlotte. "We're hardly talking."

"You and Philip? You two never stop talking."

"Since that night we've hardly talked." It had been four or five days.

Daisy began crumpling newspaper into wineglasses and wrapping them. Charlotte picked up a glass and a piece of newspaper. "When are you moving, exactly?"

"Friday." It was the day of Luis's talk. Charlotte wanted to help Daisy move, but she couldn't miss the talk. She told Daisy about Luis.

"Will you recognize him?"

"I don't know." Charlotte could remember dark hair, a hesitant but arrogant way of holding the head.

"Don't worry about helping me," Daisy said. "Pekko and Philip both promised to come. If Pekko isn't too mad at me to show up. Everybody's angry this week. Maybe it's the moon."

"He's still angry?" said Charlotte. "About that student?"

"About the student." Daisy was carrying things to the table and leaning over to put them into boxes. She was very thin. Charlotte had often envied Daisy's thinness. Her body looked fragile. It wasn't clear why fragility should seem enviable. Charlotte pictured herself strong and big, breaking things.

"So you let the kid clean for you," she said. "So what?"

"He did some work for Pekko, too," said Daisy.

"Pekko knows him?"

"He did some work at his place. He painted a rowboat."

"But now Pekko's jealous?"

"Well," Daisy said, and her arms, lifting a heavy box, looked almost as if they'd snap at a touch. Such lovely, pitiable arms. Charlotte took the box from her and carried it down the hall. When she came back, Daisy looked straight at her and said, "I did sleep with him a couple of times. When he came here to clean."

"You did? Why on earth?"

"I don't know," Daisy said. "He's attractive. Oh, I don't even know if that's true. He's young. I was flattered that he was interested. But then—this is awful—I had to give him money."

"You mean money for sex?"

"Well, no," said Daisy. "Of course not. For cleaning my house. But it felt like—"

"It must have felt bad."

"It felt terrible."

Instantly Charlotte imagined scandal, newspaper stories, Daisy's losing her job. She couldn't fathom how she and Daisy could both be so childish, with all the choices and privileges of adult, middle-class people. They deserved whatever happened to them.

CHARLOTTE WAS LATE to Luis Talamante's lecture. The man at the podium might or might not have been the Luis she knew. He had glasses and graying hair. He *could* have been forty-three; at least, he wasn't thirty or sixty. He had a slight Spanish accent. He read his lecture, which Charlotte found difficult to follow. When it was over she lingered, and after a couple of students had asked him questions, she approached him and said she'd enjoyed his talk.

"I was nervous," he said, as if they knew each other. "But I hope it was all right."

"I think I know you," she said.

"Oh, of course, of course," he said cordially. "I can't remember your name." She told him, and explained that she'd worked with someone called Luis Talamante at a youth project in Fresno in 1968.

"Merced, wasn't it?" he said.

"No, Fresno. I was the one," she said, "who took the baby to the hospital . . . and there was nothing wrong with him and there was a huge outcry? Do you remember? You left while it was still going on—that is, the Luis Talamante who was there left then. The director was Lionel Hughes?"

"Lionel Hughes?" he said. "The man who went to prison?"

"What?" she said. "Lionel? For what?"

"Oh, it was not important," he said.

"Did he hurt someone?" she said, talking fast. "It wasn't political?" Lionel's face came vaguely to mind—unless it was the face of the old man's devilish son. "Oh, my goodness!" she said. "You just helped me understand something—a problem I've been having—a man who upset me—"

But Luis was speaking. "Oh, no, not political. But small." She tried to speak, but he interrupted. "But you," he said. "Have you had a good life? You have children? I have a son and a daughter."

He took out his wallet and showed her a picture of two teenagers. Charlotte told him about Amy and Olivia. She mentioned her job and he nodded with approval. She mentioned Philip's job.

"You think I don't remember you but I do," he said. "You were lively. Flamboyant. I was afraid of you, but you were good. Energetic."

"Thank you," she said, wondering.

"Once, when my son was small," Luis said, "my wife and I panicked and drove him to the hospital. That time, too, there was nothing wrong. But how were we to know?"

For a second Charlotte thought this proved he was her Luis, and she felt as if she'd been forgiven at last. Then she remembered that she herself had just told the professor that she'd taken a child to the hospital needlessly. Luis shook hands with her. Two dressed-up faculty members were waiting to take him to dinner, and they looked impatient. She was left alone in the auditorium thinking of Luis—either this man or some other Luis—who had grown up, as she had; who had married, perhaps, and had children.

BUT CHARLOTTE WAS supposed to be helping Daisy move, and so she hurried to her car and drove to the new apartment, a first floor in a three-family house with a big porch. It was late spring, and the

streets were filled with wide, dark leaves that would not look quite
so big and moist again. Charlotte didn't see a truck at the new house,
but she parked and rang the doorbell, and then tried the outer and
inner doors, which were open. The front room—big, light, and
square—was cool and smelled of new paint. It was empty. It had
oak flooring, somewhat scarred. Like a young person looking around
to see what kind of life she was going to have, Charlotte stepped
inside. She heard someone coming. It was Philip, with a broom.

"I hoped it was you," he said.

"Hi."

"Was it the same guy?"

"I don't know," said Charlotte. "He said he was, but I'm not
sure."

"Did you ask him if he's forty-three?"

"No."

"Why not? That would prove it."

"If he wasn't forty-three," said Charlotte, thinking it out, "it
would prove he wasn't Luis. But if he *was* forty-three, there could
still be two men named Luis Talamante who are *both* forty-three."

She walked across the big room toward him, her feet sounding
loud on the wooden floor. It wasn't that she wanted to live there.
The things she had said and done, the people she knew and what
they had said and done—none of it would disappear if she could live
there.

"Oh, Charlotte," said Philip. He hardly ever said her name. She
loved it when he did. He rested his arms on her shoulders, deftly
shifting the broom in his big hands so it hung down her back but
neither hit her over the head nor got dust in her hair. "Charlotte,"
he said again. "Such an interesting wife."

CLAPPING SEASON

WHEN PROFESSOR GRADSTEIN called Rebecca for directions to her school, he began, "Exactly which bit of urban blight are we discussing?" and of course Rebecca turned defensive. He was coming to see the results of a writing project on which Rebecca and her third-graders had spent the year. They'd written books. He was coming to the publication party. It was spring: clapping season. The books were finished, Rebecca's grandson Jamie was going to play Bach in a recital the next evening, and the professor, too, it seemed, was coming to the end of some work.

"Even in neighborhoods like the one where my school is," said Rebecca, "most of the children come from stable homes."

"My paper on that topic is just out," he said. "I'll send you an offprint."

"What are you writing now?" she asked politely.

"It's almost done—a book about schools. *The Open Hand, the Tight Fist: Poor Black Children in the Nineties*."

"Not all my poor kids are black," she said. "Not all my black kids are poor."

"I know, I know. Give me directions. I'm not local. I'm spending the year at Yale."

At least he didn't ask where she lived, so she'd have to

apologize for moving to the suburbs. "Only *one* suburb," her husband, Joel, used to say. "Where else can I design a house?"

She hung up the phone and it rang. "You haven't forgotten the recital?" said her daughter, Irene.

"I haven't forgotten." Irene had two sons: Dennis, who was almost grown and a worry, and Jamie, who was twelve and took piano lessons. They had different fathers.

"What's Dennis up to?" Rebecca said. Dennis had been a perfect five-year-old. She'd had a sabbatical that year and Joel had just retired, so once a week Dennis had spent the day with his grandparents. They'd go birdwatching.

"I wouldn't know," said Irene.

"No, you wouldn't." She added, "I have to say what I think," before Irene could accuse her.

"I know you do, Mom."

They said good-bye, Rebecca in the low, glass-walled house in Guilford Joel had designed but not lived in (he had died two years ago, as the house was being finished), and Irene in her pleasantly dilapidated house in New Haven fifteen miles away. But before she could let Irene go, Rebecca asked, "Is anything changing, do you think? With Dennis?"

"No."

"Am I making it worse, asking questions?"

"Well, you are," said Irene. "Oh, stop making me say things like that!"

In Rebecca's classroom, the next morning, the books were spread out on a table, their edges bristling with staples. Some parents had come, and as everyone got ready, one man stood near the table and read all the books, though the children were going to read them aloud. It was Theodore's father—a black man with a quiet voice, like Theodore's. "Do you want to see Theodore's book?" she asked him.

"I'm curious about all of them," he said.

Theodore's book was about insects: bees, ants, mosquitoes, and tarantulas (which, Theodore had told her, were actually arachnids). Theodore stood waiting behind his father.

Rebecca had attended a teachers' seminar at which she'd learned how to help her pupils write books, and they'd talked long there about assembling them. Some favored sewing the books with yarn. You took three sheets of typing paper, folded them in half, and sewed along the crease. The outside sheet was the cover, and inside were eight pages.

But Rebecca had wanted her students free to write at length or briefly, and sure enough, one boy's book was only two pages long and in fact contained only two words—his name and the name of his mother, Clarissa, with many extra *s*'s. Another book was so thick it had to be stapled from both the back and the front. The children had begun with half sheets of paper, written and illustrated the books, then made covers, then stapled everything together. She'd had to supervise the stapling: all those skinny fingers were nearly stabbed . . . but none was. She'd let the children use all the staples they wanted, and the edges of the books were wondrous with them.

Now Theodore's father looked up from a book and said, "Some of these kids know too much," and Rebecca decided to begin, though he still hadn't read Theodore's book, and the professor was late. She gathered the books in her arm and distributed them to their authors while the children pulled their chairs into a circle and made room for the parents. Two mothers had set out lemonade and cupcakes. The children would read their books aloud, and then everyone would have refreshments. Now they all sat expectantly, with sun shining into half the people's eyes, until Rebecca, who loved sun, took pity and lowered the ugly shades. She turned to the child on her left, who happened to be Aaron. Aaron's book was a good one to start with: dull but not too long. "Once there was a horse and he lived in a barn," Aaron began slowly.

Professor Gradstein came in. He was a little man in a jacket and tie. He nodded all around apologetically. Rebecca stopped Aaron to introduce the professor. She liked him better in person than on the phone. He pulled a small chair into the circle.

"Go on, Aaron," said Rebecca.

"The horse had spots," read Aaron. When he finished, everyone clapped. Aaron held up the book, turning the pages so they could see all the pictures. The children crowded around and Rebecca had to send them back to their seats. "I didn't see the horse," one child said. "I *still* didn't see the horse."

Elena read about a car with a flat tire. Then came Caleb's story, about a boy who was beaten with a stick. "My grandma, she hit me with a stick," one child interrupted, and then a chorus interrupted.

"Let's let Caleb finish," said Rebecca, but three or four more children had to tell how they were beaten, or not beaten. Tamika had been caught doing wrong but not beaten. Rebecca glanced at Professor Gradstein, who was looking intently at each speaker in turn.

" 'The Lady's Bed,' " said LuAnn, as soon as Caleb had finished and the clapping subsided. LuAnn had written one of the longest stories. "A lady's bed was broken and a man came to fix the bed," she said, stopping to display an illustration—a bed with a piece of a leg broken off. She spoke in a loud, clear voice. "Then the lady and the man got into the bed and they fooled around. The lady gave the man money. The man took the money. The man wanted frozen yogurt. He gave the lady in the frozen yogurt store all the money. The lady in the store said, 'Hey, that's too much money.' " Here LuAnn showed a picture of a man and a woman with a counter between them. The man was eating a cone. She continued, "The man said, 'When I come, you give me frozen yogurt.' Then the man got free frozen yogurt every day."

Everyone clapped. Professor Gradstein clapped loudly and slowly, his hands hollowed.

The next child mumbled. When he was finished, Theodore's father spoke. "That little girl," he said, pointing back at LuAnn. "I don't know why these children are making up these things instead of learning," he said. "You can bet at some private school those children are *learning*."

"Doesn't this count?" said Rebecca, startled. He had spoken in a low, urgent voice, but everyone could hear.

"Folks going to bed for money!" said Theodore's father.

Professor Gradstein watched Rebecca and watched Theodore's father.

"At the seminar I attended," Rebecca said, "there were teachers from private schools, and they were planning programs just like this."

"And let those children write about sex?"

"Yes." She struggled with herself: had the teachers from private schools favored yarn sewing more than staples? Would children be less likely to write about sex if the books were made in advance, each with eight pages? Two books coming up mentioned drugs and shooting, she remembered. Maybe she had done wrong; maybe something about her, despite her neat denim dress and gray hair, encouraged license. She nodded to the next child, Jamal, to begin. Luckily, he had written about a birthday party. And next to him was his best friend, Daniel, who had written "Daniel" and "Clarissa." When it was his turn, Daniel smiled at Rebecca and opened his book and said, "Daniel," and then he turned the page and looked to see what came next and said, "Clarissa"—and the real Clarissa, his mother, was present. She stood up and waved both hands high in the air, her fingers all waving independently. Everyone cheered, including Theodore's father, but Professor Gradstein rose and rushed from the room, turning to give Rebecca what might have been a call for time out and might have been a brief wave good-bye. He would add a sentence to his chapter on writing programs in the inner city, she supposed: "And in one school, a child's entire book— his work for the year—consisted of only two words."

The classroom door opened again. It wasn't Professor Gradstein coming back, but Agnes, the school secretary. She beckoned to Rebecca, and Rebecca stood, nervous, and crossed the circle of children to reach her, aware of her dress brushing against knees. "Phone," mouthed Agnes. "Emergency."

Rebecca almost said, "But Joel is already dead."

"Can you be good for a few minutes until I get back?" she said to the children.

The children chorused that they could, and then Rebecca began to run, and slipped on a wet spot on the linoleum halfway to the office. Professor Gradstein, carrying—pointing to—a camera bag, almost bumped into her, then reached to catch her, but she pulled him down instead, wrenching her knee. She lay on the floor, the skirt of the blue denim dress up around her thighs, the little professor next to her, curved in the opposite direction. A child who had come out of another classroom stood staring. Rebecca cried, not because her knee hurt quite that badly but because she still didn't know what the phone call was about.

"Are you all right?" said the professor, getting onto his hands and knees. "I remembered my camera, in plain view on the front seat of my car." He stood and helped her up. Her knee hurt badly and she leaned on him. "I have a phone call," she said. At last, there was the receiver on Agnes's desk blotter. Agnes left her alone and she sat down in the desk chair. The professor disappeared. "Hello?" she said.

"Mom, Dennis was arrested," said Irene's voice, then before Rebecca could speak, "Now, don't go crying on me," as if Irene had already seen Rebecca crying on the corridor floor.

"What happened?"

"It was last night. I've been down at the police station."

"Was it drugs?"

"He held up a store."

"Oh, God."

"I know," said Irene. "I know."

"With a weapon?"

"They didn't tell me."

"Where is he?" Someone was keeping Rebecca's boy without her permission. For a moment she thought she'd just go down and demand him. Irene didn't answer her question but it didn't matter. "I'm his grandmother," she'd say.

"Pete's called a lawyer," said Irene. Pete was her husband. "I think we can get him out on bail."

"I have money."

"I know you do, Mom. Can you get it in a hurry?"

"Yes." The pain returned to Rebecca's knee, as though she'd been injured trying to rescue Dennis. It was not the first time he'd faced policemen. Amazing what one could get used to. But he had never hurt anyone, as far as she knew.

"How much do you need?" said Rebecca.

"Nothing now. I'll let you know," said Irene. "Oh—we're not saying anything to Jamie until after the recital. So come tonight and act as if nothing's the matter."

Rebecca stood up, knee or no knee. "But that's insane!" she said, too quickly and loudly. "And it's not fair to Jamie."

"It's for Jamie's *sake*. Jamie's been through enough of this stuff."

"Lying never works," said Rebecca, almost in tears. "When are you going to tell him?"

"I don't know. It's not the main issue, Mom. I have to go." Rebecca wanted to keep her on the phone but it would do no good. And she had to go back to her classroom.

"Do you need some ice?" Agnes said, coming in, and for a second Rebecca thought she was being offered a drink. She remembered her knee. Agnes went for ice from the teachers' lunchroom. She helped Rebecca back to the classroom. When Rebecca arrived, Theodore's father was running the readings. "Now wait until you finish the story before you show the pictures," he was saying. He whispered to Rebecca, "I'm trying to speed them up." Clarissa was pouring lemonade and carrying it to the children, two paper cups at a time, as they sat in their seats. She smiled at Rebecca. The gentle, organized people had taken over, people rightly dismayed, Rebecca thought, by excessive thought and difficult feeling. Everyone worried about Rebecca's knee, and Clarissa brought her lemonade. The children asked about the ice, which was wrapped in a towel. Professor Gradstein, tamed, was taking pictures of the children. The readings continued. Rebecca tried to pay attention to the stories instead of picturing Dennis—a short young man with smooth brown hair over his eyes—holding up a store. "Smile!" whispered Professor Gradstein. He was taking her picture, too. She glared at him, tried to find a comfortable position for her knee, and tried hard (she was almost old; why was it still so difficult?) to behave.

WHEN THE SCHOOL day finally ended, another teacher took Rebecca home with her, laid her on a couch, and gave her Scotch. A second drove Rebecca's car to the first teacher's house. They said, "Do you want to stay here overnight?" and "That knee should be X-rayed." Rebecca liked their probably excessive concern, but didn't like the way their faces tightened when she talked about Dennis. They gave her supper and offered to drive her to the recital. "Your daughter will take you home," they said, but Rebecca insisted on taking her own car.

"What happened? Why didn't you say?" said Irene, meeting her outside the music school as Rebecca limped up the steps.

"It had just happened."

Jamie helped her into the room where the recital would take place. "Are you doing this piece from memory?" she asked, trying to find a safe topic.

"Yes."

"Is that hard to do?"

"Pretty hard." Jamie was growing bigger than Dennis. His arms, supporting her, were like long sausages. He showed her where to sit. "I'm going for a drink of water," he said.

"Have you heard anything?" asked Rebecca. Irene was sitting next to her, and Pete came in and sat down, too. Rebecca put her coat on a seat for Jamie.

"He might want to be with his friends," said Irene, and Rebecca asked sharply, "What friends?" She thought Irene meant Dennis— that Dennis had made friends in jail, that Dennis might want to stay in jail.

"Jamie has *friends*," said Irene. "A boy from his school has the same piano teacher."

Now Rebecca understood, but couldn't explain her mistake. "They all have the same teacher?" she said. She looked at her program. Twelve children were going to play. The first numbers had titles like "Under the Bridge" and "My Kitten." Several children would be playing "Oh, Susannah." Only at the end of the program were there movements from real pieces of music. Jamie was third from the end.

"A very sweet guy," said Irene. Her hair was drawn tightly back into a ponytail as if she'd put her feelings there. When she turned her head abruptly, it flung itself over her shoulder, and when Rebecca leaned toward her daughter to pick a thread from Irene's sleeve, the hair, smelling of shampoo, passed pleasantly over her face.

The teacher did look sweet. He stood to welcome them. He had shiny glasses and wore a zip-up tan cotton jacket with a plaid lining visible inside—a boy's jacket.

Rebecca said to Irene, "You didn't answer. Did you hear anything?" But Irene was lifting her chin in the direction of the teacher or possibly Jamie, who was sitting down on his grandmother's coat.

Rebecca wanted to stand up and say, "Wait a minute, everybody. Dennis is in jail—we can't just go on as if nothing happened!" But of course she didn't. She looked around at the assembled parents: a dressed-up, suburban group, nearly all white or Asian. She looked at them as if she were different, as if she looked more like her black and Hispanic pupils. Jamie was not dressed up, but was wearing a plaid shirt coming out of his pants, and she considered tucking it in for him.

Now a little girl dressed in pink walked to the piano. She was one of those who would play "Oh, Susannah," and her name, the teacher announced solemnly, was also Susannah. The teacher sat at the piano beside Susannah, raised his hands, and held them tautly in the air, and then as the child doggedly played the tune, he played the harmony with a kind of joyful surprise, as if he'd only that moment encountered the old song for the first time.

"I bet I'm going to forget," Jamie whispered.

"No, you won't," Rebecca said.

"Oh, Susannah" ended and everyone clapped. Rebecca's hands already hurt from clapping—all that clapping on such a day.

"You didn't hear anything?" she whispered to Irene.

"Shh," said Irene.

"About what?" said Jamie.

Now came the little boy who'd play "Under the Bridge" and "My Kitten," and after him another "Oh, Susannah." Again the teacher sat beside the child, and again it was as though he couldn't believe what a charming tune he'd just come across—or perhaps was even making up in sprightly fashion, for his student and his audience, as he went along. It was impossible not to think the words as they played: "Oh, Susannah, oh, don't you cry for me. . . ."

"About *what?*" said Jamie again, pulling his grandmother's arm. "Heard about *what?*"

"Dennis," Rebecca said, before she thought. But it was not quite before she thought. She thought in the middle of the word. She remembered that Jamie didn't know, that she wasn't supposed to tell Jamie. "Dennis," she continued, anyway—recklessly, angrily, knowing she'd be sorry. "I want to know if she heard anything more about Dennis."

The next song was called "The Wild West," and as soon as it ended, Jamie said to her, "What about Dennis?" and she signaled him to be quiet, but he looked at her so maturely and sharply that she said to him, "Oh, surely you know. You must have overheard or something. Dennis was arrested—no great shock, I suppose, at this point. And I wanted to know—have you and your parents heard anything more about bail, about getting him out on bail?"

And Jamie said, "I didn't know. Mom didn't tell me."

Rebecca shifted in her chair and her knee suddenly hurt. She didn't want to turn her head and find out whether Irene had heard her—or whether Irene did have news. Probably she did. Probably she had news, and what she had learned—or had known all along— was that Dennis had a gun.

Another piece was already over and a new one starting, and Rebecca had not heard them. Now she was clapping for a third rendition of "Oh, Susannah" with one more to go. Jamie studied the score on his lap as if he'd never seen it before. Rebecca had hurt him, though she loved him. She loved him almost as much as she loved Dennis, who had recognized juncos and chickadees at five. But it made her angry that she had hurt Jamie—angry at him, at every-one, including herself. She glanced at Irene, and Irene looked stunned and frightened. "Joel!" Rebecca almost shouted, at her dead husband—who did nothing; nor did the little professor—what was his name? Gradstein—nor did Professor Gradstein rush in with his camera to perceive what was happening, to witness, explain, or ap-prove. Could they storm the jail? What were they doing, sitting there clapping instead of flinging themselves against its walls to let Dennis out—to let all prisoners out? Then the music teacher, his hands held high, sat down at the piano and smiled over his shoulder at the exhausted, saved audience. He was preparing to help the next little kid through "Oh, Susannah," and to discover it yet again him-self. Rebecca covered her face with her hands and the music sloshed exuberantly over her like forgiveness—as rare, as simple.

FREE DOGS

ONE DAY WHEN John Corey was measuring and cutting two-by-fours in the driveway of St. Matthew's parish house, he looked up and saw his brother Eugene, long-legged and narrow, with red hair flying, coming down the driveway with a bulky dog at his heels. There is a soup kitchen at St. Matthew's, and John and his assistant, Tom Orlando, were building a new entrance and a new bathroom there. Eugene stopped by to watch so often that he'd made friends with the people who ran the soup kitchen and sometimes he helped serve food.

The dog Eugene had brought was being eyed warily by the other people standing around in the driveway, mostly young black men in caps, smoking or talking after their lunch. They whooped when John tossed a piece of lumber onto the pile with a clatter, and then they looked at the dog again. Eugene worked at the animal shelter, and when he could, he rescued dogs. He couldn't keep a dog in his house because his lover, Albert, was allergic, but he had persuaded John to take in a little brown dog.

Their older brother, Cameron, a lawyer, also had a dog from the animal shelter—a tall black dog named Fairleigh, with long silky hair. Fairleigh was the only creature ever known to be devoted to John and Eugene's older brother.

The dog Eugene brought to the soup kitchen was a light-colored German shepherd with a big, thick tail. John watched her walk up and down the driveway; a few children shrieked, and then the cook came out and told Eugene to take her away. "She doesn't bite, Marjorie," said Eugene to the cook. "I think she's a little neurotic, but she's basically friendly." He buried his hand in the thick ruff around the dog's neck. "She's getting her winter coat already." It was October.

The dog barked twice at the cook but then she licked the cook's hand. The cook—a short, skinny black woman—ignored her, stepping briskly away as if she had no time to be licked by a dog. Then she turned back and took the dog's face in her hands, and John saw the dog and the woman look hard at each other, promising not to forget each other's faces.

The soup kitchen closed for the day and everyone left but the staff, who were cleaning up. John could hear their radio from the kitchen. He was learning their routine. The guests left by about one-thirty, and the staff was gone by two. Then he and Tom got more work done. The staff consisted mostly of people on city welfare. It was their work assignment.

One of them, a white man in his twenties named Marco, often hung around and talked to John and Tom. Marco had done some construction work, and he hinted that John could take him on, but John didn't have enough work for three, and he wasn't trying out any stranger. Tom was his brother-in-law, his wife's kid brother. Tom hadn't known anything at first, but he'd learned.

When Marco came out of the soup kitchen, the dog, whom Eugene had not taken away but who was now on a leash, began jumping on Marco and licking his face. "Does that dog know you?" said John. He wondered whether it might have been Marco's dog, who had somehow gotten lost and ended up in the pound. Marco said he'd never seen the dog before.

"Dogs know I'm good to them," he said. "I once had a dog, I taught her everything about traffic. She went everywhere with me and I never needed a leash. She knew red lights, green lights, you name it."

"Aren't dogs color-blind?" said Tom, who had come out to get the two-by-fours John was cutting.

"This dog knew red lights, green lights." Marco leaned back on his heels, watching them. He was wearing a plaid flannel shirt, and he buttoned it. It was a cool day.

Eugene told Marco the dog needed a home, and Marco said maybe he could take it in. "I have to check," he said. He wanted the dog, John could see. "She's a thoroughbred," Marco said. "Here, girl," he kept saying to the dog, snapping his fingers. The dog licked his fingers.

John thought the dog was probably not a thoroughbred, but there was no question she was a good-looking dog.

"You could call her Soupy after the soup kitchen," said Eugene.

"I'd rather call her Steak," said Marco.

Now Marjorie came out on her way home. "I thought I told you to take that dog away," she said to Eugene.

"Dogs can teach us a great deal, Marjorie," Eugene said.

"I don't want that dog messing here," said Marjorie. The dog wagged her tail at Marjorie, but the cook walked right past her, pretending they didn't know each other. "I don't know why you're hanging around here, either," she said to Marco.

THE NEXT DAY, Tom and John had another visitor on the job: Tom's girlfriend, Ida, a big blond schoolteacher swinging an old green pocketbook with buckles that flew around and knocked people on the head when Ida got excited. It was Yom Kippur and Ida had the day off, but John didn't know why she'd come, or why so many people visited them at this project. Sometimes his father showed up, too. That day Tom and John were working indoors because it was raining, installing the light fixture in the bathroom and a red electric exit sign just above the new doorway.

Ida kissed Tom, who was kneeling on the floor opening a carton. When she leaned over, her bag thumped him on the shoulder and her hair fell past her face and onto his face, and Ida laughed and flipped it back. She had a loud laugh that made John laugh when nothing was funny. Tom sat back on his heels and said, "I think I just had a mystical experience."

They were working in a corridor right off the dining room, which was full of guests. It smelled of wet clothes. One man recognized Ida, who had been his teacher in high school, and he left his tray to come say hello. Ida hugged him. John thought she must be upset that her old student was eating in a soup kitchen, but if she was, she didn't let on. Then Marco came out of the kitchen, bringing a tray of clean mugs. He set them on a cart near the serving table and then came over. "Will your brother be here today?" he asked John.

"I never know when I'll see him," said John.

Marco said, "I really want that dog. You don't think they already put that dog to death, do you?"

"I don't think so," said John.

"What dog?" asked Ida.

"I don't know why I didn't just take that dog yesterday," Marco said. "She was such a good dog."

When Ida heard the story, she said, "Let's not take any chances. Let's just go get her."

"I don't have a car," said Marco.

"I have a car," Ida said.

"I *had* a car," said Marco. "The muffler place stole it."

"They stole your car?" said Ida. John wished they would all clear out and let him and Tom work, but he didn't like to say anything because Ida was Tom's girlfriend.

"Stole it," said Marco. "I left it to be fixed and they said they junked it. That was that. I paid a lot of money for that car."

"What kind was it?"

"It was a Chevy," said Marco. "It was an '81 Chevy. It still had a lot of good miles in it."

"Did they pay you?" said Ida.

"No, they didn't pay me," Marco said. "Of course they didn't pay me. They wanted me to pay them for junking the car."

"You should see a lawyer," Ida said.

"I'm thinking about it," said Marco. "Do you know a good lawyer?"

Ida was buttoning her raincoat. John glanced at her. He figured there was no harm in Marco, but he was surprised that she had no qualms at all about taking a strange man into her car. And Marco was going to be in trouble at the soup kitchen if he sneaked out, but John was not going to give anyone his opinion about that.

Then Ida said to John, "Isn't your brother a lawyer?"

"I thought he worked at the pound," said Marco.

"Not that brother," said Ida. "Your other brother is a lawyer, isn't he?"

"My brother Cameron," said John. "My older brother."

"Maybe Marco should go see him," said Ida.

"First things first," John said. "I think first you better go get that dog."

Marco and Ida came back with the dog forty minutes later. Marco had already named her Katie. He was so happy he brought Katie right into the soup kitchen. Marjorie screamed and screamed at him for first disappearing and then bringing in a dog. By now the guests were almost all gone and the rest of the staff was cleaning up. The dog sniffed the dirty trays piled on a table.

A man was mopping the floor, and he yelled at Marco about the mud the dog was going to spread. Ida said, "Not to mention if the health department hears about this, you probably get closed down." She walked into the middle of the nearly empty dining room. John had stopped working and was standing under the new exit sign. He watched Ida.

"I apologize," Ida said in a loud voice. "I apologize to the Neighborhood Soup Kitchen, its guests, and its employees." She hustled the dog outside and told Marco she and Katie would wait in the car. "I'll drive you home," she said.

"Was she making fun of something?" John said to Tom.

"No," said Tom. "That's what's interesting about her."

John was a little afraid Ida would drop Tom in favor of Marco, but she didn't, and Tom didn't seem to be worried that she would. "She likes getting things done," Tom said to John, and sure enough, Ida rescued the dog for Marco and then she got Marco to consult Cameron, John's older brother. That was something John wasn't sure about. When he thought about it afterward—weeks afterward; after Thanksgiving—he wasn't sure how it had come about, whether it was his fault or not, if fault was even what they were talking about.

IN FACT CAMERON would say nothing bad happened. Some people came into his office determined to make things worse for themselves and there wasn't much he could do to change their minds. Some people can't stand it when they have only a little money. Of course *some* people who have only a little money can't stand it unless they get more, but mostly those weren't the people who showed up in Cameron's office. His clients were often people who were simply determined to lose what little they did have.

When Cameron came into his office one day in October at tenthirty in the morning, his old father was sitting in the waiting room like a figure in a dream. "You don't come earlier than this?" his father said. Cameron was late because he had taken his dog to the vet. Fairleigh was middle-aged and had hip problems. The vet had said pills might help or they might not. Cameron didn't want to discuss all this with his father. Fairleigh was now outside in Cameron's car.

When Cameron was a young lawyer, the night before the first time he had to argue in court, he dreamed that the judge was his father. It would have been a funny story to tell, except that Cameron didn't like to tell funny stories on himself, and also, in the dream his father had said to him from the bench, "Tell me, son, how did you do it? I may want to kill someone myself sometime."

Now his father had brought fish. "I defrosted this yesterday," he said, standing. Cameron's father had been a thick, ruddy man with reddish hair, but he was paler and less substantial these days. It kept happening or Cameron didn't get used to it: he always noticed. Cameron's secretary, Marie, was smiling at his father, which annoyed Cameron. His father took a package of fish, wrapped in plastic, from a grocery bag. "But last night when I went to cook it," he said, "I just didn't feel like fish. So I opened a can of cream-of-mushroom soup. With milk, it's very nutritious. I was going to cook the fish today, but Eugene called me first thing. He and Albert want me to come to dinner tonight. Tell Albert to hold the garlic, I said. My son-in-law the cook! With three sons," he said in an aside to Marie, "I did not expect a son-in-law. The fish will spoil by tomorrow," he went on, turning to Cameron again. "Put it in that little refrigerator where you keep milk for the coffee. But make sure you eat it tonight."

"If you would let me buy you a microwave," said Cameron, "you wouldn't have to defrost food in advance."

"The walk here did me good," said his father. After his father left, Cameron carried the package of fish into his office and threw it into the wastebasket, and then a client arrived. While he was talking to the man, Cameron began to imagine that the fish had already begun to smell. He was sure the man was sniffing and trying to place the odor while they talked. The client, who knew John, was a square man in a plaid flannel shirt that made him look more square. He claimed that a car repair shop in Hamden had junked his car without his permission.

"Don't they owe me? Seems to me they owe me," he said.

"Do you have any proof that you didn't tell them to junk the car?" Cameron said.

The man had no proof. He was on welfare, but he had a few hundred dollars. Probably he'd lied to the welfare department about the money. He kept going on about his money and his car, but Cameron was listening to the sound of barking from outside—the wild barking of a dog with a point to make, and Fairleigh's slower, deeper barks.

"That's my dog, Katie," said the man. "She's barking at a dog in a car. There's a big, skinny black dog in a car."

"My dog, Fairleigh," said Cameron.

"Katie's a great dog," said the man. "I just got her, but I trained her already. She knows red lights, green lights."

"Very impressive," said Cameron. He could still hear Fairleigh's steady woofs. He wanted Fairleigh to destroy this man's foolish Katie, but Fairleigh was locked in the car.

"I think a jury would be sympathetic," said the man. He claimed his car was worth three thousand dollars. Of course the repair place would say the car needed expensive work and the man had authorized them to junk it. They'd say he had signed something giving them the right to settle things over the phone, and that he'd told them over the phone to junk it. Cameron ran his hand through his hair. Surely the man didn't imagine Cameron was going to put on a jury trial over the junked car. Cameron could see into the man's mind, and he was angry at the fantasy there: justice, triumph, the abasement of the mechanic. He told the man he couldn't do anything without a retainer. Luckily the man had that money. Cameron sent him to Marie to work out the details, and he himself hurried outside to the garbage cans behind the office with the package of fish. Fairleigh had settled down in the front seat of his car. He didn't see the client's dog.

There were things Cameron let himself do, as if a road went straight but Cameron suddenly drove his car off the road, not very far, but through a yard, and back onto the road. There was a certain pleasure in it, though when he questioned himself Cameron had a practical reason for everything he did. And sometimes Cameron did something splashy and generous. He'd bought his father a toaster oven and a coffee maker. He would have bought him a microwave in one minute if his father hadn't been so stubborn. He'd be hitting the counter at Caldor's with his credit card before his father knew what was happening.

JOHN AND TOM were almost finished with the job at the soup kitchen and it was a good thing, because some of the work was outdoors, and it was getting cold. After a while they had fewer visitors, and John was surprised when Eugene walked in one morning while he was painting trim. Eugene stood at the foot of the ladder, watching, while he told John that he and Albert wanted to make Thanksgiving dinner for everyone. John looked down at his younger brother, who seemed to sway on his long legs as he spoke. "I know Barbara always does it," Eugene said. Barbara was John's wife.

"It'll be a relief," John said. He and Barbara had a new baby, their first child, Carolee. Barbara was worn out, and she had already said she didn't see how she could do Thanksgiving. Since his mother died, he and Barbara had always had the whole family plus her family: his brothers, his father, her parents, and Tom.

"You and your folks, too, of course," Eugene was now saying to Tom. Then Eugene stood for a while longer, quietly watching John, and John knew he was saying silently that he hoped nobody was going to get tense about him and Albert being a gay couple. Inwardly, John told Eugene that he for one was not interested in judging what his fellow humans did as long as they didn't hurt other people, and Barbara definitely felt the same. He thought Eugene probably knew he was saying this, but they remained silent and so did Tom. Then Eugene said, "Well," and left. He'd been on his way to work with the van and a stray he'd picked up.

John and Tom had one more visitor that day—John's father. He'd been raking his leaves, he said, and stuffing them into big brown paper bags, which was what the city now required. But he had filled eleven bags and a lot of leaves were left.

"They sort of disappear by spring, don't they?" said Tom. Now he was up on the ladder. "After all, nobody rakes leaves in the forest, but you don't see trees buried in piles of dead leaves."

John's father kept talking. The city permitted leaves to be raked directly into the gutter, but only just before the public works trucks came around sweeping. The city would be sweeping on John's father's block the day before Thanksgiving. Or you could put your leaves into a free compost bin, which you could request from the city. John's father had done that, but the bin was too small. "You call," he said to John. "Ask for another bin and give it to me. I'd have Cameron do it but a lawyer can't be too careful."

"Careful about what?"

"About claiming he's using a compost bin when he isn't."

John wrote down the number to call on a scrap of paper and promptly lost it. "Does everyone have to deal with stuff like this at work?" he asked Tom.

"It's because you're a nice guy," said Tom.

"Not anymore," said John. The next job was out of town, and nobody would bother to follow them.

WEDNESDAY WAS EUGENE'S day off, and on the afternoon before Thanksgiving he started making an apple pie because it wasn't fair for Albert to have to do all the cooking. Albert was an optometrist. He'd tried to clear his Wednesday afternoon that week, but if he didn't come home soon, Eugene would have to make a pumpkin pie as well. As he was slicing apples the phone rang. It was Cameron, who had had a free hour when a court appearance was canceled. He'd gone and bought a microwave oven and taken it to their father's house, but while he was inside persuading their father it wouldn't cause cancer, Cameron's car had been towed away.

"Street sweeping," he said.

"Didn't they put up signs?"

"Oh, there were signs. I never noticed. Dad was more excited that he got all the leaves into the gutter than he was about the microwave. I don't know about him, Eugene."

"He's all right," said Eugene. "Do you want me to take you to get your car?"

That was what Cameron wanted. Eugene left his pie and picked up Cameron at their father's house. Cameron was furious. He'd have to pay for the towing, plus a parking ticket. "I'm just looking after the old man," he said. "Nobody else bothers. I didn't bump into John at the check-out, paying for a microwave for Dad."

Eugene didn't answer. They'd caught up to the street-sweeping trucks, a few blocks from his father's house. The street was empty of cars. One truck was pushing leaves into a pile and another was scooping them into a dump truck. Then a truck with rotating brushes wet and swept the street. Eugene always liked street sweeping. Life was still civilized, it said. Gay people and straight people, black and white, all had their leaves scooped up.

When Eugene got home, Albert was making the pies, and he looked Eugene over with amusement. "Scared off by a pie," he said. Albert was dark and curly-haired and just a little fat. He liked making puns about eyesight. He said when he was in optometry school the annual dance was called the Eye Ball, and he'd been looking for eye puns ever since. "Outta sight!" he teased his nearsighted patients. Or "A true visionary!" Eugene wished Albert were not allergic to dogs. He had asthma.

Albert cooked into the night and all the next morning, and at one the family began to arrive. Barbara and Tom's parents had gone to an aunt's, but Tom came with Ida, who walked in carrying a tray of crackers and cheese, grinning because it was too full and she was just barely managing not to tip it, while Tom held the door. Eugene brought Albert from the kitchen to meet her, and Ida and Albert talked optometry and cooking while John and Barbara came in with Carolee and a sweet potato casserole. Eugene took his niece from John's arms. "Should I take off her jacket?" he said.

"Just support her head," said Barbara.

Eugene looked into the baby's face. "You want Uncle Eugene to take off your coat?" he said. His hands tingled with the pleasure of holding her. Carolee was barely awake. Her head wobbled above the pink puffy jacket. She had hardly any neck.

The doorbell rang again and Cameron came in, but he had brought his dog. "But Albert's allergic," said Eugene from the sofa, where he was working Carolee's arm out of her jacket sleeve. "Why did you bring Fairleigh?"

"He has to take a pill at two o'clock," said Cameron.

"But what about Albert?" said Eugene. He had always liked Fairleigh, a smart dog who looked like a black Irish setter. Albert, coming in with drinks, said he'd probably be all right, but then he said maybe the dog should stay in the car for part of the time.

Cameron said sure, but he sat down and took a drink, saying, "You talked me into adopting the dog, Eugene." Fairleigh lay down at his feet. Cameron leaned over to look at Carolee on Eugene's lap, then tugged at her foot. But Carolee was sleepy. "A little out of it," said Cameron.

John moved over to stand protectively in front of Eugene. "That's what they're like," he said.

Then the phone rang in the kitchen. "It's probably Dad," said Cameron. "Insisted he'd walk, but now I bet he wants a ride." But Albert said the call was for Eugene and he didn't know who it was. Fairleigh followed Eugene into the kitchen, where Albert was making gravy, and Eugene tried to push the dog away as he reached for the phone. Fairleigh looked at Eugene as if he understood almost everything.

It was Marco on the phone—Marco from the soup kitchen, where they were also having Thanksgiving dinner. Marco was crying. His dog had been hit by a car. She wasn't badly hurt—it sounded as if her leg was broken—but Marco was afraid the animal control people would somehow grab her and destroy her. Marjorie, the cook, was out in the driveway guarding Katie. She felt bad, Marco said, because she had shooed Katie away from the door.

"Can you get her to the hospital?" Eugene said. New Haven Central Veterinary wasn't far, but Marco couldn't. "I'll come and take you," said Eugene.

But when he went into the living room and explained, Ida jumped up, reaching for her big turquoise bag. Cameron raised his arm to keep from being socked in the forehead by one of its dangling buckles. "I'll go," she said. "Katie's a friend of mine. *Marco's* a friend of mine." Tom left with her. "Start without us," he said.

"Dad's not here yet," Eugene said. "We won't sit down without Dad."

His father was quite late, in fact. Barbara thought someone should go get him, but he had wanted to take his usual walk. He wanted it even more than he ordinarily did, he'd said to Eugene, because he was going to have a big meal in the middle of the day. "He has to fortify himself with exercise," Eugene said.

"Your father's a character," said Albert.

"A character," said Cameron. "That's a nice way of looking at it." Everything he said sounded tense. Eugene was afraid to mention Fairleigh again. He went to the phone to call his father, but the line was busy. "Doesn't mean a thing," Cameron called out. "Leaves the phone off the hook half the time. It's a miracle he remembers to put on his pants in the morning." He settled himself in front of the cheese tray and ate several crackers rapidly. "Try him again," he said, but the line was still busy.

"He knows where you live?" Barbara said, when more time had passed.

"He's been here," said Eugene.

"He's slow in the morning," said John. "I'm not surprised he's late."

But their father had still not arrived when Ida and Tom came back. "The dog's going to be okay," said Tom. "But it's expensive, and Marco doesn't have any money."

"They didn't turn him away, did they?" said Eugene.

"They demanded a deposit," said Tom. "They asked for a hundred, because Katie has to be hospitalized. I don't know what it will run to in the end."

"So what did you do?" said Eugene.

"Well, I gave them my credit card," Ida said. "The dog was in pain," she said, as if people were objecting. "What was I going to do?"

"I think that was nice of you," said Barbara. Ida ran her hand under her long hair and lifted it as if it were caught in the shoulder strap of her bag, although it wasn't. She patted Tom's arm.

"Listen," Cameron said, and Eugene noticed that Fairleigh raised his head as if he was indeed making sure to listen. "I'm going to pay that bill. Let me know what it is, and I'll pay it."

"That's not necessary, Cam," said Eugene. "Maybe we can all help out." Other people murmured appreciatively.

"Well, I think probably it *is* necessary," said Ida in a loud voice.

Cameron was standing. "We'd better go look for Dad," he said.

Eugene was already putting on his coat. "What do you mean?" he said to Ida. "I think this is very generous of Cameron. Marco was an idiot to let the dog run loose."

And Ida said, "Your brother Cameron took all of Marco's money. I sent him to consult with Cameron about his car, and Cameron relieved him of every dime he had. So I think Cameron ought to pay the bill."

Cameron's head snapped around in Ida's direction. "I *beg* your pardon," he said. "I somehow missed hearing that you're an attorney. I somehow missed hearing that you know more than I do about how to run my own practice."

"Wait a minute," said Tom.

"Maybe in this instance I do," Ida said, playing with a strand of her hair. She didn't seem to be afraid of Cameron. "You haven't done a thing for him so far, and I don't think you're going to."

"Look, lady," said Cameron, "if someone's determined to sink his money into a losing proposition, beyond a certain point there isn't much I can do about it."

"I feel terrible about this," said Ida. "Marco just told me what happened, in the car. I'm the one who sent him to you. I feel responsible."

"You feel responsible!" said Cameron. "Well, maybe you *are* responsible." He was opening the door and pushing Eugene ahead. "You drive along Whalley and I'll go on Edgewood," he said as they reached the sidewalk. "If he's not at the house, we'll go back along Elm." Fairleigh was just behind him.

Eugene nodded and moved toward his car. He tried to recall the whole conversation that had just taken place, what Ida had said, what Cameron had said. Cameron was difficult, he'd known that all his life; somewhere in Eugene was a three-year-old who knew that his older brother Cameron was difficult. But what Ida had said was different. Eugene drove slowly, looking from one side to the other, but did not see an old man making his way along Whalley Avenue, which was windswept, unusually empty. Everyone was inside eating turkey. Eugene turned at his father's street and saw Cameron's car in front of the house. He parked behind it.

His father had the downstairs apartment; it was where they had all grown up. The front door was unlocked and Eugene went in. The inner door was also open, and it opened out while the front door opened in; all his life, it had been hard to squeeze past first one and then the other. And then there was a third door in the narrow, dark hall. He tried the third door—the apartment door—and it, too, was open. Now he heard voices, so he knew his father had not died of a heart attack on the windy streets, and had not been mugged.

"So I forgot," his father was saying. "To me it was just Thursday. I forgot it was Thanksgiving." His father's apartment door opened onto a corridor. At the end was a small, dark dining room that had hardly been used since their mother died, and beyond that was the kitchen. The light was on in the kitchen. Cameron's back filled the doorway between the dining room and the kitchen, but when he shifted, Eugene could see his father all the way at the other side of the kitchen. His father was sitting at his small table, bringing a spoon to his lips. He must have returned to his food—probably cream-of-mushroom soup—after letting Cameron in.

"So will you hurry?" Cameron was saying. He had not seemed to hear Eugene come in, and Eugene didn't call out to his father and brother.

"You want me to waste this?" the father said.

"They've got all kinds of food for you—turkey, stuffing," Cameron said. Fairleigh came slowly down the corridor toward Eugene, swinging his plumy black tail in restrained sideways sweeps.

"Look, Eugene's bad enough," Cameron now said sharply, and his voice turned sarcastic. "My brother of the *gay couple*! We don't have enough problems; now we've got this *gay couple*—and in addition we've got *you* to deal with? You can't even be bothered to *remember?*"

But the soup had gone down the wrong pipe and their father was coughing and sputtering. Cameron moved forward, but when Eugene stepped into the kitchen, his brother was not patting their father on the back or holding a glass of water for him. He was grasping the old man by the shoulders and shaking him like a piece of laundry, shouting almost tearfully, "Just stop it! Just *stop* it!"

The spoon fell to the floor. Fairleigh hurried into the kitchen ahead of Eugene. He sniffed the fallen spoon and sniffed the old man's leg. Then the dog turned his long, mild face toward Eugene, as if to report what he'd learned and offer his sort of help. "Use me," Fairleigh said, or seemed to say.

THE DANCE TEACHER

PAID BY A program to foster the arts in public schools, Marta Lowenstein taught dance after school every day at a New Haven high school, almost always to girls. In college, twenty years earlier, everything Marta did felt foolish and conspicuous. Then she took a dance class, two more, and became serious. In large part it was embarrassment—even humiliation—she became serious about. She wasn't a natural and she was always being yelled at. She fell during a performance. Worse, she wasn't hurt; she had to stand up, dance some more, and bow. When she was alone that night, her shame was mitigated by ambition: she would learn not to care. Marta is not easily injured, and sure enough, after a while nothing troubled her. That is how, of all her classmates, she became a dancer. The others wore out.

Last year she had a lump in her left breast. The doctor said it was nothing, although Marta should have a mammogram anyway. "I don't have time for problems," she told the doctor.

"Neither do I," said the doctor, a kind woman with two-year-old twin sons whose photograph, across the room under the doctor's elbow, caught Marta's eye while the doctor examined her. "Luckily, we don't have to worry about this one." Marta searched the doctor's happy, intelligent face. The mammogram, a few days later, showed she was fine. The next day, naturally, she read a story in the paper about false results from mammograms.

In the dance class, some girls had crushes on Marta. The girls crossed the floor diagonally, stretching or leaping badly, and then she did it: faster, more grandly, her huge arms and huge legs taking up all the room they wanted, eating the air around them. The girls— black girls, white girls, Latinas—hugged themselves and stroked the dusty floor with their bare feet. They were chilly and self-conscious in their little leotards. Marta glanced at the group and without pity took in the looks of those who loved her: that one, that one.

Last year one was Rosemary, called Rosie. One evening after class Marta's car wouldn't start. It was almost dark, and Marta wasn't sure what to do. She flooded the engine and made herself wait and try again. Then she couldn't stand waiting, and she knew it wasn't going to start anyway, so she set out on foot for a public phone. She walked fast in the dark. A car pulled up beside her with a girl and a woman in it. "Marta, do you need a ride?"

Marta got in without looking hard at who was helping her. She thought it was a girl called Jen. She said, "I thought you had to go play the flute," because Jen had left early for an orchestra rehearsal, infuriating Marta. When the blond, skinny girl in the front seat turned and looked at her, her tangled hair hanging down over her forehead, Marta saw that it was Rosie. She thought Rosie would be defeated by the pain of being confused with Jen, but Rosie looked at her steadily and said, "This is my mom, Marie."

"Where are you headed?" said Marie.

"A phone. My car won't start."

"What do you mean, it won't start?" Marie said. "I don't like that attitude."

"My attitude or the car's attitude?"

Marie turned around to look at Marta, even though she was

driving. "I can start any car," she said. She drove back to the school. "From what Rosie tells me, I wouldn't think you'd be afraid of cars."

"I'm not," said Marta.

"Ma," said Rosie.

Marie was wearing a dress and heels but in the dark she looked as young and thin as Rosie. When they got to the car, Marie bent over it and looked under the hood. Then she sat in the driver's seat and listened shrewdly while she held the accelerator down and turned the key. The car wouldn't start. They went out for pizza. Marta phoned her mechanic. Back at the table, she could see in the light that Marie's skin was older than Rosie's; Marie was Rosie with a lot of makeup and, even so, lines around her eyes. She smoked.

"I can't stand it when you smoke," Rosie said.

"I know," said her mother.

"You'll get cancer and I'll be an orphan," said Rosie.

Marta started to say, "I have a lump in my breast," which she would not have expected to say to someone she didn't know, but Marie was already talking. "Then your father will have to show up," she said, but she put out the cigarette, took the pack from her purse, and handed it to her daughter. "I just quit," she said.

"Do you quit once a week?" Marta asked. "Are you one of those?"

"No, I never quit before," Marie said. "When I say something, I mean it."

Marta didn't want to say, "But you didn't start my car." She said, "I have a lump in my breast."

"Did you go to the doctor?" said Marie.

"She says not to worry," Marta said.

"So you're not worrying." They both laughed.

"Well, I'm not," said Marta. "I'm not a worrier."

"Lucky you," said Marie. "Pass that on to Rosie, would you?"

Rosie blushed.

"She worries plenty about your class," Marie said.

"Shut *up,*" said Rosie.

IN THE DANCE class, Marta told the students to find stories they could dance to. In a rash moment she had agreed to let them perform in a benefit for the PTO, along with jazz musicians and poets. "Find stories with action," she told them, "not just love and thinking." At the end of the following class they sat on the floor in a circle and told their stories, with gestures and little demonstrations. Most of the stories couldn't possibly be danced. Rosie's was the best, though she was the worst dancer. She had invented a story. A man and a woman are driving together, quarreling. They dance an unhappy dance.

"How do they dance while driving?" someone said.

"The dance is what they feel," said Rosie. "Now and then, they can pretend to drive." She mimed driving. It was acceptable. "A girl will play the man." It went without saying.

A hitchhiker appears. He dances a dance of independence, solitude, need. Rosie stood and struck a pose, her thumb out like a hitchhiker's. For the first time, her movements had authority. This was what she'd do if she wanted a ride—but it was more interesting.

"Or maybe it's a girl hitchhiker," said one of the other students.

"Okay, a girl hitchhiker." The couple stops for the hitchhiker. "They all dance together," said Rosie. "But then one of them leaves with the hitchhiker, and the other is alone."

"The hitchhiker doesn't get into the car?" said Marta.

"No, the hitchhiker steals the woman. Steals one of them."

Marta said Rosie's dance would be one of three they would do at the show. Rosie said, "Can I play the hitchhiker?" Marta was caught off guard. There was an obvious person to play the hitchhiker, a good dancer, a tall black girl named Lakeesha. But Marta paused and then said that if Rosie stayed half an hour after class each day, Marta would teach her to be a better dancer, and maybe Rosie could play the hitchhiker.

MARTA CONTINUED TO feel the lump. She thought she could make it out through her bra and leotard, just at the bottom of her breast. She thought it might have changed. "Feels the same to me," said the kind doctor, who had had her hair streaked since Marta had been there last.

"Surely you can't remember it," said Marta, irritated that the doctor wasted time coloring her hair.

"Of course I do," said the doctor.

Marta got dressed. In the waiting room she met Marie, who saw another doctor in the practice. "Wait," said Marie. "I'm just picking up a prescription."

They went to the drugstore. Marie needed a new diaphragm. "I can't believe I've gone back to it," she said. "Did you ever use one?"

"No." They stopped for coffee.

"I hate that thing," said Marie.

"Hate what?" Marta looked at her coffee mug.

"The diaphragm."

"You have a boyfriend?" said Marta. Marta was alone and she liked other alone women.

"My boss asks me out now and then so people won't think he's gay."

"Is that a problem, going out with your boss? What's his name?"

"Cameron Corey," said Marie. Marta didn't know any lawyer of that name. "You bet it's a problem. Of course, he's difficult to start with."

113

"Are you in love with him?" Marta said.

"No, I'm certainly not in love with him," said Marie. "All right, yes, I'm in love with him."

Marta snorted. "Did you really give up smoking?" she said.

"So far."

"Why?"

"To please you."

"To please *me*?" said Marta. "Why?"

"I liked the cut of your jib," said Marie. "Whatever that means."

"Listen, do you think I have cancer?" said Marta (but she knew she meant, *Are we friends?*).

"No," said Marie (which meant, *We are*).

ROSIE STAYED FAITHFULLY after the dance class every day. She waited, sitting on the floor, her legs crossed, or she did stretches. Marta saw the others out and went to the bathroom, and then she took Rosie through some of the exercises and worked with her, wishing she had not made this offer. Rosie had no line. She had no strength. But she sometimes became lively, almost hysterical. She whirled swiftly across the floor, all shyness gone. She wrapped something around her head and impersonated a scared old woman, then a frightening man. One day when Rosie was in an antic mood of this kind, a man in office clothes came into the room where they were working and sat on a folding chair near the window. Marta guessed that he was Cameron Corey, Marie's boss and boyfriend, coming to call for Rosie. Mr. Corey did not tap his watch or breathe out loud, but she knew he was impatient and annoyed. She felt protective, and even joined Rosie in a zany routine Rosie was inventing.

*　　*　　*

ONE DAY MARTA was alone in Marie and Rosie's house. She took a bath. She had an elaborate fantasy of breaking in like a burglar, but that wasn't how she'd come. They'd gone out for pizza again and Marta had mentioned that her apartment was being painted. Marta had a part-time job as a copy editor for a journal at Yale, and she worked at home. Now the paint smell bothered her. Marie had turned to Rosie. "Give her your key," she said, tilting her head toward Marta.

"My key?"

"You don't need it. I come home before you."

"Not always," said Rosie, but she took out a key on a chain with a small stuffed bear on it and handed it to Marta.

"Work at our house," said Marie.

After her bath Marta wandered from room to room. The rooms were messy, which interested her. Working there had seemed like a good idea, but Marta couldn't decide where to sit.

In Rosie's room she found a diary. Without hesitating, she turned the pages until she saw her name. Rosie had written:

> Marta stays every day whether she feels like it or not, and if she feels like it, so much the better for me. She looks better and I think maybe she isn't ugly. Maybe she's even beautiful. If I talk she doesn't slap my shoulder but writes down the first word of what I say on the blackboard. If I say "What do you want me to do?" she writes "What" on the blackboard, maybe at a slant, maybe even banging into a word she already wrote.
>
> When Marta doesn't want me to be there she doesn't write on the blackboard and she slaps my shoulder if I talk— not hard. Once she cried. Just a little. This is how I know she isn't mad at me.

After she checked to make sure there was nothing more, Marta put the diary exactly where she had found it. She tried to think about writing on the blackboard. Sometimes she made diagrams to show direction, and unlike some dancers she liked words; she might write a word like "shoulders" as she spoke. Why would she write the first word that Rosie said? Why would she write "What"? And of course she hadn't cried.

She heard a noise and walked quickly to another part of the house. Marie came in. "I'm early," she said. "Cam sent me home to change. There's some kind of political dinner."

"Should I do something with your hair?" said Marta. She didn't know much about hair but she wanted to touch one of these women. She tried to remember the feel of Rosie's shoulder.

"What for?" said Marie. "He could care less."

"I didn't like the look of him," Marta said.

"When did you see him?"

"Wasn't that Cam, picking up Rosie last week?"

"Oh, right. Did he do anything obnoxious?"

"No," said Marta.

Marie sniffed. "When he wants me to sleep with him, he doesn't say a word. He brings me flowers. Heaven forbid I have my period when he brings me flowers." She was tidying the kitchen while she spoke. Marta laughed at what Marie said. When Marta stopped talking and laughed, she thought of Rosie's diary. The thought hurt, but it was interesting.

"He liked the look of you, though," Marie said.

"Your boyfriend?"

"Mmm. He said you had decent breasts."

"Decent!" Marta saw in Marie's look that she herself was a somewhat frightening person. She slapped Marie's shoulder quickly and then saw what she had done. And recognized the bony arm, like Rosie's.

*   *   *

MARTA AND ROSIE faced each other and Rosie tried to imitate her stretch and reach. Then Marta walked around Rosie and molded her arm into position, and pressed down on her shoulders. Rosie was obedient but what she did was always wrong. It was hard not to pummel and squeeze and pull her to get her right. Marta's hands hurt when she watched Rosie flutter irresolutely across the room, turning. She slapped her own sides and it made a sound and Rosie stopped, breathless, and looked at her, waiting to be criticized some more.

Marta looked at the clock. She should keep Rosie another fifteen minutes. But she said, "This isn't working."

She thought Rosie would say, "I know," but Rosie said, "Do you want me to do it again?"

"I'm afraid you can't play the hitchhiker."

"But you aren't sure?" said Rosie, coming toward her quickly.

Marta walked to a chair where she kept a sweater and put it around her shoulders. "You can't be the hitchhiker. I'm going to ask Lakeesha to do it."

"Who do you think you are?" said Rosie. "You *can't*."

"Rosie, listen to me," said Marta. "It's a fine dance, and you made it up, but I want the right person."

Rosie stood opposite her in the grimy, empty room. She wore a leotard but no tights and her bare legs were thin. She stood with her feet straight ahead of her, not like a dancer. "Whatever," Rosie said. Then with a swift gesture, she pulled her leotard off. She stood in a pink bra—she barely had breasts—and white cotton panties, which had slipped partway down. She pulled them up and stepped out of the leotard and kicked it toward Marta, and then she ran from the room in tears. Marta reached down for the leotard but then she stopped, put on her sweater, and left. She was being cruel, but sometimes people are cruel.

117

The next day the leotard was gone, but Rosie did not disappear forever. She missed one day of class but came on the next, wearing shorts and a T-shirt. One dance included an ensemble, and Marta asked Rosie if she wanted to be in it, but Rosie said, "No, thanks." Then Rosie volunteered to direct her dance. "I want Lakeesha to do something different when she first comes in," she said to Marta as they were all leaving one afternoon.

During the week of the performance, Rosie spent extra hours at school rehearsing the girls in her dance. The dancers dropped the question of whether they were playing men or women. Lakeesha was good. Rosie followed Marta around, keeping lists of costumes and talking about music. Marta saw almost as much of her as before. They worked calmly together, selecting music for the dances and copying songs from tapes brought in by the other students. Rosie set about making a master tape, which she offered to play at the performance, since she was the only student who wasn't dancing. She insisted the tape would even have silences of the correct length on it. She was quiet and careful with Marta, as if she imagined each meeting in advance and relived it when it was over.

The night of the performance, Marta arrived early and sat in a classroom near the auditorium. She'd thought there would be things to do but there weren't. Rosie kept bustling in. Lakeesha was late. Marta had a fantasy: Lakeesha doesn't show; Rosie dances after all; Rosie is terrible and Marta comforts her, telling her of her own early misfortunes as a dancer. Then Rosie came in to report that Lakeesha had arrived, but it was freezing in the dressing room, and she was going in search of someone to turn on the heat. "I can't have this," she said. Marta followed Rosie into the hall and watched her hurry away. Rosie landed hard with each foot when she walked, like someone running.

People were beginning to arrive. A woman sat at a table outside the auditorium collecting money—two dollars a person, five for a family. People dropped money into a box.

Marta wasn't sure what to do next. She and Rosie had planned to run through the tape one more time. She stood in the classroom holding the tape recorder, and at last Rosie appeared. "Sorry!" she said cheerfully, and sat down on a desk top. Marta had been running her finger against her breast again, and moved it quickly away from herself. She and Rosie played the tape. Rosie had never recorded the silences, and now she admitted it was better just to turn off the tape recorder between sections of the dances, which was what Marta had thought all along. Rosie had a notebook in which she made complicated entries.

Marta watched Rosie rewind the tape. Rosie was in jeans and a black bodysuit. Her blond hair, as usual, fell in a floppy curl on her forehead. Marta picked up her coat so they could get going.

Then a man burst into the room—a furious man, whom Marta recognized after a moment as Marie's boss and boyfriend, the lawyer Cam. Mr. Corey. Cam was in a suit and coat, and in his right hand he grasped a fistful of bills, which he released on the desk top next to Rosie. "Royalties," he said to Rosie. "Your goddamn royalties. I'm paying you for making up the dance. Your mother just told me you're not even in it. And you people"—he looked at Marta—"are in addition too *stupid* to keep your eyes on your money. That woman at the table turns her back to gab with her girlfriend."

Rosie jumped up and stared at the ones and fives now scattered on the desk.

"Take it!" shouted Cam. "You earned it, and you got cheated. Take it!"

"Cam!" Marie was coming in behind him. "I couldn't figure out where you went." Marie was dressed up, wearing higher heels than she wore to the office. She had that flowery smell some women can manage, a smell that joins with heels and hairspray and the flash of jewelry to make a new presence. Marta knew she should deal with this crazy lawyer, but she needed to think about Marie's festive skinniness, or maybe Marie's daughter, this nearly identical creature now backing away from the bills on the desk, moving like her mother, as if Marie had lain down on plaster of Paris and used the indentation as a mold to make Rosie. And she remembered that they loved her—or something.

"We're not interested!" shouted Marta to Cam, and Cam gave a half shrug and backed away.

"He's impossible," Marie said, but she sounded indulgent. She was gathering the money and shuffling it into a pile. Rosie reached for a bill that had fallen. Then Marie called after Cam, "I didn't mean it like *that*."

"What?" said Marta. "What?" She had not been troubled by Cam's first sally, because it made sense for Rosie not to dance, nor by his second, because *Marta* wasn't in charge of the money. She faced Marie.

"We were talking in the car," said Marie.

"What did you say?"

"Well, I said it wasn't fair—but I didn't mean he should go steal the money and give it to Rosie!"

"What wasn't fair? Have you ever seen Rosie try to dance?" said Marta, much too fast, and she felt Rosie flinch, while Marta's hand went toward Marie's shoulder. She did not strike Marie but seized her shoulder—as if she were going to yank Marie to a place from which the view would be clear—and Marie tottered on her heels before she shook Marta off and caught her balance, saying, "She dances fine." Then she said, "And what did you want with her leotard?"

Marta had never talked to Marie about what had happened. She had forgotten to be friends with Marie.

But Cam, apparently, had turned back. He came into the room again. "You simply know nothing about kids!" he shouted—to Marta, who had *been* a kid. "You don't even *have* kids!"

"Oh, neither do you," said Marie, to Cam's departing back. Marta reached for her but Marie followed Cam in her heels, holding the money high to show that she for one was not stealing it.

"Marie!" said Marta. But now she was alone with Rosie. It was time to go into the auditorium and see the show.

"Why didn't you tell her?" Rosie said.

"Tell her what?"

"What's wrong with my dancing." Rosie was trying to keep from crying, but she said, "Don't cry."

"What makes you think *I'm* crying?" said Marta.

"You do this thing . . ." Rosie said. "I watch you." She touched her own cheeks and Marta imitated her gesture. Her cheeks felt pulled out of shape, and she ran her fingertips over the details of her own face, identifying something—the grimace that precedes crying. How alone she was. She held out an arm to Rosie, and in a moment Rosie was holding tight—oh, probably stunned at her luck—pressing her hair into Marta's face and catching tears.

"WELL, THE WORST THING," I said, sitting up in bed on one elbow, still naked and damp, "was when my goldfish died. I substituted my dead goldfish for my sister's live goldfish."

"That's bad, Tom." Ida thought for a while. "They had separate bowls but they looked alike?"

"Right." We were in her bed on a Saturday morning. I'd stayed over. We woke up, had coffee, and went back to bed. "So what was the worst thing *you* ever did?" I said.

"That was bad, letting your sister think her fish died." She lay on her back with her blond hair spread out and the red blanket up to her neck.

"I said it was the worst thing."

"Did she ever find out?"

"I can't remember. What was the worst thing for you?"

"One thing I *must* do today is my laundry," she said.

"But what was it?"

"I fucked a student's father," said Ida.

Ida is a high school teacher. As a matter of fact, she was *my* teacher at one point, some time ago. She's six years older than I am.

I didn't know what to say. "You did?" I said.

"Yes."

"You had sex with a student's father?"

I was cold, and I pulled the edge of the blanket around me. That pulled it off Ida, and I looked at her breasts and belly. She is fat and lovely.

"I fucked"—slight pause—"a student's father."

I wanted to undo the last minute and let her change the subject. I remembered the year I was in her class. I pictured my dad going up on report card night, hat in hand (he doesn't wear a hat, but the situation seemed hat-in-handish), waiting in line, then bending over the desk to confer with Ida about my B+, then kneeling—while removing his jacket and spreading it out—and stretching out on the classroom floor to make love to her as she slid off her chair. "Ida, it wasn't *my* father?"

She laughed. She *laughed*. "No, dummy, it wasn't your father. It wasn't that year."

I stood up. "How could you do that?" I put on my shorts, turning away from her.

She laughed again.

"Don't," I said. And then I cried. I hadn't cried since my grandmother died, and I hated the sound I made, a silly oohing. I cried standing up, without putting my hands on my face. She hurried out of bed. "Tom, sweetie, I'm sorry!"

But I was angry, and soon she was angry, too. "What is this? We were just talking," she said.

"Some kid," I said. "Some kid sitting there in your class—"

She got back into bed and pulled the blanket over herself, as if she were going back to sleep. "Stop being stupid," she said.

"I don't know why it bothers me so much . . ." I said.

"I'm a decent person!" she said, and vaulted out of bed (a flash of her large, naked breasts, her wonderful buttocks) and walked to the shower. The blanket dragged on the floor and she yanked it around herself.

It was cold—January—and in Ida's house the wind blew in

around the old window frames and between the frames and the old glass. It would be simple to replace those windows with nice, tight, well-made ones. I'm a carpenter; I renovate old houses. I stood there in my shorts, freezing, and looked through the wavery glass at a fence and a yard next door.

Ida didn't come straight into the bedroom after her shower and I heard her talking to her roommate, Kitty. Kitty is also a teacher. She is newer and was never my teacher. I said to the bare tree outside, "Did I hear you inquire what they are talking about? They're planning the next meeting of the Teachers' Sex Ring." I put on my pants. "They're working out the agenda." I went to the bathroom, now that Ida wasn't in it. On the way I heard her say, "Basically, maybe." I didn't like that. Someone in a good mood would say it. And she was wrapped in that red blanket like a kid playing Indians.

In the shower, I accused myself of being young and naive. Ida was older than I was, and so naturally she had gone to bed with more people. Maybe she just knew that sometimes workmen bring a bed to your classroom, or the UPS man delivers you in a brown van to the house of your student, where no one is home but his dad.

No, I assured myself. Maybe I feel naive compared to Ida, just because I wasn't around when interesting things she remembers happened: men walking on the moon or whatever I just missed. (I was actually around for men walking on the moon, but too young to remember it.) But I'm not naive; I'm simply a *nice guy*.

I dried off with Ida's red towel, got dressed, and found Ida in the kitchen, also dressed, cooking an omelet for us, which was friendly. Kitty sat at the table eating an apple. She had been out shoveling snow in front of the house, and Ida had felt bad when we went back to bed with our coffee instead of hurrying to help her. They only rented, but nobody else shoveled, and it had snowed over and over again. Now Ida was promising that we'd finish shoveling the snow. Kitty was tired, and her boyfriend, Martin, was coming for her, so they could do something with friends of his. Kitty thought the friends might not be interesting.

"Just because he himself is boring," Ida said, "doesn't mean his friends are boring."

Kitty pretended she was going to throw the apple at Ida, but this was old talk between them, and I knew Ida liked Kitty's boyfriend. I thought he was unusual—I wouldn't say boring. I am not in favor of anybody's being described that way. Martin's a big, hairy, sleepy guy. "I've been sitting halfway down the block for half an hour," he said, yawning, when he arrived. "A car in front of me got stuck partway out of a parking space and I couldn't go around it."

"You didn't help dig it out?" said Kitty.

"The lady wouldn't let me," he said. "She said thank you, but God would do it."

"And did God do it?"

"At last." Now that wouldn't have happened to anyone but Martin.

Ida and I put on our boots and went out to shovel after Kitty and Martin left. We had to dig out the porch steps, a little walk between the porch and the sidewalk, and the sidewalk in front of the house. They had a lousy shovel with bent corners, and a fairly solid hoe for chopping ice. It was a tremendously cold day—it had been cold all week—and I thought we couldn't do much. Kitty had shoveled a little piece of the sidewalk, which nobody was walking on anyway, because so much of the block hadn't been touched. People were walking in the middle of the street.

Ida took the hoe and I took the shovel, which I used to chop ice. I started on the steps while she went to the sidewalk. I chopped and chopped and every so often there was enough broken ice to scoop up. After a while I got tired of that and began shoveling fast down the walk. It was quiet on the street. A man and a woman walked by on the sidewalk and Ida straightened up, puffing and red-faced, to let them go. She went back to chopping. Her rhythm seemed to say, No, no, nonono, no, no. She was behind me. I was tossing snow over my shoulder, happy—or happier—because I was good at it. When I turned to watch her, she looked great, in her blue jacket with a hood and some of her hair coming out, and that hoe, which she held in both mittens and banged up and down.

But then she stopped abruptly and carried the hoe past me and toward the house. "Never mind," she said as she came along.

"Never mind what?"

"Don't bother doing any more. Thanks, but never mind. It's too hard."

But I was doing fine. I had cleared a path the width of one shovel, and I was wondering whether I couldn't widen it. I was looking forward to the sidewalk. I was warm now. "But look how much I did!" I said.

"I can see it," she said. "I don't want to wear myself out with this. I have to read a stack of tests and I *have* to do my laundry."

She went into the house. I didn't want to go with her. I wouldn't have enjoyed shoveling at my parents' house, where I lived, but this was different. I was liberating Kitty and Ida to meet the community, as if they couldn't leave unless I shoveled a path. Ida, good now, would walk out into the world.

I WENT INTO the house much later—too late. I had made a path two shovels wide, both on the sidewalk and the walk, but my back hurt and I was cold deep inside myself. Ida looked up from the tests she was marking and said, "That was childish."

"I wanted to do it," I said.

"You have a mechanical soul, Tom," she said. "Now I see why

you're a carpenter. You like achievements that can be lined up and counted. I bet before you quit work every day, you count how many goddamn screws you put in."

"Not as many screws as you, apparently," I said. I said it because my feet were heavy with cold.

Ida stood and the papers in her lap fell down, though she grabbed at them. She came toward me and I saw she was too angry to speak. Her face was ugly with it, and that was something I never thought I would think. She walked past me into the kitchen and began making coffee. She knew I hardly ever drink coffee, but I wanted something hot so badly, coffee would be fine. Except that it made me additionally angry: she'd probably drunk coffee with her married lover, at cute little coffeehouses.

Maybe at least he was divorced. "Was he divorced?" I said.

"I don't know why I should talk to you about it," she said. "Do you think I did wrong on purpose?"

"You went to bed with the father of a student by mistake?"

"I didn't know who he was."

"You didn't meet him on report card night?"

"I guess the mother came up." I tried to remember whether my mother or my father would have gone up. "When I realized," she said, "I knew I had known all along. But I didn't know I knew."

"That just doesn't make sense, Ida."

"Well, sorry," she said. She poured milk into her coffee and put the container back into the refrigerator so I had to go get it for myself. I felt awful about everything. I ordinarily like winter, but right then I hated the cold and snow. There were great things I could have done on a Saturday in January. I could have gone cross-country skiing. A friend of mine had said it wasn't hard and we could rent skis at a store nearby and ski in a park or on a golf course. If I hadn't been sitting there, I pointed out to myself, I'd have been cross-country skiing.

Outside, a dog walked by. The fences between the backyards weren't tight and he was ambling from yard to yard—over one fence with the help of a snowdrift, through a gap in the next. Ida and I both love dogs, and for a minute we almost made up, talking about him, but then we had another fight. We argued about whether dogs are (a) a nuisance but worth it, which was my position, or (b) not a nuisance at all, which was what Ida said. "People who don't appreciate dogs have little minds," she said.

"I *love* dogs," I insisted.

What would happen if we lived together or got married? Ida was so sure dogs have no faults, I began to think that she'd want four or five dogs. To me, children are faultless; *children* are perfect. I decided, then and there, that I wanted four or five children. Ida would want to substitute dogs for my children!

Now was the time of day I'd absolutely intended to leave. It was getting dark. My parents were having company and I'd promised to show up and say hello. And Ida had to go to the laundromat. It would have been smart to leave, but I couldn't. I wanted to fix things. When Ida walked past me to get her laundry together, and came back into the room, stuffing the sheet we'd slept on into a laundry bag, and then leaned on the sink, watching me drink the last of my coffee, she looked farther away than usual. Once, my boss and I put kitchen cabinets where a lady's coat closet had been, and she said that corner was where she stared when she talked on the phone. "Now while I talk, I'm thinking pots instead of coats," she said. "Cooking instead of going." Carpenters had apparently come through Ida's kitchen and widened it. Everything in the room looked dangerous. I'd never noticed how many knives she and Kitty had.

I didn't leave, and it took Ida so long to get her laundry together while fighting with me—about sex, about dogs, about everything— that we got hungry. Eventually we had a pizza delivered, which took longer than we expected. But we couldn't leave to do the laundry once we'd ordered the pizza. It took a long time to eat it, too. Ida was afraid we wouldn't make it to the laundromat on time. She said there was a sign on the door: LAST WASH: 8:50 P.M. And both our cars were socked in with snow. The plow had come through and buried mine, but it was less buried than Ida's, so when we finally did get moving, we took mine. At some point it became clear that we were both going to the laundromat, if only to finish the various arguments. I'd probably missed my parents' visitors anyway. My car required only minor digging. I shoveled it out while Ida put her bag of laundry into the back seat and then remembered her detergent.

"His wife walked by while we were shoveling," said Ida, as we finally drove away over the hard, bumpy snow. The big old turquoise bag she always carried was between us, and she'd stuck her box of detergent into it.

"Whose wife?"

"The man. My old lover."

"You recognized her?"

"That's why I got so upset with you for shoveling. She walked by with another man. Maybe she's cheating on Parker."

"Who's Parker?"

"My lover." I hated her saying that—twice—and so I blew it. I didn't let her make up with me. I should have said, "Oh, baby," and hugged her.

"That was his name, *Parker*?" I said, instead.

"Forget it, please."

"His poor kids," I said. "How many kids?"

"Will you *stop* it?"

I drove around a corner—carefully because it was a narrow street with a lot of snow wedged up against the curb, and I didn't want to get stuck—and then, all of a sudden, somebody was *dancing* in front of my car: a happy hitchhiker, a guy my age in a hooded sweatshirt—no coat in that weather—leaping and waving a shovel at me as if flagging me down was a terrific joke. As if he knew me. As if he were my brother! I just have one sister. He had straight dark hair over his face and wasn't very big—I'm not big either—and I stopped the car where I was. One thing about a heavy snow: everybody stops cars anytime they want, and nobody crashes into you. I jumped out to hear what he wanted, as if he might say, "I'm your new brother! God decided you needed a brother!" Which I did, which I did.

He touched me on the arm, smiling. He had a long nose and a pointed face. "I gotta get this car out," he said, waving the shovel. "You gonna help me get this car out?"

I looked. There was a little old car, deep in the snow, as if it hadn't been used all week.

"Why, do you need a ride? I could take you somewhere," I said. "Soon as I take my girlfriend to the laundromat. I mean, if it's an emergency . . ." I guess I thought that you wouldn't just stop someone if it *wasn't* an emergency. I was even thinking that if it was a serious emergency, I might have to take him to the hospital or something and forget the laundromat. But he looked fine. He didn't need a ride to the hospital.

"No, I don't need the car until later. You just gotta help me dig it out," he said. Then I thought maybe I did know him and I hadn't recognized him. You might say what he'd said to a friend, maybe an acquaintance. Maybe he knew me, or even knew my car. Maybe we'd gone to high school together, or played softball together.

"I have to drive Ida to the laundromat," I said. "They have Last Wash."

"Fuck, man, I've been digging for so long . . ." His car looked sweet and helpless, tucked away there.

"You stopped me because you just couldn't stand digging alone anymore?" I said.

"Right, right."

"What's going on?" It was Ida, getting out of the car. She looked at the guy. She didn't seem to know him.

"He needs help," I said.

"A ride?"

"I just need somebody to help dig, or push while I start the car," he said.

"I could do that," I said. I'd stopped to help people dig out a couple of times in the last weeks, and people had stopped to help me.

"Tom, I know this is of no interest, but the laundromat—"

"Could you just take my car to the laundromat?" I said to Ida. "I can walk from here, after I get him dug out. I'm Tom," I said to him.

"Hey, Tom. Denny."

"Glad to meet you, Denny." I figured I'd better not say, "This is Ida."

"All right," said Ida.

"I'll drive him, I'll drive him," Denny called to her. We were five or six blocks from the place. It was *cold*.

Ida got into my car. I was standing in front of it, and I stared at her through the window. She moved a little closer to me but it was just because she was moving the seat forward to reach the pedals. She looked exasperated, and reset the rearview mirror and the side mirrors as carefully as if she were driving a hundred miles away from me. She drove slowly down the bumpy street.

Denny and I started to dig. I didn't mind. At last I was away from the fight with Ida. I was good at digging, unlike fighting. Denny hadn't accomplished much, even though he'd worn himself out. He had shoveled in the wrong places—making a lane for the car to go straight out. I thought it would be easier if we turned the wheels and drove out at an angle. No, he said, it definitely wouldn't. He couldn't stop talking to me while I dug, talking about his girl-friend, whom he was going to visit, if he ever got the car out. "A very cool lady," he said. "She's cooking a fine soup for me. It's almost done. I don't want it to get overdone."

"I don't think you can overcook soup," I said.

"Of course you can. Overdone soup, yuck."

It irritated me that even though I was helping him, he kept contradicting me, but I liked him, too, maybe just for being so bold. He next told me he could make more of a contribution if he sat in the car and tried to drive it instead of shoveling, which was nonsense. He said the wheels would push the snow a little at a time. He demonstrated, but of course the wheels spun.

"They were spinning," I said when he got out.

"They *appeared* to be spinning," said Denny.

I decided he was a nut or on something, but at least he was cheerful. "You live here?" I said, pointing to the nearest house.

"Naw, I wouldn't live here," he said. "I'm staying with friends a couple blocks down. I parked here because somebody had just dug the space out—boy was *he* mad! But then it snowed on me all week."

"You drove in when he drove out?" I had been tempted to do that, but some of the old men in my neighborhood acted as if they owned the spaces once they dug them out. They'd put up string barriers or leave a chair in the middle of the space.

Finally we moved the car a few inches. I was tired. I'd done a lot of shoveling. I got Denny to dig while I drove, and I rocked the car, moving it slightly back and forth, and made a little progress that way. At last I drove the car into the street, and Denny jumped into the passenger seat, shaking his head in wonder as if we'd dug up Troy. "Hey, man, you are one helluva guy. And *I* am one helluva guy."

I started to get out, but he said I should drive to the laundromat. I figured by now Ida should be almost ready to put the clothes into the dryer. We drove a couple of blocks and he suddenly said, "No, wait, wait, turn down here," and obediently, before I thought, I made the turn. "I want to show you something," he said. "I really got to show you something. This is something all my friends got to see."

I was afraid he meant drugs, and I said, "I'd rather just go to the laundromat, if you don't mind." I thought I'd make another turn and circle around to the street we'd been on.

"No, wait a minute. I don't mean nothing bad. Listen, man, I know you're not that kind. I'm not going to get you in trouble."

The next cross street, the one that would start to take me back where I'd begun, looked so choked with snow I wasn't sure we could make it, and there was no possibility of a U-turn on the street we were on, which was one of those narrow old streets lined with three-story houses. It hadn't been plowed much. So I kept going, figuring I could wait in the car while he went in wherever it was. He took me a lot farther out of my way than I wanted to go—maybe eight blocks—and I didn't know what to do next. We were coming to a large intersection and I figured I would make the turn there, but just before it Denny yelled, "Stop here, Tom, stop here."

And then I went into the house with him. Reasons: I was freezing. I was curious. I was so upset about Ida I'd have gone anywhere with anybody. And it was too far to walk back to the laundromat in the cold.

Also, though I knew Denny wasn't some harmless potential buddy of mine, I thought I also knew where he was coming from. I didn't think he'd be any trouble. He looked basically civilized, under all the craziness and street smarts, as if he had regular parents somewhere. His teeth were good—I could see when he smiled that he had no missing teeth. Teeth is the key, I've been told. I wouldn't have gone up those mildly cabbagy narrow wooden stairs with a guy who had big gaps in his teeth.

"Is this where you live?" I said.

"Almost, but not exactly."

"Is this the house a couple of blocks from the parking space?"

"Of course not," said Denny. "This is no couple of blocks."

Denny seemed to have a key, or he knew where they hid the key, even if he didn't exactly live there. He was scrambling around in the dark and then he opened the door. "Is this where your girl-friend lives?" I said.

"No, she lives in a much nicer place than this," he said. "She lives in the country, like my grandma."

"Your grandmother lives in the country?"

"A million birds," he said.

In the apartment, which was dirty but all right, not too different from places I'd lived in, was what he wanted me to see—and it was a pile of dolls on a sofa: an enormous heap of flimsy pink and red doll clothes and plastic smiles, and arms sticking up as if they were stretching toward me for help. "Where did you get those?" I asked. They looked new.

"A friend of mine gave them to me," he said. "He was going out of business—he had this real nice toy store, and he was going out of business."

"Did you steal them?" I tried to think whether I'd seen anything in the *Register* about a recent break-in at a toy store.

"Why would I steal them?"

"Why do you want them?" I said.

"Why do I want them?" He pulled off the thin, brown, woolen gloves he was wearing and thrust his hand into the pile of doll arms and legs and bodies and chiffon, or whatever that thin scratchy cloth they use is. "Don't you like them?" And he straightened up and smiled as me as if he'd been showing me dirty pictures.

"They're great," I said. I was depressed. He waited, watching me, and finally I thrust my hand in, too. I could feel the rough net of the ballerina cloth and the slippery cloth of their other clothes, and the hard, rounded plastic bodies and fake hair. My hand worked its way down among the dolls and then I pulled it up. "Cool," I said hesitantly, though I was a little sick to my stomach.

But Denny had turned away. "Take off your coat," he said quietly.

"I have to go."

"Take it off."

"I need to get back to Ida," I said.

"In a minute."

I unzipped my jacket. I didn't want him to have anything to complain about.

Denny had taken off his sweatshirt at some point, and I saw that he was wearing a white T-shirt. I saw it because he had turned his back and was fiddling with something on a table in the middle of the room—a round table with clutter on it. His back was hunched a little. He was a small man with a tense back, and from behind he looked young and questioning. The T-shirt was strange on such a cold day. His arms were thin.

"I think you better give me money," he said. Of course.

"What did you say?" But I'd heard him. Except I wasn't certain. Maybe he had said something else and my mind had changed it around.

"I guess you better give me your money."

"You're asking me for money?" I said.

"Right."

He shifted or I shifted and I saw what was on the table in front of him: three things about the same size. A light bulb, a black plastic thing that was probably the remote for a TV, and a gun. It was a small, squarish automatic—it looked like stainless steel. Denny was pushing the three things around on the table a little, moving first one, then another. Of course, it could have been a toy gun, but it didn't look like a toy.

"I don't have much money," I said.

"Neither do I," he said. He let the light bulb roll, and it rolled off the table and shattered on the floor. It was important to cheer him up, to get him friendly again, to get him talking about different things, but for a long time I couldn't think of anything to say. "I had a fight with my girlfriend today," I said at last, while I reached under my coat for my wallet.

"The blond lady?"

I took my wallet out. All I had on me was a ten-dollar bill. I put it on the table.

"You're giving me this," he said seriously, turning to face me again and putting it in his pocket. "I'm not *taking* it, I'm *asking* for it. It's a present."

"Sure," I said. Anything.

"What did you fight about?" he said.

I was too scared to make something up. "I asked her what was the worst thing she ever did—"

"What did you ask her *that* for?" Denny moved closer to me and I stepped back and stiffened, but he didn't pick up the gun. "What did you ask her something like that for?"

"I don't know. It was a game," I said.

"Some game. What did she say?"

"Well, see, she's a teacher." I wished I hadn't started this, but I didn't know what else to say. "And she said she went to bed with a student's father."

"She did? A teacher? Wow, that's something," he said. "Did she send home a note with the kid, or how did it start?"

"I don't know," I said.

"You'd think she'd be afraid the principal would find out; she'd lose her job."

"I didn't think about that."

"Sure, man, that's a big thing to worry about," said Denny. "You tell her, watch out, the principal could fire her just like that. He could walk into her room where she's teaching and say, 'Lady, you're history.'"

"English," I said.

"What?"

"She teaches English." Then I saw what he meant and I laughed but I felt stupid. Being scared you're going to die makes you stupid. "I had a fight with her about it. I didn't think she should have done it." And right then, I thought, What if it doesn't work out for Ida and me? What if it doesn't? Since the day we started seeing each other, I was sure we'd get married and be happy forever, but now I was suddenly thinking, What if it doesn't work out?

"So, she's glad she did it?" said Denny.

"No, I guess not," I said.

"So what did you fight about?"

"I don't know," I said.

"Did she do it when you guys were already—"

"Oh, no," I said.

"So you wanted her to save herself for you?"

"No, it wasn't that."

"So what was it?"

"I felt bad for the kid," I said.

"The guy's kid?"

"Right."

He considered. "I could see that," he said. "Do you love her?"

"Of course I love her!" I said. "I love her—you can't imagine how much I love her!"

"Even my girlfriend—hey, I gotta get over there, I gotta get you back to this lady." He put on the sweatshirt and gloves again. "You *gave* me the money, right? Gave. Because we're friends. Brothers."

"Gave."

"I mean, if you need it, I'll give it back to you anytime, just not tonight."

"Right," I said.

"The worst thing. You know what the worst thing I ever did was?" By now we were walking down the stairs. He was ahead of me.

"What?"

"I shot this guy," he said. "And it was bad because he never did nothing to me. He was nice to me—he tried to help me out, and I shot him."

"Did he die?" We were down in the street by now, walking side by side like members of the same Boy Scout troop.

"I don't know, man." He got into the driver's seat of his car. I considered walking the mile or so back to Ida, in the snow, but it must have been zero out, and I was pretty sure the gun was upstairs. I got into the passenger seat.

"You love her?" he said.

"I said yes!"

"I mean, *love* her?"

"Of course I do! Of course!" He made a three-point turn in the snow, and I was sure we'd get stuck, but we didn't; and as we faced this way, then that way, in the turning car, I felt as if we were turning to look at the vastness of my love. I loved Ida in every direction and in every object on that dark, wintry city block.

Then Denny drove back the way we'd come, turned the corner into the route we'd left, and stopped the car when we got to the laundromat, right behind my car, which I was amazed to see there, as if I'd found it on the moon.

"Thanks for helping me dig out," he said. I could see Ida inside, moving around, stretching her arms wide. Folding, she was already folding.

I got out and waved a little and closed the door and watched while Denny drove away. Then I went into the laundromat. Nobody was in there under the bright lights but Ida and an old woman. Dryers were turning and thumping, turning and thumping. Ida was slowly folding a sheet, and I recognized the sheet on which we'd made love that morning, light blue with dark blue flowers on it. She was holding it out as far as she could with both arms, as if she wanted to wrap me in it. Then she folded it once and folded it again. "What took you so long?" she said. She sounded tired, not angry. She sounded glad to see me.

"And another thing," said the old woman. I looked at her. She was a dignified old lady, not a bag lady or anything like that. She had on a coat with a fur collar and a fur hat on her white hair. I expected her to say, "And another thing, you gave that fellow all your money!" But instead, the old woman said, "Another thing. When a lady refuses to give you a recipe for something delicious you have just eaten in her home, quite often it is for a surprising reason. Quite often there has been a disaster in the kitchen and she has served the food anyway. You know! Probably you've done it yourself! You put the last spoonful of flour into the cake batter, and you see that there is a bug in it." The lady stared into an imaginary bowl of cake batter. "You *scoop* out the bug"—she acted it out— "but! You continue baking the cake! You don't throw out the batter! And when you receive compliments, you think that perhaps the cake was improved by bug urine. Now, haven't you ever done that?"

"No," said Ida, looking at me and keeping her back to the old woman. Her face was red and she was trying not to smile. I know it was because of the old woman, but she was smiling at me, too. "I don't think I've ever done that," she said. "Can't remember doing that." One of the dryers flopped a last time and settled.

"Well, if you're going to marry this gentleman and set up a household," said the old woman, while Ida crouched and opened the dryer and took out an armful of clothes, "sooner or later, you'll do it. We all do it, sooner or later. Right?" She turned to me. "Am I right?"

I was smiling hard at both of them. "Sure," I said, hardly knowing what I was agreeing with. "Right you are," I said, watching Ida stand up, her arms full of clean shirts and underwear, while socks fell to the floor on all sides of her.

FOR YEARS EUGENE lived alone, even when he had a boy-friend. Now he lives with Albert, an optometrist. Eugene works for the dog warden. Albert is educating him about movies: they rent old movies; they go to the movies. They went to the York Square to see *Remains of the Day* and then they argued about it. "How could you not like that movie?" said Albert, and Eugene said he did like it, he just didn't love it.

"Anthony Hopkins was really like a butler in that movie," he said. "He was so stiff."

"That's the idea," said Albert. "They paid him to be stiff." They had coffee. Albert had real coffee and Eugene had decaf.

Walking to the car, Eugene recognized two people he knew from volunteering at the soup kitchen. "Downtown is all street people," he said.

"Yalies," said Albert.

"Yalies and street people," said Eugene. "That man crossing the street. Middle class looking, white, nice clothes. I see him eating at the soup kitchen all the time."

"Maybe he *is* middle class and he just likes getting a free lunch," said Albert.

"I don't think so," said Eugene. The man didn't take

care of his face the way middle-class people did. He thought of Anthony Hopkins' careful face in the movie.

In the morning there were no juice glasses and Albert scolded him. "You are a person who breaks glasses. At least drinking glasses, not eyeglasses." Albert patted the temple of his glasses.

"But I sweep up the glass."

"This is true." Albert paused. "The juice glasses I used to have were made of tempered glass," he said. "They were harder to break, but when they did break, they broke into a million tiny chips. They made me nervous. They were holding themselves together too tightly."

"Anthony Hopkins," said Eugene. He didn't say, "Who did you live with then?" because whoever it was—well, Albert had had one boyfriend who left him, and one who died.

It was Eugene's day to go to the soup kitchen, where he had once broken a tray of mugs, which was serious, because there weren't very many. Mugs walked out the door there, everyone said. Eugene had brought a tray of clean mugs from the kitchen into the dining room, and he had no place to put it because there were already mugs on the serving table, so he balanced the tray against the table with his body, taking mugs out. The mugs were white, with the words "First Constitution Bank" on them. The soup kitchen had received hundreds of them when the bank went under and changed its name, but there weren't many left. The tray slipped and all the mugs fell. The noise made everyone look at him. Eugene bent down to look at the fallen mugs, but every one of them was broken in half, or had a big chip or no handle. Going for the broom, he was deeply ashamed.

This morning, before Eugene went to the soup kitchen he rinsed six large yogurt containers he'd saved. Albert liked yogurt and granola for breakfast, and Eugene had been storing the containers under the sink, trying to remember to take them with him. At the soup kitchen, leftover food was given away at the end of the meal in plastic containers. "Have fun," called Albert as Eugene went out with his yogurt containers, and, in a way, working at the soup kitchen *was* fun. He had lived with Albert for just a few months; leaving him in the apartment, saying good-bye only casually because they would be together again soon, was like taking a cool bite of something smooth and sweet. Eugene touched the doorknob, the mailbox, and the porch railing as he passed, and then he was on his way.

The line of people waiting for lunch stretched out the door. Eugene squeezed past and went inside. He brought his yogurt containers to the bin where they were kept. Elizabeth, the dining room manager, walked up behind him as he was putting them into the bin. She wore purple skirts to her ankles, but had sense. "Here you are!" she said, smiling.

"The breaker of cups!" It had happened months ago. After a while, he had stopped apologizing.

"Break any more and I'll break *you*," she said in a friendly way. "Serve dessert, okay?"

Today there were all sort of pastries, somewhat squashed. Eugene took his place behind the serving table. Now the first server put a scoop of mashed potatoes onto the first stainless-steel tray. She handed it to an old man who was first in the line that stretched around the room and out the door.

"Potatoes make you sexy," said the old man. He held out his tray to the next server for chicken stew. "Make you lose all control."

"They do *not*," said the server of the potatoes, a young black woman with highly organized hair. Eugene couldn't remember her name. "That's the first time I heard *that*."

"What happened to 'The customer is always right'?" said the second man in line, taking his tray. "If my uncle here says potatoes make you sexy, they make you *sexy*. I'm feeling sexy already."

"He's not your uncle," said the server.

"How do you know?"

A different old man, whom Eugene had seen here often, was coming along the line. While Eugene served the guests ahead of the second old man, he tried to figure out how the old man had changed. Eugene had once told Albert about him. He was lame and blind and had no teeth. "Remember that sign in the hardware store?" he'd said to Albert. " 'Lost dog—three legs, no ear, one eye, half a tail, answers to Lucky'? Something like that? Well, this must be Lucky." Lucky reached Eugene and pointed to a doughnut, and Eugene said hello and gave it to him. The old man was less old or less something. He wasn't blind. Maybe it was a different man, not Lucky.

Eugene couldn't remember whether Lucky was black or white. This man was a light-skinned black man. Many people who ate here and worked here were black, but not all by any means. Eugene, who was white, liked forgetting about race and having to think. And so many people weren't exactly black or white, anyway; they were just light brown people. Eugene went for more pastries, and when he came back nobody was serving salad, so for a while he did both; then a woman named Shirley took over the dessert, and Eugene served salad. A lot of people didn't like salad, but the ones who did liked it a lot.

It was a day on which people burst out with things. One man said to Shirley, "Look at that plain cake you gave me. No icing. No sugar. You are always mean to me."

"Joey, I'm not mean to you!" Shirley said. "Which one do you want?"

"I don't want none, now. You know what I wanted, Shirley."

"Oh, stop," said Shirley. Eugene didn't know if she was angry or only pretending.

"You made me so unhappy!" said the man. Now his voice rose sharply, and people stopped talking and looked at him. "I loved you!" the man shouted. "What did that mean to you? Nothing!" It was remarkable shouting.

"Oh, you never loved me," Shirley said.

"Oh, I did love you." He paused, and his voice dropped. "I do love you." He faced the room. "I love her!" His voice boomed. At last he took his tray—without dessert—and went to a table.

"Was he *serious*?" Eugene asked Shirley. She shook her head and smiled. "I thought he was," said Eugene.

"What do you know about it?" said the man serving stew, a tall man Eugene hadn't seen before. The staff was people on city welfare—they came and went. Sometimes there were other volunteers like Eugene, often not. "*You* wouldn't know."

"I guess not," said Eugene.

Shirley looked at Eugene. "Because you're white or because of something else?"

"I mean something else," said the tall man.

"Oh, leave him alone," said Shirley.

"Nah, I didn't mean nothing," said the man. Eugene wondered if the man meant because he was gay—or because he was a baby. "You're such a baby!" people said. An innocent. The line had slowed, but now there was a burst of new people and the servers were too busy to talk for a long time. When the salad was gone, Eugene went back to serving dessert; Shirley took a break. He emptied the dessert tray twice more and refilled it with pastries from donated Entenmann's boxes.

Then it was the cook's turn to burst out. Ten minutes before quitting time, she stuck her head out of the kitchen. "Bring the food in!" she called.

"It's way too early," said Eugene, surprised.

Marjorie, the cook, came out of the kitchen. She could be grumpy and Eugene was a little afraid of her. The day he broke the tray of mugs, Marjorie hadn't said anything, but she'd looked at him without any expression in her eyes at all, as if she'd stuck dull nickels into her eye sockets. He had thought that if he were black, like her, she'd have yelled. Now she said, "I said, last tray, Eugene!"

"It's too early."

"It's twenty past," said Marjorie.

"It's only eight past on my watch."

Marjorie said, "It's twenty past in the kitchen and I said last tray!" She went back to the kitchen. No one was waiting on line, but if they carried the food in, five people would turn up.

Eugene shouted, "No, Marjorie, it *doesn't make sense*!" He had never shouted there. Everyone shouted except Eugene.

"You're right, man," said the tall man—whose name had turned out to be Graham. "That clock they got in there stinks. Sometimes it goes backwards."

Shirley and the woman with the organized hair laughed. "Oh, it doesn't go backwards!" Shirley said. Now she was serving green beans.

"Time for fireworks," said Graham, looking toward the kitchen. But Marjorie didn't come out, and when they finally carried the food in, ten minutes later, she shouted at Eugene, who was leading the way, "Who told you to bring that food in?" So they backed up and served another man who had just come in and was already shouting at them for not serving him. "You white guys," he said to Eugene, choosing a doughnut. "You don't know what it's like."

"Oh, quit it," said Eugene. He felt disorderly, a little excited. He had yelled and been yelled at. One more person was coming, an old man. "I already ate," said the old man. "I came back for another doughnut." Of course—it was Lucky again. How could Eugene not have recognized him? He remembered that once he'd carried Lucky's tray to a table for him, because Lucky obviously couldn't see. But this man could see. Now the angry man said to Lucky, "You eat too many sweets, Kent." So Lucky's name was Kent.

Eugene carried the rest of the pastries into the kitchen. He was still fascinated that he'd yelled, though nobody else seemed to have noticed. He took the least ratty broom. Shirley and the woman with the organized hair were wiping the tables, and Graham was sweeping at the other end of the dining room, so Eugene went over to sweep near the door. His eyes were on the floor, and as he swept, the feet of the last people went out of the dining room past him.

And then suddenly he was not sweeping. The broom clattered to the floor (but he was aware of having made it clatter in a safe direction) and Eugene's arms were clutching a woman he had seized, it seemed, before seeing her.

"Let's take it easy," he was saying. His arms were around a small, thin black woman. He was holding her up, and holding her close to him as if they were friends or lovers. A last woman had come in late, he began to understand, and collapsed as she walked past Eugene, and he had knocked the broom aside and caught her just before she fell, and now he was supporting her light body—it was delicate and spare—and they were walking together to the nearest chair in the dining room. Graham pulled the chair away from the table, and Eugene eased the woman into it and knelt to make sure she didn't topple off, releasing her slowly and then laying his hand lightly on her arm.

"It's just my medication," said the woman. She had a dark, still, intelligent face.

Elizabeth hurried in. "Isabel, shall I call 911?"

"No, thanks," said the woman clearly. "I'll be fine. I hurried to get here before you closed."

Graham brought her two of Eugene's yogurt containers, filled with food. The woman was saying, "They wouldn't see me at the health center. They said I didn't have an appointment."

"Shall I call them?" Eugene asked her.

"They gave me an appointment for Monday. That's all they'll do for me."

149

Elizabeth said, "Isabel, I want to call the EMTs."

"Oh, I don't want to go to the hospital," said the woman. "I'll walk home slowly. This happened because I hurried."

"I hate hospitals, too," said Eugene. He said to Elizabeth, "Shall I walk her home?"

"And what will you do if she collapses in the street?" said Elizabeth.

Eugene was embarrassed. He was not thinking. He knelt. "Let her call," he said, stroking Isabel's arm, as though because he'd held her, he was allowed to touch her.

"Well, I'm calling," said Elizabeth. She strode into the other room, her long skirt swaying.

"Do you have a cigarette?" Isabel asked Eugene.

"A cigarette!" said Eugene. "Of course not!" He stayed with her, neither of them speaking, until the EMTs, two earnest men he'd seen there before, arrived. He didn't move away when they asked Isabel questions. "Date of birth?"

She was thirty-four, Eugene's age.

"She's on medication," said Eugene.

"Have any liquor today, Isabel?" said one of the EMTs.

"A couple."

"Smoke?"

"Yes."

He took her blood pressure. Sixty over seventy. Eugene hadn't known blood pressure could be so low.

"Isabel, I want you to go to the hospital," said the EMT.

"I hate the hospital," said Isabel.

"I know, I know."

"Go," said Eugene. "I thought you shouldn't, but now I think you should."

"Where's my purse?" said Isabel. "What happened to my purse?"

She had no purse. "I don't think you brought it," said Eugene.

"Of course I did. It's brown. One of you took it."

"Isabel," said the EMT.

"All right, I'll go, but I want my purse."

And now she insisted on a cigarette. She walked out to the driveway, just a little wobbly, carrying her containers of food. Eugene followed. The EMTs stood nearby, waiting for the ambulance. Isabel asked everyone standing there for a cigarette. Eugene went back to say good-bye to Elizabeth. He found her at her table in the corner, writing numbers on the charts she kept. He watched for a moment. "How many did we serve today?" she said.

He considered. The soup kitchen owned 204 regular trays, and 75 had been washed and used again. And they'd used most of the kids' trays, which were smaller. Nobody ever seemed to know how many kids' trays there were. Thirteen? They agreed on a total of 288.

"It felt like more," he said. "Oh, and Isabel. One more."

"Two eighty-nine. A quiet day." She was joking. Two eighty-nine was a lot, not the most they'd ever had, but a lot.

"I thought it was a hard day," he said.

"So did I."

"Wild."

"A little wild."

"Sometimes I like wild," he admitted. "Letting loose."

She nodded. "It has pleasures and pains."

"I never heard of blood pressure so low," he said.

"Oh, sure."

He turned away and turned back. "I thought she just had the flu or something. How did you know?" If Elizabeth hadn't been there, he'd have tried to walk the woman home and anything might have happened.

"I know. And I know *her*. I think she has AIDS."

"She's trying to bum a cigarette," he said. It hadn't occurred to him that Isabel might have AIDS. Of course he should have thought of it.

"Of course she is."

"I guess she can't stop smoking."

"I guess not."

Eugene went outside. The ambulance had backed into the driveway. Isabel was lying on the stretcher with her containers of food propped next to her; "Stop & Shop 100% Natural Plain Lowfat Yogurt," they said—as if one could know that much about anything. The stretcher was a terribly clean, tightly made bed on wheels, and the woman lying on it looked dark and ordinary in her street clothes, and very thin. She looked self-conscious. Eugene wanted to go to her but he didn't. After all, she might not exactly have noticed him. The woman looked completely different from Eugene's lover, Albert, but as if Albert had come in smiling from the grocery store with his arms around two big yogurt containers and had suddenly lain down to rest, Eugene imagined *him* lying there on the stretcher, smiling, and the containers in the crook of Albert's arm, not Isabel's. Now the ambulance workers wheeled the stretcher to the ambulance.

Eugene stood in the doorway. His arms felt light and strange from holding Isabel, and he thought he might cry if anybody touched him. Then he saw the man he'd thought was blind, the man called Kent, formerly Lucky. "I know what's different about you," Eugene said. "You have new glasses."

"That's right," said Kent. Now Eugene remembered. One lens of the old glasses had been covered with Scotch tape. It must have been broken. These new ones were bifocals with thick lenses.

"They're great." Maybe Albert had prescribed them. It was possible.

"Thank you," said Kent. The old man sat down on a low wall

near the driveway and Eugene sat with him. The doors of the ambulance closed and it drove slowly down the driveway past them
and moved into the street. Eugene thought of leaning over and crying on the old man's shoulder, but of course he didn't. It helped to
sit there. A man passed and looked at Kent. "Hey, pal," he said.

"You got a cigarette for me?" said Kent.

"Not today," said the man. "I'm fresh out." He waved at both
of them, as if they were two panhandlers.

Then Kent told Eugene a story. One night he'd been panhan-
dling in front of the Store 24. He'd lost a button from his shirt cuff.
He had a coffee cup for money, and when he held it up his cuff fell
away and his arm was cold. But the cup was not comfortable in the
other hand; that was for his cane. A man in a denim jacket walked
up Broadway and Kent said, "Change?" though what he wanted was
a cigarette. The man touched his pants pocket and said, "In a minute."

It was a good night—just a little cool. The lights in the parking
lot dazzled into lines. It wasn't rain; it was the tape on his glasses.
Soon Kent would walk home. Not a good idea to walk too late.

A car double-parked in front of the Store 24 and a man got
out. "Hey, would you watch my car?" he said to Kent. "No problem," said the old man. He liked facing a different way for a
change. Kent moved across the sidewalk and between the parked
cars, and he leaned on the man's car. He saw the man in the
denim jacket come out of the Store 24 carrying a container of
milk. The man stopped and looked around. "Here!" called Kent.
Then the man came over to him and gave him a twenty. And the
second man, the owner of the car, came out and gave him a five.
Kent just had time to buy liquor before the store closed. All the
way home, holding the package of booze, leaning on the cane, he
thought about what had happened. He had cigarettes, too. He

thought, "Maybe it will happen again," but he knew it wouldn't. He went home and got drunk and smoked, and finally he went to bed. It was hard to go to bed, because until he went to bed he was living in the same day with his luck, and leaving it was like leaving a room with a friend in it.

MY DAUGHTER'S NAME is Tabitha but sometimes I say Plumjam, Pebblesweet . . . even now; she's a high school senior. "Where do you *get* that stuff?" shouted Christopher once. "Pebblesweet!" Christopher is a man I've loved for twenty years—when I've thought of him—but I don't sleep with Christopher. My husband, Parker Stillman, has gone to bed with other women. (Yes, I knew. My anguish fastened on trivialities: Who heard Parker's rare jokes?) Now Parker wouldn't do what he couldn't discuss with Tabitha. Their voices rise through the heating ducts in our mellow, wood-worky old house, which Parker and I bought last year, recklessly, with all our money.

Something is wrong with Tabitha's eyes. Our son, Brian, discovered it when he tested everybody's visual perception for a psychology assignment. When Tabitha covered her left eye, straight lines swooped sideways no matter what Brian was demonstrating. "I have a warp in my right eye," she said.

The doctor asked if she'd stared at eclipses. She hadn't. She has macular degeneration. I thought only old people got that, but it turns out they get the "wet" kind and this is the "dry" kind. "The wet kind sounds sloppy," said Tab. It may get worse; it won't go away. Tabitha says reading is peculiar lately; light hurts. She has special glasses.

"What's it like *exactly?*"

She looked up at me from the *Times*. "I shall look out the window," she said. "I shall close my left eye and curve the telephone pole. Curve, telephone pole! I have curved the telephone pole." She bowed.

I cannot curve the telephone pole. "But the street around it, Plumjam, that looks right?"

"Unless I look directly at something straight. I can curve the edge of that roof if you want me to."

"I want to straighten the telephone pole!" I said. "Or at least I want to see it your way."

"What a mother," said Tabitha.

Perhaps you are picturing white people saying these things, but we are light-skinned black women, Tabitha and I. Parker is white. Brian has very light skin and describes himself as "Other."

Eyes were the main topic here, besides college applications and financial aid forms, when Christopher (a big man, light brown skin, hair getting gray) came for the weekend in the middle of January, a wintry January. I had first met Christopher when he and Parker shared an apartment on Chapel Street. Chris was a graduate student in political science at Yale and Parker was in the school of architecture. Parker is a New Haven architect, but Christopher lives in San Francisco and writes for magazines—mostly, he says, *The Pig Farmer's Newsletter* and *Modern Sewage,* but now and then I spot his name and read something cranky and interesting about politics or city life.

When Christopher came for the weekend, Tabitha was finishing applications to Oberlin and Vassar. Both had to be postmarked on the Saturday. Brian was thinking hockey, and Parker had promised to drive him and some teammates to a game on Saturday. Christopher came on Friday in time for dinner. "I'm writing two good stories," he said. " 'Lying' and 'Dying.' " Parker had cooked Indian food. "Suicide," Christopher said, and swallowed. "In India—"

"Lying down or telling falsehoods?" said Tab.

"Falsehoods. I'm here to interview a grand old liar at Yale."

"There are a number of grand old liars at Yale," said Parker.

"This is the prince of lies," Christopher said. "Retired philosophy professor. Wrote a great book. I'm lucky to get him before he drops dead."

"Then you could interview him for the other story," Brian said.

The prince of lies was named Markowitz and he lived not far from our house, in a richer direction. The interview was Saturday afternoon, and Parker was taking our only car to the hockey game, but Christopher could walk to the professor's house.

"It's supposed to stay cold," I said.

"The cold is interesting," said Christopher.

The temperature had been close to zero or below for several days—unusual for us. I didn't mind, but I was shy with this serious weather, conscious of when I went outside and who knew I was going. I told Chris I'd walked to work twice when it was zero.

When I said work, Christopher remembered what I'd been worried about at the office the last time he'd come. "Did you have to shoot anyone?" he said now.

"One."

"What happened? Tell me the whole story." I will love any man who says that, but now Tabitha asked about Christopher's article on suicide. "Well, I read one of those dumb pieces about depression," he said. "Send Grandma to a shrink if she's sad because Grandpa has cancer. One of *those* pieces. I can't leave them alone. The worst thing is checklists. If somebody prints a checklist, I have to test myself."

We were all suckers for checklists. Brian went for his psychology textbook, full of checklists. Christopher kept talking. "So I read the symptoms of depression, and one of them is 'suicidal thoughts.' I mean, it's a symptom of depression to *think* about committing suicide. Well, I don't know about you, but every *week* I think about suicide. It didn't say try it. It just said think of it."

"You think about suicide every week?" I said. "You think about it as a topic or you think about doing it?"

"Doing it. I think, I wouldn't have to write this if I were dead. How shall I kill myself? For example, I'd never jump out a window. Never."

I was clearing the table but I stopped. "Every week?"

"Is this a story about putting a plastic bag over your head?" said Parker. "Dr. Kevorkian?"

"No, no, I'm not writing about committing suicide, just thinking of it."

"I know what you mean," said Tabitha.

"No, you don't!" Parker said, and he almost shouted at her. "You're the happiest little person I've ever heard of. You don't have suicidal thoughts."

"I think Chris is right," said Tab. "I think everybody does."

"If I were a science-fiction writer," said Christopher, "I'd do this as fiction. A universe in which you could die just by deciding to. If you could lie down and cross your arms on your chest . . ." And Christopher lay down on our dining room floor, though it has no carpet. He closed his eyes.

"Watch out for splinters," said Parker.

"Say if I could make up my mind and just die," said Christopher from the floor. "Would the death rate go way up? Isn't it because it's trouble that most of us don't do it?"

"No," I said.

"Anyway," Christopher said, sitting up and opening his eyes and looking at me, "I want to find out whether everyone thinks this, or just me," but now Brian brought in his textbook and began showing Christopher checklists. They sat on the floor together. "This is how I diagnosed Tab," said Brian, showing Chris a vision test he'd used.

"What's wrong with Tabitha?" said Christopher.

"I'm a macular degenerate," said Tabitha.

Parker explained.

"Is this some tragedy and you guys didn't tell me?" Christopher said.

"It's not a tragedy," said Tabitha. "It's not what makes me think of dying, if that's what you mean."

"What makes you think of dying, baby?" said Parker, and I stopped stacking plates and sat down next to him and touched his shoulder, watching my husband think the thought he was thinking.

THAT NIGHT I went to bed early and heard Parker and Christopher talking through the heating ducts. "The military," Parker said.

"Of *course* the military," said Christopher. "I have something so good—I have found someone who knew about the bombing of Cambodia."

"Unless *he's* lying."

"Right, but that's different, a different impulse. Lying to Sherry is creative—but bad. People who lie institutionally do not feel guilty. This is in the book. Markowitz's book."

"But if I tell Sherry a lie . . ."

I am Sherry.

"I think in some families everyone lies, and in others nobody ever does."

"I think I do lie to her," Parker said more quietly, "because when I had a reason to, it was easy."

"When you were fooling around," said Christopher, and I tried to stop listening. I had told Chris myself, but I didn't know Parker had told him, too.

"Well," said Parker.

"But what about the children?" Christopher was saying. "Would you lie to keep them from pain? Say you knew Tabitha's eyes are worse than she knows—"

"How could I know that?"

"I don't know. Doctor confides the result of some test. Would you tell her?"

"They're *her* eyes," Parker said.

"You mean you would?"

"I can't imagine the scenario you're inventing," Parker said. "I can't imagine knowing more than Tabitha about her own eyes."

"I'd lie," said Christopher.

"I don't think lying is ever right," said Parker.

"But you lie to Sherry. You don't know *what* you think!" said Christopher with a laugh.

"Hush. I didn't say that."

"I *remember* you lying to Sherry," said Christopher. "I remember the occasion. It had to do with apples."

"Do you have to talk so loud?" Parker said.

IN THE MORNING Parker and Brian left before I got up. I had breakfast alone with Christopher, and I didn't ask him about the conversation I'd overheard, though I wanted to. It's always that way when he comes: emotion at breakfast. Maybe *that's* what I love. "If Tab doesn't wake up and write those applications," I said, "we'll be walking to Brewery Street in the dark."

"The post office?" said Christopher. I explained that Tabitha had until four to mail the applications in the neighborhood. Downtown, the last pickup was at six. But she had until eight P.M. if we went to the main post office on Brewery Street.

"Won't Parker be back with the car?"

"I don't know."

"Can't we fax them?"

"Oh, the whole world isn't like you journalists," I said. "Some of us still use those blue mailboxes."

"Show me the rest of your new house," he said, and touched my cheek. We stood at the window in Brian's room, looking out, and Christopher touched my back and traced the line of my spine through my sweater, starting at my neck and stopping halfway down my back. Then my shoulders. "Here you are in Connecticut, owning your bones," he said.

"What was that conversation you had with Parker last night?" I said.

"I'll tell you sometime," he said, patting my shoulder. It's as far as we go.

Tabitha woke up about ten and panicked by eleven. Vassar wanted to know what books she'd read lately and what they'd meant to her. *"A Guide to Low Vision,"* she snapped. We tried to remember books. She'd read *Wuthering Heights* and Paule Marshall.

"Wuthering Heights . . ." said Christopher, coming unbidden into her room, where I was trying to help. He'd put on a tie for his interview. "Feel like walking me there, Sherry?"

I wore a woolen hat and tied a scarf over it. It was five below. Snow had fallen a week before and it lay in gray, apparently permanent heaps. In the cold air, we didn't talk. We were so wrapped up, we could bump each other, and we did. Christopher stepped gingerly on the ice. He was nervous.

In front of the professor's house I socked his arm and turned back. I had been cold but now I was warm. Whenever I passed a mailbox I checked for the last pickup, but most of them had no Saturday pickup at all. We could call a taxi. . . .

"I don't want to call a taxi," said Tabitha, at home. "Don't you sort of want to walk to Brewery Street in the cold with me?"

I sort of did. She and I could do anything. "Plumjam, just fill them *out*!" I said. "Isn't the downtown post office far enough for you?"

"Sure," she said. "I forgot about it."

Before I'd taken off my boots, Christopher came back. "He wouldn't see me," he said. "The bastard wouldn't see me."

"Did you have an appointment?"

"Of course." He sounded angry with me. "His wife died."

"You mean, today? Oh my god."

"I don't know. I don't know when."

"Suicide!" said Tabitha brightly, from the stairs.

"I don't think it was suicide," he said coldly.

"I'm not making light of it!" she said.

"Maybe he was lying," I said, worried that they'd fight—drawing his anger from my daughter to myself. "Maybe he never had a wife." Christopher stared at me; then he did laugh.

TABITHA MISSED THE four o'clock deadline at the neighborhood mailbox. She was sure she'd be done for the six o'clock pickup downtown, but she wanted to send along a short story she'd written, and she had to print it out twice on her computer. Her printer is slow. I typed address labels on my typewriter while Tabitha and Christopher hovered over the printer, but we missed the six o'clock pickup anyway.

"I can't think with him in the house," she said when we met in the kitchen, looking for crackers. "Why did you let him come?"

"Of *course* we let him come."

"Right." She hurried from the room.

I lingered and Christopher came in. "It's still below zero," he said.

"If Parker comes after we leave," I said, "send him to Brewery Street to rescue us."

"But I'm going with you."

"You are? Why?"

"To keep you company. And to help fend off criminals."

"Outdoor crime drops when it's zero," I said.

Tab finished at six-fifteen and came down with her two fat manila envelopes. "My mother and I are walking to Brewery Street," she said to Christopher from the staircase, "and I'd appreciate it if you could keep from telling us how crazy that is."

"It's not crazy," said Christopher. "It's picturesque. I didn't know they still *had* post offices. I thought everything was faxes and e-mail."

"Stop it," said Tabitha.

"Do you mind if I come along?" he said. He'd been walking around in his big stocking feet and he was pulling on his boots again. I didn't think Tabitha would let him come, but she did. We left a note for Parker.

We walked on ice like black iron. Setting out, I was frightened. The cold air might damage Tabitha's eyes, I thought wildly, though it wouldn't. She walked ahead of me in a parka with the hood up and a scarf over her mouth and big mittens, gripping the two manila envelopes, to which we'd affixed all the stamps in the house.

I walked second and Christopher came last. His voice sounded from behind me. "What's the short story about?"

The air felt empty, not cold but roomy. Tabitha turned to look at Christopher and pulled the scarf around her mouth down a little. "My story?"

"Mmm." He'd stripped the perforated edges off the sides of the computer paper.

"A girl who works in a frozen-yogurt store," said Tabitha.

"I love frozen yogurt."

"This high school girl works in a frozen-yogurt store," said Tabitha, "and a man comes in, and he gives her money. First a quarter, and it's like a tip, except this isn't the sort of place where people leave tips?"

"Uh-huh," said Christopher.

"And then ten dollars and twenty, and she realizes he wants her to sleep with him, in exchange for the money."

"Does she?"

"She goes to his apartment. She wants to return the money, but she doesn't have enough, and she sleeps with him and becomes a prostitute."

Tabitha was silent and none of us spoke for a moment. "I worked in a store like that," she said then. She turned to me. "Don't worry, it's not true." She'd never shown me the story. "I didn't let Pekko see it, though."

"Who's Pekko?" said Christopher.

"My boss."

"I knew someone called Pekko when I lived here in the old days," Christopher said.

"I'm afraid he might think it's true," Tabitha said. "He thinks I'm pretty innocent. I don't want him imagining I was turning tricks out of his yogurt store."

We had reached Olive Street. We had to cross the railroad bridge, where nobody had shoveled and we could hardly scramble over the snow.

"What does Pekko look like?" Christopher said.

"He's big," said Tabitha. "White. He has a long white beard."

"I think he had a beard," said Christopher.

"When did you know him?" I said.

"Maybe I better not tell you," said Christopher.

"Now you have to tell me," I said. But it was blocks and blocks before he did.

"At the end of my story," said Tabitha, after a long silence, "the girl is planning to kill herself."

"Heavy story," said Christopher.

"Yes," I said.

"The colleges won't think it's true, will they?" said Tab.

"Of course not," I said.

"You mean it's not *true?*" said Christopher, with mock incredulity.

"The store is real," Tabitha said.

"How does the girl plan to kill herself?" said Christopher.

"She hasn't decided."

"Now, lying down in snow is a good way of committing suicide," Christopher said. "If we all lie down right now, that will do it."

"I think maybe the police will find us," said Tabitha. "Or Dad. Dad will come and save us."

And then Christopher told us the story.

Years and years ago, when Parker and Christopher shared the apartment over a store on Chapel Street and Parker and I were falling in love, Christopher got into a conversation in a coffee shop with a man called Pekko. Pekko had dropped out of graduate school or college. He'd been in Vietnam and had turned against the war. He had a car. "Want to pick apples?" he asked Chris.

Christopher was from the crowded part of Long Island and he had no idea you could pick apples. He thought all fruit was picked by oppressed migrant laborers, and people like him merely boycotted it, or marched outside supermarkets on picket lines. Pekko did plenty of marching, but he explained that he also liked to drive into the country on a nice fall day and pay to pick apples in an orchard. They went on a Saturday, and Parker went along.

They loved picking apples. They picked bushels—mostly McIntoshes, Christopher thought he remembered, some Jonathans, some Delicious. Pekko sang blues songs while picking and the two graduate students joined in. They paid for their apples and loaded them into the trunk, but now Pekko said he was tired, and tossed Parker the car keys. Pekko went to sleep in the back seat and Parker drove home.

Parker got lost, and became tense because he was confused. Suddenly thinking he knew where he was, he made a turn without signaling and caused an accident, banging into an old car driven by a middle-aged black man. Both cars were slightly damaged. Pekko woke up and Christopher told him what had happened. Parker paced nervously until the police came.

The white policeman gave the black driver a ticket and let Parker go, and Parker said nothing. (Neither did the black man.) Furious, Pekko called the cop a bigot and demanded that he give Parker the ticket, but the cop said he was crazy. "This is your *buddy,*" he said.

Parker paced for days, Christopher said. "How could I let the cop give the ticket to the black man?" he asked Christopher over and over again.

"What did you say to him?" I said now, as we walked on the ice and snow decades later.

"I said, 'Next time you'll know better.' "

"You decided to forgive him?"

"I don't know what I decided," said Christopher. "Here I am."

"And here *I* am," I said.

"Well, he didn't tell you, of course," Christopher said. "He lied to you. He kept saying to me, 'If I tell her any of it, I'll tell her all of it, and she'll never speak to me again.' He told you somebody gave us the apples. Don't you remember?"

I remembered apples. I made applesauce and apple pie in their rudimentary kitchen. They didn't have a vegetable peeler and I left the peel on, not knowing if that was all right. I loved Parker's love of the apple pie.

Christopher finished the story and Tabitha and I were silent. We reached the bottom of Olive Street and turned onto Water Street, a dark, silent street made harmless by cold. No one was out but us. We carried Tabitha's applications down Water Street, under the highway, and onto Brewery Street. In the light of a streetlamp, I looked over at Tabitha. She was looking at me and her eyes were dark and startled. I took her arm, and then I took Christopher's arm. "You shouldn't have told us," said Tabitha.

I held on to both of them as we reached the post office. We stepped inside carefully, because the floor was wet, said, "Ta-*da*!" and approached the out-of-town slot. "Wait!" I almost said, but Tabitha was shrugging and mailing the applications, and she did a restrained dance step in her boots so we'd know she wasn't scared of the adult life she was beginning—it seemed—at just that moment. Then she led the way outside. But I don't know what she was thinking or seeing, looking down the icy street with her oddball eyes—where Parker's car was just coming into view, coming to rescue us and drive us home.

WHAT IS THERE TO CRY ABOUT?

AT A BORING lecture about writing grant applications, Pam Shepherd changed her seat twice, always sitting in an aisle seat so she could stick her big feet out. Pam has trouble sitting still. Her legs cramp—her very soul cramps—and she imagines she will pay attention more easily elsewhere.

"Patience," breathed a note-taking woman next to her when Pam began to rise yet again. "My friend! Patience!" When the lecture ended they laughed and talked. The woman was Charlotte LoPresti, a social worker from a program for old people. Charlotte's glasses magnified pale blue eyes. She scrutinized Pam, who loves to be scrutinized. Soon they *were* friends, but Charlotte can't always be with her.

Until recently Pam was a massage therapist, so she should know stillness, but massage is performed by someone who stands and moves. She misses the muscular work and the privilege of touching others' flesh, but she makes a little more money in her new profession, as a psychiatric social worker. For months, Pam worked to open a group home for psychiatric patients. She secured a grant, she figured out the structures of several bureaucracies, she held back her impatience through many phone calls, and she reassured her clients, some of whom had lived only in hospitals for years. Of course, she told them, they would do well in the house, and there would be staff to help them. "You'll plant flowers," she said to one or another of them. "You'll make popcorn."

The house was almost ready, but now some people who lived near it wanted to talk to Pam. "We have our children to think of," a man on the phone said. "We're considering calling a lawyer." Pam suggested they all meet at the house, an old frame one-family, newly renovated by carpenters who'd put in roomy bathrooms, steadied the banisters, stripped the dark woodwork, and stained it Golden Oak.

"The house has no furniture," said the man on the phone. "We'll meet at my office. I'm a podiatrist."

"Oh, I used to be a massage therapist," Pam said. "I love feet." The podiatrist coughed, then told her the address.

"Maybe he thought you meant the other kind of massage," Charlotte said later, on the phone. "Prostitutes." Charlotte had never been massaged until she met Pam. When Pam first brought up the subject, Charlotte said a massage would be New Agey and upsetting, but a few months later she nervously agreed to have one on her birthday. She even said she liked it.

"He thinks I'm going to run a whorehouse?" Pam said now.

"He thinks ax murderers," said Charlotte.

TEN PEOPLE WERE squeezed into the podiatrist's waiting room. Pam insisted on standing. The podiatrist apparently liked Norman Rockwell: prints of benign people carrying fishing poles or wearing scout uniforms were partly visible on the walls above the neighbors' thickly coated shoulders. The neighbors, who didn't smile, looked at Pam as if she had kept them waiting, and she involuntarily checked her watch, but she was early.

"I just don't know why it's *allowed*," said a woman.

The podiatrist said, "Of course, we sympathize with these people, but there are appropriate and inappropriate—"

"They're nice people," said Pam cheerfully. She dropped her briefcase and pushed up her coat sleeves. "Well, a couple of them aren't. But they're not *dangerous*."

"That's just it!" said a man who looked friendly, almost like the Norman Rockwell characters. "Nobody can be *sure* they're not dangerous."

"But there's no guarantee about anybody!" said Pam, smiling too.

"I know! I know!" said the man happily. "*You* could be a murderer! *I* could be a murderer!" Most of the people didn't talk. Pam and the man went back and forth.

"I know, I know!" said Pam.

"So you see," said the man, "we *can't* take chances!"

Pam said, "But then you couldn't live near me, either."

"Oh, I don't really think *you*—"

Whatever she said led to trouble. The friendly man was worse than the others. She shouldn't have come alone.

"If you think my children are unimportant to me—" a man shouted. Suddenly nobody was quiet anymore.

"But what will they *do* to your kids?" Pam said.

"Oh, please," said a woman in a puffy pink coat buttoned up to the neck. "I read the papers."

Other people shouted. Pam wanted to strip them and massage them. At home she had a folding massage table, and it might have fit in the small open space in the middle of the waiting room. She'd start with the podiatrist and proceed clockwise around the room, ordering them one by one onto the table, pounding everybody's backs and legs and asses and bellies.

"Zoning—" they said.

"We don't hold you personally responsible," they said.

Finally Pam shouted, too. "My clients are just like you!" she shouted. "They are indistinguishable from you! No, that's wrong.

They are saner than you, more reasonable than you, and—" She was going to say "more attractive than you," but it wasn't true. Half the clients were more attractive than these rather ugly people. That is, they had stopped trying to look a certain way, and their natural faces, even charged with pain and anger, were beautiful. Half had become ugly with fear, like the bundled-up people here in this stuffy room.

CHARLOTTE LOPRESTI HAS a husband and two daughters—one in college and one in high school—and Charlotte's friend Pam, divorced so long ago that Charlotte has never heard Pam's ex-husband's name, seems like a jaunty, solitary, interesting creature in contrast to herself; Pam is like a lanky clanking knight—girl knight—outlined against the sky. She might say or do anything.

"Massage, for example," Charlotte said to her younger daughter, Olivia. "How did she get into that?"

"What's wrong with massage?" said Olivia.

"There's nothing *wrong* with it," Charlotte said.

"I thought Pam was your friend."

"Of course she's my friend."

"Then why are you criticizing her?" Olivia was combing the dog with her fingers. The dog lay on the sofa. She rolled over so Olivia could rub her belly. "Let's send Rags for a dog massage," said Olivia. Olivia was wearing an ankle-length dark red dress with little cream-colored flowers on it, the kind of dress that existed only in storybooks when Charlotte was a girl. If Charlotte owned such a dress she'd save it for parties, but Olivia had worn it to school and to her baby-sitting job. "Or Rags could *do* massage," said Olivia. "She could use her tongue."

She began to laugh in an adult way, girlish dress or no. "That sounds like X-rated," she said. But Olivia kept on laughing, and suddenly she was crying hard. Charlotte moved closer but Olivia pushed her away. Charlotte knew better than to say, "You are a beautiful young girl in a beautiful dress. What is there to cry about?" She didn't say it, but to her surprise—for she'd been studying hard truths all her life—she had to fight her lips not to say it.

Philip, her husband, came into the room. It was evening and he looked tired. He was carrying a stack of papers to mark—he is a teacher in a community college—but Charlotte knew he would lie down on the sofa, lean the papers on this month's *Harper's,* then read the magazine instead. Olivia smiled at him with tears on her face. "Mama thinks Pam is weird because she does massage."

"Is *that* why you're crying?" said Charlotte.

"No," said Olivia, reaching her hand toward Philip, who took it.

"I almost asked her to give me a massage when I hurt my back," he said, settling on the sofa, letting go of Olivia's hand—how lightly he could let it go—and reaching for the magazine.

"But you didn't," said Charlotte.

"I felt foolish," said Philip.

"It's something like being a dog," said Olivia, who had gone back to scratching Rags's belly.

"So are you in love, or what?" Charlotte said recklessly.

"Love," said Olivia. "You could call it that." She pushed Rags away and went upstairs.

PAM MET WITH a lawyer from legal aid named Brenda. "You shouted at the angry neighbors?" said Brenda. "Tell me you didn't shout at them."

"I shouldn't have gone alone," said Pam.

"You're damn straight you shouldn't have gone alone."

"So what can we do?" said Pam.

Brenda took out a yellow legal pad. "If necessary," she said, "we will haul their asses into federal court. But I wish you hadn't shouted at them." She wrote vigorously on the pad but Pam couldn't see it. Maybe it said, "1. Haul asses into federal court." Pam pictured the bare-assed, newly massaged angry neighbors shuffling resentfully up a broad marble staircase. "They sound crazier than your crazy people," Brenda said.

"My mental health consumers," said Pam. "Or my psychiatric survivors."

"Right." Brenda asked her a hundred questions and said she'd talk to the neighbors' lawyer. "He's not a real sharp guy."

"You know him?"

"Cameron Corey?" Brenda said. "A little. He specializes in obnoxious law." The next day when Pam came home from work the phone was ringing and this time it was the neighbors' lawyer himself, who had found out her phone number. She tried to give him Brenda's number, but he kept talking. "You want to prove my clients aren't classy?" he said. "Well, you're right, they're not classy. If they were rich maybe they wouldn't mind living next door to a bunch of raving lunatics. They'd just take a trip to Bermuda."

After he hung up, Pam walked through her apartment, shifting objects: a ceramic bowl was too close to the edge of a shelf, a book seemed about to fall from the arm of a chair. She got into bed, fully dressed, pulled up the blanket, and fell asleep. When she woke up, she was hungry. She went into the kitchen and took eggs from the refrigerator. Then she put them back and phoned Charlotte. "Have you guys eaten?"

"We're just eating."

"Is there any extra?" It was a cold night, but Pam wrapped her scarf around her neck and went over there, was given a plate of spaghetti, and made a fool of herself right away. "You all love one another!" she said. She told Philip and Olivia the story of the patients and the house. "You're such a good family! Just looking at you helps." They looked uncomfortably back at her. Olivia was a dramatic girl in a wonderful long red dress. When Charlotte had interrupted the part of the story about the lawyer to say, "That name sounds so familiar," Olivia shook her brown hair from side to side and said in an audible undertone to her father, "She always says that! She thinks she knows everybody!" Now Olivia left the room and Pam was sorry she had spoken extravagantly. She and Charlotte talked, clearing the dishes. Philip excused himself.

Charlotte began to complain about Olivia. "She cries half the time," she said, and Olivia rushed back into the room, screaming, "That's not *true*!" Then she stopped screaming and said to Pam, "You probably think I'm like your clients." Pam said Olivia was not like them. Olivia left the room. In fifteen minutes she returned. "I don't suppose you need furniture for that house," she said.

"I do," said Pam, wondering if Olivia was about to donate her bed and run away from home. But Olivia had a boyfriend—"sort of a boyfriend"—whose grandfather had died. His family didn't know what to do with some of the old man's furniture.

"Can I really have it?" said Pam. She had a budget for furniture, but it wasn't enough.

"I'll make sure." Olivia went to her room and was not seen again, but next day at work Pam got a phone call from her. She was at her boyfriend's house, and his mother got on the phone and told Pam she was glad someone wanted what was in the apartment. Pam and Olivia were so pleased to have made this useful connection that they decided to meet at the group home in an hour. Olivia and her boyfriend didn't have a car, but they could get a ride there. They would all drive to the grandfather's apartment in Pam's car.

Pam's office was in the hospital, and on her way through the corridors she met one of the people who was going to live in the house, a woman named Mary Jo. Mary Jo had a pass for the afternoon, and Pam brought her along. She had tried to find a way for all those who would live in the house to see it. Some of the others had met the carpenters and toured the house, but Mary Jo hadn't been there. Pam put Mary Jo into her car and told her about the furniture.

"Mind if I smoke?" said Mary Jo. Pam did mind. When the group met to discuss living arrangements, smoking was the biggest topic. Mary Jo was irritated when Pam said no, but she didn't lose her temper.

They found Olivia and her boyfriend sitting on the front steps of the house. Olivia, once more, was in her Louisa May Alcott red sprigged dress, which stuck out under her winter jacket. Her boyfriend was called Angus, and he was dreamy and shy. They climbed into Pam's car and Angus gave them directions. Mary Jo talked about the rights of smokers, and Olivia agreed with her emphatically, though she didn't smoke.

In the apartment they found a television set that worked and a worn but not dreadful green-and-yellow sofa, along with smaller items. Olivia sorted through silverware while Mary Jo tried the chairs. "Forget this one," she said, standing up. "I think the old guy wet his pants in this one." Pam looked at Angus, who was looking out the window, his features twitching a little.

"Did you come here a lot?" Pam asked him, and he nodded. "You must miss him."

"I do." He smiled at her. She went to look over the bedroom and meanwhile, before she had a chance to discuss it with them, Angus and Olivia got the sofa through the door and out onto the sidewalk. Of course it wouldn't fit in Pam's car, especially with four people.

"I'm so dumb!" said Olivia.

"It doesn't matter," Pam said. They piled the cushions in the trunk and drove to the house with lamps, pots, and dishes, leaving the sofa on the sidewalk. Pam and one other person would come back for it.

At the house, Mary Jo counted closets. She asked Pam if she could have the room with the biggest one, and Pam was feeling so good she almost said yes. They had brought a surprising amount of stuff. When it was time to go back, Olivia and Angus waited while Mary Jo went alone with Pam.

They still couldn't fit the sofa into the car. Pam would have to find someone with a truck or a van. Meanwhile they took a few kitchen chairs, two lamp tables, and the TV. But when they reached the house again, Angus was alone. Olivia had walked home. It was several miles.

"Why didn't she wait? I'd have driven her," said Pam.

"She wanted to go."

"But she was so interested."

"I said something that upset her," said the young man. He was confessing bravely, his shoulders squared.

"What the hell did you say?" said Mary Jo. "What did you say to that great kid?"

Angus looked even more miserable, and Pam said, "You don't have to say, Angus," just as if she were leading a therapy group. Angus looked grateful and helped carry in what they'd brought. Then he raised his eyebrows, staring at Pam, until she realized that he wanted to speak to her alone. When Mary Jo was in the house and he and Pam met on the steps, he said, "Something else happened. After what happened with me and Olivia."

Pam rested what she was carrying on the step.

"A woman came over and started asking us questions," Angus went on. "She thought we were moving in."

"Tell me."

"She asked were we moving in, and Olivia said yes."

"She said *yes?*"

"She said we weren't moving in today, but we were the people who were going to live there."

"She did?"

"She told the woman a long story about how she was married to a sailor and he left her," he said. "And then her baby died in a car accident, and she had a nervous breakdown, and had to go to the mental hospital. They both cried."

"The woman *cried?*" said Pam.

"They both cried," said Angus. "Olivia is a very good actress. But when the woman went away, Olivia couldn't stop crying. Then she left." Now Mary Jo came out of the house. Pam touched Angus on the arm. What Olivia had done scared and delighted Pam, who'd say almost anything, but not what Olivia had said. They finished quickly, and Pam drove Angus home and took Mary Jo back to the hospital. For the first time, she let herself wonder how it would be if she, too, lived at the hospital, if she'd been out on a pass and had to be back for supper. At home, she phoned Olivia and reached Charlotte. Olivia had come home and gone out baby-sitting. "She's wonderful," Pam said to Charlotte. In the middle of the night, she remembered the sofa.

THE NEXT DAY Charlotte came home chilled and tired. Philip sometimes taught evening classes, and he would be home late. The house seemed dark and empty, but Rags did not greet Charlotte as hysterically as if she had been alone all afternoon. "Where's Olivia?" Charlotte asked the dog. She went to find her. None of the lights had been turned on, and as she walked through the house, she turned on lights in the halls and in the living room. Olivia was in her bed in the dark. As Charlotte opened the door, she heard Olivia crying.

"What is it, honey?" She sat down on the bed.

Olivia would not speak for a long time. "I'm a stupid idiot," she said at last.

"No."

"I'm such a stupid idiot."

"No."

"Yes." She was lying on her side. She pulled the comforter more tightly around her and brought her knees to her chest, so her feet were farther from her mother.

"Olivia, you are a brilliant, wonderful girl."

"No, no." The sobs were half shouts.

Charlotte stroked the curved form through the comforter. Olivia put up with it for a while, then shouted, "Will you stop that, *please?*"

"Of course."

"With your clients you're so cool, but at home all you do is intrude and poke around and humiliate me."

"You know that's not what I want to do," said Charlotte. She sat with her arms folded to prevent herself from reaching out.

Olivia was silent.

"Did something happen with Angus?" Charlotte asked.

"It's none of your business."

"Maybe I've been through something like it."

"Oh, sure." Sobs.

"I'm going to make supper," said Charlotte, but she didn't stand up.

After another long silence, Olivia said, "Did you talk to Pam?"

"Last night I did," Charlotte said.

"What did she say?"

"She said you were great."

"Yeah, right—we left a sofa out. It's probably slashed. Ten alcoholics probably threw up on it last night."

"Where did you leave it?"

"Outside Angus's grandfather's house. We pulled it out and

then it didn't fit in Pam's car. She went back for it but I know it didn't fit."

"You think it's still there?" said Charlotte. "Maybe it would fit in the station wagon."

She went downstairs to make supper and called Pam, who hadn't found anyone to help move the sofa. Charlotte offered to come after supper with her station wagon, and Pam was grateful. Charlotte went back to Olivia's room, turned on the light, and told her what she'd done. "Come eat," she said. Water was boiling and sauce was reheating. She just needed to cook some spaghetti. Olivia didn't answer.

"Doesn't that make you feel better?" Charlotte asked. "It didn't rain or snow last night. The sofa will be all right. There aren't a lot of drunks throwing up on sofas in the middle of winter."

"No, that does not make me feel better!" shouted Olivia, flinging herself out of bed. She was in her underwear. "No, that does not solve everything, social worker mom! You think you can just make this call and make that call and life will be absolutely perfect. Well, it's not. Things happen. Things *happen* to people." She glared at her mother, then looked around. "I don't have time to eat," she said. "I'm baby-sitting tonight. I told you. They're picking me up in five minutes."

"You can eat quickly," Charlotte said without thinking.

Olivia had picked up the red sprigged dress, which she'd worn almost every day since she found it at a funky boutique and spent weeks of baby-sitting money on it. She clutched it in her hand, screaming at Charlotte, "You think making a call solves everything! You think food solves everything! Clothes solve everything!" Charlotte was surely the least clothes-conscious mother in the city, but suddenly she saw herself as her daughter must see her—a person with nothing to offer but actions and objects, who claimed to fix what nobody could fix. And then Olivia yanked the fabric of the

dress between her hands, ripped it with a terrible noise, and flung
it at her mother.

"Oh, baby," Charlotte cried, and then there was the sound of a
car horn. Olivia pulled on sweatpants and a sweatshirt and was out
the door in half a minute, and Charlotte hadn't even urged her to
take along a sandwich.

Charlotte didn't follow her. She sat where she was. Then she
stood, straightened the bedclothes, and folded the red dress without
looking at it. She went to the kitchen and put a handful of spaghetti
into the boiling water, stood and watched the strands soften, and
ate her supper.

PAM CLIMBED INTO Charlotte's station wagon and gave directions. The night was cold and the heater in the car was slow. When
they reached the street where Angus's grandfather had lived, at first
Pam didn't see the sofa, but then, there it was, right on the sidewalk,
looking colorful and pitiful in the night: a very indoor object. It was
hard to get it into the station wagon. Pam lifted one end over a
piece of broken sidewalk while Charlotte, bundled in her hat and
driving gloves, swinging her purse over her shoulder, pushed the
other end hard. She looked a little ladylike for this job, but she was
strong. They'd never worked together before, and Pam liked grunt-
ing and shoving with Charlotte. They had to lay the passenger seat
in front flat, because the sofa was as long as the station wagon, and
so when they drove away, Pam was riding in a corner of the back
seat with the sofa pressed against her shoulder.

"Now I feel like a little girl," she said to Charlotte's back. She
had spent much of her childhood squashed in the back of someone's
station wagon, her mother's or somebody else's mother's.

"So do I."

"I mean, riding in the back seat. You're the mother, in front."

"Oh, I'm the mother all right," Charlotte said. By the time they reached the group home, Pam was stiff. She unfolded herself slowly and climbed out. "I had a bad fight with Olivia," Charlotte said, but then they turned their attention to getting the sofa out of the wagon. Somehow they had wedged it in too tightly. It was stuck, but at last a car slowed and a woman rolled down the window. "Moving in?" she said.

"We're just bringing a sofa," Pam said. In the dark she couldn't tell whether the woman was one of the people who'd been at the meeting. And she didn't know whether this was the woman who'd spoken to Angus and Olivia.

Charlotte came up behind her. "Do you live near here?" she asked the man and woman.

"Right there."

Pam didn't want the people's help. She didn't want the wicked neighbors—if these *were* the wicked neighbors—to know there was anything she couldn't do. But the couple parked and came over to look, and then the man crawled into the station wagon and managed to shift the sofa slightly so that Charlotte and Pam could pull it free. The woman stood near them calling, "Take it easy." Then they all carried it into the house and shoved it against the longest wall. Next, in the dark, they looked at one another. Pam plugged in one of the lamps but the bulb was shot.

"I can see it's a nice big room," said the woman.

"Would you like to see the rest of the house?" said Pam.

"We should go," the man and woman both said.

Instead, they talked with Charlotte about big pieces of furniture they'd managed to move. Pam didn't speak. She didn't want them to be the wicked neighbors. Maybe there was a second, quieter set of *good* neighbors. "Well, you certainly seem nice," Pam said at last, against her better judgment. "Not like some of the people I've met

182

around here!" The couple said nothing at all. "You weren't at that meeting, were you?" Pam said. "There was a meeting."

"He was there," said the woman. "I was coming down with a cold."

"Oh," said Pam. Brenda the lawyer would want her to shut up, and Pam did try. But when the couple still didn't leave, and didn't speak, Pam finally said, "You ought to give my clients a chance. I don't know what people around here are so nervous about."

"You can't be too careful," said the man. "Something in the paper yesterday about an ex–mental patient who killed an old lady."

"Still," said the woman, "that girl I talked to yesterday, she was the sweetest thing."

"You know," Charlotte said brightly—Pam saw that Charlotte had been trying to change the subject for a while—"I knew someone once who lived on this block!" The couple didn't know Charlotte's acquaintance, and as soon as that had been made clear, Charlotte opened the door for them, and they were gone.

"I said the wrong thing," Pam said.

"Oh, I don't know," Charlotte said. Then she said, "Look, I'm so upset about Olivia, I can't pay attention to anything else."

"What's wrong with Olivia?" said Pam, wondering what she'd told her mother.

"She cried again tonight," Charlotte said. "What do I do? Do I sign her up for therapy?" Then *she* began to cry, standing in the cold, dark, almost empty room. "She really doesn't like me," she said.

"Oh, no."

"You don't know . . ." Pam didn't have children; it was true. "You side with her," Charlotte said. Then she said, "Pam, she ripped that dress. On purpose. Her favorite dress."

"That long red dress?"

"She was angry. She was upset. But what was she punishing herself for?"

"I wish I'd been there," said Pam.

"What good would that have done?"

Pam pulled Charlotte to the sofa, put the cushions in place, and pulled her friend down. She searched in her pockets for a clean Kleenex. "I don't want to sit here in the dark," said Charlotte. "It's too cold."

"All right." Pam couldn't keep from thinking that, right now, she could surprise Charlotte. She could tell Charlotte truths she didn't know about her own daughter. She could explain what the neighbor woman had meant about the sweet girl. Maybe the woman would persuade her husband and the others to change their minds. "What did Olivia say about yesterday?" she asked Charlotte.

"Just that she left the sofa out."

It was tempting, and then Pam did it. She told Charlotte everything Angus had told her: that he'd upset Olivia and she had left, that Olivia had talked to the neighbor, that Olivia had told the neighbor she was a psychiatric patient. She told Charlotte the story Olivia had told—how she'd married a sailor, how the sailor had left her, how her baby had died.

"A sailor!" Charlotte interrupted. Then, "She said she had a baby? She said her baby died?"

After Pam finished, Charlotte didn't speak for a long time. Then she said, "I don't think you had a right to tell me."

Pam was chagrined. Of course that was true. Olivia would have trusted her not to tell.

"I wish you hadn't told me," said Charlotte.

There was a long silence. "I have no self-control," Pam said.

"No, you don't."

At last Pam said, "Let's go." They locked the house and yanked the passenger seat in the station wagon into place. It seemed even colder in the car than before.

"She let that woman think she was, you know, damaged," said Charlotte as they drove. She sounded sad, not angry. "And such terrible things. A dead baby."

"I know."

Then Charlotte said, "Would you give me a massage?"

"Now?"

"Yes."

Two blocks later, Pam said, "Maybe it was *good,* what Olivia did."

"Not the dress."

"No, not the dress. But the neighbor. She changed the woman's mind. Maybe she'll talk sense to the others."

"But, Pam—the story she told!" They went to Pam's place, where Charlotte stripped off all her clothes in the warmth, crying only a bit, and climbed onto Pam's massage table. Pam played her tape of whales singing and spread a clean sheet over Charlotte's naked back. Then she plunged her fingers into Charlotte's fine, light hair, reaching for her scalp, and through her scalp reaching into Charlotte's imagination—or wherever she kept that double pain: knowing, not knowing.

SELFISHNESS

WHEN A MAN I like touches my arm or my hair, I want to know if he'll touch the center of me, and whatever I learned in school—I went to school for a long time—I seem to believe that my center can be reached best with the tip of a penis, as though that happy poke permits what I am to radiate through my body and out, like warmth from a dear little stove with a Pennsylvania Dutch design on its iron surface. Pre-AIDS, nobody considered me promiscuous. I am forty-three.

I went to a Fourth of July picnic at a house in the woods in Guilford with a lawyer named Gary, who knew the woman who lived there. We were outdoors under trees, and all anybody talked about was Lyme disease. I was chided for wearing sandals. It was the third time I'd gone out with Gary. The first time he was funny, but the second time he told the same stories, and he was about to tell them again. One that I'd taken to be about someone's charm was really—I saw now—about her stupidity. So I was restless, and then a slight, tough-looking young fellow with dark hair came out of the house carrying a big wooden bowl. He set it on the table, reached in, and bit something: a lettuce leaf. I walked over. "Did you make the salad?" I said.

"I tossed it," he said. "People think oil and vinegar matter—but salt and pepper *really* matter."

The gray-haired woman whose house we were at was going around introducing people, and she came over and put a hand on my shoulder and one on the young man's. She had an unfussy denim-and-chambray look. "Have you met?" she said. "This is my grandson Dennis, and in a second I'll remember your name." She did. "Daisy. Gary's friend Daisy."

"Stay away from Gary," Dennis said, and I looked at him, surprised. "I prefer to be called Denny," he said. His grandmother patted our shoulders and moved on.

"What's wrong with Gary?" I said.

"He warned my grandmother about me."

"Are you dangerous?"

"Not to my grandmother."

Someone came over and Denny walked away, but later he came back to me. "You look interesting," he said. "Are you a psychologist or something?" Then his grandmother asked him to go and buy some more pita bread. "Want to come?" Denny asked me.

We took my car. Gary and I had come in it, and maybe I was stranding him on purpose. As we drove down the driveway, I said, "I'm a teacher at a community college in New Haven."

"No kidding! I can't believe that."

"Why not?"

"It's just interesting."

"Actually," I said, "you remind me of some of my students."

"I don't remind you of bad guys on television?"

I laughed. "Oh, that too, that too."

"Does that community college of yours teach philosophy?" he asked—and he kept on asking questions. "But if your students just don't have time to read something," he was saying when we reached a convenience store, "if they have a job, let's say, and they just don't have time—you mean you don't give them extra time?" I saw a baffled innocence—the students' innocence—cross his face, while his own face, not innocent, somehow showed through underneath.

"We manage," I said. "I'm nice." The place had no pita bread. We never found any. We went to Friendly's for iced coffee, and Denny made up stories about teenagers in the other booths. "Now, she shoplifts underpants," he said of one ordinary-looking girl. "Dozens of pairs. Do you know how to fix it so the alarm doesn't go off when you carry something out of a store with that plastic tag still on?"

"No, how?"

"Well, it's not worth it. You have to get the tag off later."

"But how, really?"

His hair hung in front of his eyes and he looked through it over his rather large nose at me. "Oh, it has to do with magnets. I'll show you sometime." I looked into his intelligent blue eyes while we laughed.

By the time we returned to the picnic it was over. We walked up the driveway while Denny's grandmother strode toward us, her skirt swinging. "I gave them English muffins," she called. "Somebody drove Gary home."

"Oh, good." I kissed each of them on the cheek, walked back to my car, and drove away, done with Gary.

Denny had looked at me man to woman, not son to mother, and he was that way with his grandmother, too. She was one of his girlfriends. A few weeks later, I saw the two of them come out of a Thai restaurant and walk down Chapel Street. His grandmother, in a long flowered dress that day, matched his loping steps.

The night after we met, Denny called me. I got a little scared because I hadn't told him my last name, but he said he'd called the college that morning and persuaded somebody to read him a list of faculty members. Finally one of them was named Daisy. By evening, when he called me, he'd begun to believe what he'd told the woman on the phone: "So if I want to take a class with you, how do I do that? How much does it cost?" Before I could answer, he said, "You know, there are scholarships for people like me—people who've done time, like me, or been crazy. Prodigal-son scholarships."

"You've done time?" I said.

"Hey, could I come over?" he said then. I said yes, but when he arrived I asked about his parents, to keep him at a distance. His father owned a restaurant in Washington. "I've bussed tables for an hour, cooked for an hour," said Denny, "but we've never made it to the Social Security number stage."

"They're divorced?" I said.

"Very divorced. She married Pete when I was six." He sat opposite me, drinking a beer. "You learn a lot about beer with a dad in the restaurant business." He lifted the bottle and gazed at it: a joke—it was ordinary beer.

"You grew up with a stepfather."

"Step by step," Denny said. "Stepping on his toes, being stepped on, stepping out to a friendly guys' basketball game."

I stood up and sat down next to him and combed his hair away from his eyes with one finger. He put the bottle on the floor and clutched me, and in a moment we were embracing as tightly as if we'd spent hours in search of each other in a forest full of dark shadows. Then I led him to my bedroom. "You let people like me in here?" Denny said.

"I let you."

MY BEST FRIEND is a man, Philip LoPresti, another teacher, and we have long talks on the phone at night. Philip says he'd be as likely to go to bed with people he hardly knows as to turn cartwheels in the street. "How do you make it happen?" he says, not that he's looking to cheat on his wife, Charlotte, who's my other best friend.

"It's just like turning cartwheels in the street," I tell him. "I do something risky and clear. One time out of three I'm humiliated. The other two times he's so relieved that *he* doesn't have to do the risky thing that he's unzipping his pants in two seconds."

"I don't know . . ." he says.

"You *could* turn cartwheels," I say. Philip could—he learned for a play in college. But sex is more fun for me than for some people. I'm more motivated. All I had to do with Denny was fix his hair. Once I left a guy sitting in a bar, went to a drugstore, bought some condoms, walked back to the bar, and handed him the package.

I told Philip about Denny a few days later, on the phone at night. "How old is he?" Philip said.

"He's over twenty-one," I said. "But not much."

Then he said, "I have fantasies of following you and a man to a bar and pretending I don't know you, just watching to make sure nothing bad happens."

"To me or to him?"

"To you."

"To me?" I said. "No, I'm the perpetrator. The perp." But I was pleased. "Protect me from myself, Phil," I said.

"I'll try," he said. "Now let's hang up and both go to bed."

A few days later Denny showed up at my house as I was about to go out for groceries, and he came along, urging me to buy good cheese, nuts, and dried fruit. Back home, we cooked extra-wide noodles with vegetables and soy sauce. "I love extra-wide noodles," he said. We didn't make love that day, but the next time he came he leaned on the sink and said, "Come here. I'm reading your thoughts."

"What thoughts?" I crossed the room and took his hand.

"How terrible you are to fall in love with me."

"I'm not in love with you!" I said.

"Fall in love with me," he said, kissing me lightly. It was a hot night and his face was pleasantly moist. "Don't fall in love with me. Fall in love with me. Daisy."

One night at the end of July we went for a walk. "Let's get frozen yogurt," Denny said suddenly, steering me in a different direction. As we walked he remarked, "Lots of parked cars. We could play car alarms."

"What's that?"

"We can't really. You need about six people. Each one stands between two parked cars, and you all count to three and bang the cars hard, or kick them."

"Will the alarms go off if you just bang on the cars?"

"Oh, sure."

"But not every car has an alarm."

"You'd be surprised."

"Did you ever really do that?"

"Lots of times. Mostly my kid brother does it. It's a kid thing."

And then we reached the yogurt store. I'd been there once or twice, and I remembered the bulky man with a white beard who owned it. "Pekko, Daisy," Denny said, while Pekko reached over the counter to shake hands with me. "You were both reading *The Great Gatsby* last week." So Denny was friends with him.

"I was thinking of teaching it," I said to Pekko. "Why were *you* reading it?"

"You're the lady who lends Denny books," he said. "Where do you teach? I've been a teacher. I've done everything." He took our order. "I read a Fitzgerald novel every summer."

I liked that. After he served us our cones he came out from behind the counter and looked Denny over. "Keeping your head on straight?" he said, touching Denny's hair. He looked me over, too.

When I meet a lover's friend I always think he's wondering if I wouldn't rather be with him. Maybe it's part of being a mammal, or maybe it goes deeper and is part of being a vertebrate. I wasn't really Denny's girlfriend, but I thought we had that recent-bed look. Pekko didn't wear a wedding ring.

In a few days, I went back to the store alone, and Pekko and I talked. He was divorced, with a grown daughter. He lived on the water in Guilford. He'd fought in Vietnam, then turned against the war and done left-wing political things ever since. He'd been to Nicaragua.

"Look, are you seeing anybody?" he asked me, and I said no. It was true. I hadn't seen Denny since the night of our walk. I never did have a phone number or address for him—he'd just call, or turn up. Pekko invited me to dinner, and within days we were driving to the country, taking walks, and buying large quantities of fruits and vegetables at farm stands like an old married couple about to serve string beans to crowds of children and grandchildren. Then we'd try to persuade each other to keep what we'd bought. We'd go to his place or mine and make love, then go out to dinner, feeling guilty about the string beans or the blueberries. You can eat blueberries for breakfast, and we did, but if you eat dinner out, what can you do with string beans?

"When I was going around with Denny," I said on the phone to Philip, "I *cooked* string beans. Now I'm throwing them out covered with white fuzz. A nutritionist would say I was doing better before."

"No," said Philip. "This is better. Bring him to dinner. Where did he get a name like Pekko, anyway?"

"It was his grandfather's name."

"Where did his grandfather get it?"

"Denmark? Finland? I forget."

"So what does he think about you and Denny?" he asked.

"We haven't talked about it," I said. "Nothing bothers him."

Yet I was a little uncomfortable, waiting for Pekko to talk about me and Denny, waiting to get it over with.

I still hadn't heard from Denny. Maybe I never would again. I was glad I hadn't mentioned him to Charlotte. I thought Philip wouldn't. I'd been keeping Charlotte for later. You shouldn't wear out your confidants with too much truth. That August I spent a lot of time at Pekko's little house on the water. I had been teaching summer school but now I was free. The weather was hot and I lay in the sun, or read, or talked on the phone. Pekko spent long days at his store, and I liked being alone at the house, aware of him.

CHARLOTTE INVITED PEKKO and me to dinner, though she is too busy and serious to give real dinner parties: they'd feel trivial and yet worrisome to her. She has surprised blue eyes (lighter than Denny's) behind glasses. When I met her she stared at me so attentively I thought she didn't like me. It was years ago, at a department party at the college. Charlotte's younger daughter, Olivia, who was then about two, walked up my body with her bare feet braced against my legs while her hands gripped my hands. I loved the feel of that bold child pushing away by holding on, and I still love Olivia, who's now in high school. Charlotte watched this scene from across the room, while I somehow thought she might be disapproving, and then she came over to rescue me, but I didn't want to be rescued.

"You are a welcoming person," she said.

"Do you mean I'm a whore?" I said, and as her daughter dropped my hands and ran off, Charlotte put her own hands on my arms and said, "What is in your head? *What* is in your head?"

Never in our long friendship, I believe, has Charlotte thought I might go after Philip. Maybe they talk about it. I love Philip but can keep my hands off him easily except when he wears certain clothes—some faded canvas pants, for example. If he wore those every day, what would happen? Are they tighter than his other pants?

The afternoon of our dinner at the LoPrestis', Pekko came to my house and we baked a cake to bring along. It had peaches on top, sliced by Pekko. He was wearing a bright blue shirt with the sleeves rolled up. With his white beard and belly (not a big belly, but a belly), he was always noticeable, and when he cooked, with a dish towel tucked into his pants, he looked like a cook on television. I was pleased with myself, about to bring him to my friends' house, which I did as soon as the cake came out of the oven. I was slim beside him, in a red skirt and a red long-sleeved shirt. I'm blond. My hair had just been cut. Maybe I looked a little older than usual, next to a gray-bearded man, but in a good way: like someone growing more interesting as I aged, with the scent of my alarming youth about me.

It was a relaxed, unfancy meal. I could see Charlotte trying to make a good impression on Pekko—she knew he'd like informality—while Philip judged him, pushing his chair back as if he wanted to see Pekko from a few yards away. He was drinking a beer and he kept looking at it when he wasn't looking at Pekko, and I thought of Denny—that night we first went to bed—turning the bottle of beer in his hand.

"Hey, I *know* you," Pekko had said to Charlotte the minute we arrived. They worked it out that twelve or thirteen years ago—around the time Olivia walked up my dress—Pekko had visited a parent-cooperative day-care center, and there he met Charlotte, the parent on duty. "You were reading to a bunch of children on a big mattress," Pekko said. "One kid had on a feathered hat and nothing else. I wanted to lie down on the mattress and hear the story."

"I can't believe this," said Charlotte.

She was wearing a blue T-shirt and it made her blue eyes more noticeable; I reached to touch her. "Pekko would remember you," I said, loving her hard. "You're so beautiful."

The LoPrestis' older daughter, Amy, was away at college, but Olivia came in while we were eating the peach cake. "Maybe you were the kid in the feathered hat," Pekko said. Then Pekko and Charlotte and Philip talked on about what they'd done in those days, the groups they belonged to, the marches and rallies.

"We were fixing the world back then," Charlotte said.

"Not now?" said Pekko. When he wasn't in the store he was always at a meeting or writing a press release.

Charlotte sat back and considered. "Well, sure—I'm a social worker," she said. She cut a little triangle of cake and ate it off her palm. "But in those days I listened to entire long speeches."

"Now it's easier to write a check," Philip said.

"At least you do that," I said. "I'm just selfish."

"Are you?" said Philip.

But Pekko was saying, "Oh, I don't know what's good and what's not, these days. I just spend time with people I like."

"You do more than that," I said.

"Look," he said earnestly, "I'm on committees, boards—and there are young ruffians in this town I've helped raise from pups. And with the kindness I've shown them, they now have the confidence to commit not just shoplifting but armed robbery."

"Oh, I doubt that," said Charlotte.

"I don't know *how* to write a check!" boomed Pekko.

"Well," said Philip, with a little irritation, "I wrote five yesterday. To various nonprofit organizations."

I looked to see what Pekko would say next, but it was Charlotte who spoke. "You wrote five checks yesterday?" she said. She stood there holding the coffeepot: the decaf pot, they called it. "*When* did you write five checks yesterday?"

"You weren't here," Philip said.

"But where *are* they?" The air in the room shifted, or stiffened.

"I mailed them."

"But we didn't talk about them," she said seriously.

"But I know what you think."

"That has nothing to do with it." Charlotte looked at Pekko. "Here is this new person—"

"It's all right, Mom, I watched him do it," Olivia broke in. "Your favorite causes."

That made Charlotte angrier. She raised her voice. "Am I invisible?" she said. "Am I nothing?" She and Philip don't fight often, but when she loses her temper she can't stop herself. At last Olivia left the room and the fight subsided, as if it had more to do with their daughter than their money. When Charlotte stopped shouting, I saw Pekko decide that we should leave, and he stood up, patting the front of his thighs energetically.

I'd been staying at his place several nights a week, and when he turned his car that way I was pleased, though I knew I should go home and clean up the baking pans. "Sweet people," he said, shaking his head sadly.

"I was afraid you'd think I was trivial or something, having friends who fight with other people around."

We were silent, driving over the Q Bridge. I looked at the harbor, the lights of ships. "You have guilt to spare," Pekko said.

"I guess." And suddenly I decided that he meant Denny. I'd thought of Denny when he spoke of young ruffians. "All that virtue," I said. "Fighting over whether to send money to Amnesty International or the ACLU."

"That wasn't what they were fighting about."

"Mmm." But I didn't want to discuss Philip and Charlotte. I was finally ready to talk about my sins, to have Denny's name mentioned, to have Pekko say he considered it a little irresponsible of me to have slept with someone so young and mixed up.

"I wish I were more like them," I said. "Instead, I do things that make problems worse."

"You throw out leftovers!" Pekko said, teasing. He was looking at the road ahead, but he glanced affectionately at me for a second. "Once, I saw you toss out a jar that should have been recycled!"

"And I sleep with juvenile delinquents," I said, trying to match his tone.

"Juvenile delinquents?" He was changing lanes, a little distracted.

"One in particular," I said, looking away. I was going to like being scolded.

But instead there was a long pause, and suddenly Pekko was gripping the wheel, staring straight ahead. "Daisy," he said, "you don't mean you've been to bed with Denny Ring?"

"You didn't know?"

"How was I to know?"

"I thought he told you—I thought you assumed. He introduced us."

"If a man introduces me to a woman, I'm supposed to assume they're sleeping together?" he said. Then he didn't say anything for a long time. "If I assumed you were sleeping with him, you think I'd start up with you?" he said at last. "Daisy, this is a very fragile"— his voice was shaking—"kid. Almost twenty years younger than you."

Oh, I cried. Pekko was more than upset, he was frantic. I thought he might drive back to New Haven in search of Denny to make sure I hadn't done him some special cynical harm. I was afraid he'd break up with me—but he didn't. He didn't break up with me, and he was so damned mature he didn't even make me miserable. We stayed at his house that night, although we didn't make love. I was wretched at what I'd done—not about the sex with Denny as much as about the telling. I thought I'd destroyed my own happiness, but I hadn't. It was the end of our headlong time, but the beginning of our seriousness. Baking a cake together had been playing house. Now, when I drove through a stop sign and caused a fender bender, I called Pekko before the cop arrived, and he came rushing from the store, not even stopping to put on a jacket, and stood beside me with that bushy beard, looking like a biblical prophet, his shirt sleeves flapping in the wind. The cop—whom Pekko knew, somehow—continued writing me a ticket, but respectfully.

Philip said Pekko was full of shit—"Likeable . . . I mean, he's wonderful. But full of shit." I guess he meant Pekko was theatrical. Charlotte (quickly over her fight with Philip) guessed that Pekko might be moody. In the next months I lived in his moods. Sometimes I'd stay at his house for a week and then for a while I'd hardly see him.

FOR TWO MONTHS after Pekko and I met, I didn't see Denny. I assumed he was watching me from someplace. I didn't know if Pekko ever saw him. But when my doorbell rang late one night in October I knew it was going to be Denny and I was excited. It was raining, and Denny had rain in his eyebrows and eyelashes. I pulled him in and made tea.

"I went for a walk to think things over," he said, talking fast, "and I remembered I didn't know how your teaching was going"— as if he were the dean of faculty.

"I've been a teacher for centuries," I said. "I am a fine and happy teacher." I was thumpy in the chest and a little trembly, setting out the Red Zinger, as if I'd been waiting for this moment, imagining it just as it was.

"How's Pekko?" he said.

"He has a cold."

"Did he go swimming?" Denny said. "It's October."

"No."

"An airborne virus," he said. Then, "Any of your students writing term papers? I thought if they wanted to write about underground figures, they could interview me."

I didn't want him to be crazy and strange. I wanted him to be someone I might reasonably have slept with, and also someone who didn't seem likely to talk about it. I thought of asking him not to, and I was tense; maybe that was why I wanted to keep him there. I did want to keep him there. I drank my tea slowly, and I started on new topics when the conversation stopped. Mostly Denny talked about my job. He thought I should refuse to go to faculty meetings or turn grades in on schedule. "Why do you put up with that?" he kept saying. His sense of injustice was overdeveloped. Maybe that happens to people who do time. I remembered that when we met he thought I'd be unjust to my students, not that somebody would be unjust to me.

"The college has to be run," I said primly. I stayed on my side of the table and we didn't talk about bed. After that, for a month or so, when I was staying at my own place, every few days I'd hear from Denny. When I was at Pekko's I didn't hear from him, and neither of us spoke of him.

The phone would ring late in the evening and Denny would say, "Take a break from marking papers." We'd meet for coffee or a drink at about midnight. He had a car now and we'd arrive in our own cars. Sometimes he'd just tell me to drive to a street corner and then he'd get into my car; we'd sit and talk there. I'd be terribly happy when he tapped on my car window. I'd reach over and pull up the lock and he'd step into the warmth, blowing on his hands. He wore a hooded sweatshirt, no coat, and the hood would be up. He'd ask me questions and tell me what he thought about everything I said, but he didn't say much about what he was doing, how he'd spent the day.

One night, in a pizza place, he said, "See that woman? See those three women together? The short one is hoping the blonde will invite her home, because the blonde has this great mother, and the other one has a thing about families. Cozy stuff."

"Did you overhear something?"

"No, I didn't overhear anything except what they ordered, which was very greasy, but I can read minds. Test me. I'll tell you your secrets. One, sometimes I bore you. Two, you're dying to know whether I'm doing anything criminal these days. Three—I know you don't just think about me—you wish you had kids."

My eyes teared up. "Are you doing anything criminal these days?"

"Yes."

"SO HOW'S PEKKO?" he said, late on another night. He'd gotten me to drive out Route 80. He said he wanted a whole-wheat dough-nut from a Dunkin' Donuts, and we'd stopped at several, but they didn't have whole wheat. "You can get to my grandma's this way," he said, interrupting himself.

"I don't think Dunkin' Donuts makes a whole-wheat dough-nut," I said.

"Sure they do," he said. "You know why there are so many Dunkin' Donuts on Route 80? Commuters' nostalgia. People get sad, driving from city to country, country to city. Sweets are con-soling."

"Denny," I said, risking his mood. "Are you on drugs?"

"Another one!" he said. I put on my turn signal. This Dunkin' Donuts didn't carry whole wheat, either. We settled for cinnamon doughnuts and milk. I asked again. "Are you?"

"The whole-wheat ones are glazed," he said. "Very nice. How about you, Daisy? Do you do drugs?"

"No."

"Did you ever?"

"I tried stuff in college," I said.

"Well, there you are. But how's Pekko? You didn't tell me if he got over his cold."

I had to think before I remembered Pekko's cold. "He's fine."

"And the store?"

"The store is fine. He works hard."

"He does. He works hard, but he's foolish," Denny said. "That store isn't secure. Have you noticed that?"

I admitted I hadn't.

"That little back window doesn't lock," he said. "I'm surprised, because it's not an old building. I think that window was replaced at some point."

"What do you know about the back window?"

"I help," said Denny. "I've washed that window. Anybody could climb in that window."

"Let's go, Denny, I'm tired," I said. That night, I didn't like him much, which alarmed me. If I wasn't spending time with him to please myself, I didn't know why I was there.

"Let's drive past my grandmother's, just see if everything's okay," he said.

"No." I turned the car back toward New Haven, though I liked his grandmother, and I liked the way she looked near him. Maybe I, too, looked that fine way, near Denny. Maybe, after all, it was selfishness that made me spend time with him. That night, I wanted it to be selfishness.

*　　*　　*

AS IT GREW colder I stopped hearing from Denny. It was a cold winter. I told Philip it was a relief that Denny had disappeared from my life, but then, in December and into January, I'd wake in the night and drink Red Zinger—at my place or Pekko's—and remember how we'd sit in my car talking and how I'd say, "I'm starving, you want to get something to eat?" even though I wasn't starving.

When he called me again it was registration week for the spring term. "How do I sign up to go to your college?" he said.

He'd been busted for parole violation, but now he was working for a cleaning service and he was going to take courses and go straight. I thought that was good. "What do you want to take?"

"You."

"No." But he did, and there wasn't any way for me to stop him. He began to appear in our hallways in his sweatshirt, hair hanging over his eyes. He met Philip. And there he was in my Composition and Literature class. I assigned "Tell Me a Riddle," by Tillie Olsen, and he loved it, and chattered in class about the elderly people in the story. "Old people! I love old people!" Denny proclaimed. He wrote his autobiography, full of mischief. The young women fell for him, and there was I, feelings uncatalogued, seeing Pekko weekends and a couple of weeknights, too.

Denny hung around my office cubicle. "Maybe your colleagues would like to have their houses cleaned," he kept saying. Although he and his partners worked for a cleaning service, they did extra work on the side, not telling their boss, so as to be able to pocket all the money. I said, "What if the cleaning service gets mad and complains to your parole officer?"

"I don't think that will happen," he said.

"But it might."

"My parole officer would think it was wonderful," he said. "What he minds is—you know. Bank robbery. Arson."

"Dealing drugs."

"Hey, Daisy, I'm not dealing."

"Sorry."

I promised I'd ask around about cleaning, but I didn't. I did tell him he could clean my apartment, thinking he'd come with the group. But on the appointed afternoon he showed up alone. "Where are the rest of them?" I said.

"For an apartment you get only me."

And then we went to bed right away. I remember walking slowly with him to the closet where I kept the vacuum cleaner, and then we joined hands and swung our joined hands as we walked, without saying anything—like actors following stage directions—into the bedroom. He was a swift, intense, humorous lover, and when we made love I felt a strange excitement rise from him, a feeling so high-pitched it was almost a sound.

It was the first time we'd been alone together in the apartment since the night of the rain and the tea. Denny didn't clean anything—and I didn't really want him to—but he did ask me for money, which felt awful, and was new. I gave him a ten. He said he needed it for food. He wouldn't tell me where he was living.

At that time Pekko and I were talking about moving in together. My landlord raised my rent and I decided to move. That started it. Pekko didn't have room for me in his place—it was really just one big room. We had talks about geography in which the true subject was ourselves. He'd propose that we live in towns far from my job and I'd think he wanted to back out; I'd talk about downtown New Haven neighborhoods, knowing he liked the country. "I must be able to walk to an independent bookstore," I'd say. In the next weeks Denny came to clean a few more times, and, each time, we made love.

Pekko knew that Denny was in my class, and he asked me if I was sleeping with him. I said no.

"I should have known you weren't. You're not a selfish person."

"This time I'm really coming to clean," Denny would say. "I clean well," he'd tell me. "Most people don't vacuum thoroughly enough. You should push the vacuum cleaner back and forth seven times on each spot." Once, he actually did vacuum the living-room rug, leaving the vacuum cleaner in the middle of the room when we went off to bed. Each time, he asked for money, and I hated that but gave him some. A ten, a twenty. It was all hasty—a look at the vacuum cleaner, into bed, money, out the door.

Pekko wouldn't live with me. Every place we saw had something wrong with it. I told Charlotte that Pekko was jealous of a student of mine, and she was disgusted with him. Then, the next time I saw her—I'd been wanting badly to do this—I told her that I really had slept with the student, who had come to clean my house. I spoke as if it were a one-time thing. She was upset with me. She's loyal, but I knew she thought I had done something wrong.

IN THE SPRING, I finally rented an apartment on my own, not far from my old place, and Pekko and Philip and Charlotte helped me move in. Of course Pekko stayed on in the house on the water—where, in fact, he mentioned one day, he'd had Denny come and paint the rowboat. Now it was clear to me that he would never give up that half-winterized rental with the smell of salt water and the sound of wind. Meanwhile, Denny finished the course and I gave him a B. He'd done A work for a month and a half and nothing after that. At the end of the term he sometimes came to class, but he stopped hanging around my cubicle and we didn't see each other outside of class. And then the term ended. At Pekko's one evening in August—just over a year from the day we'd met—Charlotte and Philip and both their daughters came to dinner. I'd been alone there all day, and before anyone arrived I started a fire outdoors and sat in a slight breeze, in back of the house, tending it. I sat on an old kitchen chair that had been left out all winter and was stippled by sun and salt and water. When I picture myself on the chair, I, too, am mottled with weather, older and more breakable than I know. I lean forward, elbows on my bare thighs, staring at the burning charcoal and feeling its heat added to the day's heat.

Charlotte and Philip and their daughters arrived wearing bathing suits with shirts open over them, and I was touched by that: they were so energetic and citylike I hadn't imagined them lying in the sun or going swimming off our swampy shore. Olivia and Amy did go swimming. I roasted corn. Charlotte never took off her long-sleeved shirt, and she arranged it over her thighs so she wouldn't get burned. Then the sun went down. Pekko was late, even for him. Philip tried to argue with me about books, but I wasn't in the mood, and just agreed with everything he said. There was a bedspread and a tablecloth on the grass, and we sat there, drinking beer. It was getting dark and cooling off. The girls were out of the water, wrapped in towels. They went into the house to change and came back. Mosquitoes bit us. Charlotte pulled the bedspread around her like a blanket. In the twilight, the water—Long Island Sound— looked sad. I always think that.

At last I heard Pekko's car on the other side of the house. I went into the house for the salad, and to say hello to him. Pekko came into the main room, that big weather-beaten room, and looked at me. His beard was white and full in the dim light. I'd have turned on the light, but the switch was across the room and I had a big bowl of salad in my hands. He looked around as if he were confused. I thought he'd forgotten we were having company. "The LoPrestis are here. Remember?"

"Now I do."

"You forgot?"

"I just wasn't thinking about it."

"Why are you so late?" I said. Then, "Do you feel sick?" He gestured vaguely, and looked as if he were searching for a place to lie down. "Would you rather eat inside?"

"Outside is fine," he said. He went outside and shook hands with Charlotte and Philip, and Charlotte introduced him to Amy. He nodded. He picked up a bottle of beer. He said hello to Olivia.

"Shall I open your beer?" I said. "Charlotte, do you want a jacket or something?"

"Never mind," Pekko said, and sat down on the grass. He put the beer bottle beside him, ignoring it.

"You look so tired," I said.

"How are things at the store?" Charlotte said.

Pekko said, "You didn't hear anything?"

I was turning to go into the house to find a sweater for Charlotte. "About what?" I said, turning again.

"When I got to the store this morning," he said, "it had been broken into."

Of course we asked questions and exclaimed, but he shook his head. "Nothing was taken. Nothing was broken. The back window had been pried up. The alarm was turned off. But there's something else."

"What is it, Pekko—would you tell us what it is, please?" I said sharply.

"The person who did it was Denny Ring," he said. "He—" But then his voice went funny and he made fists of his hands in the dark and I could just see his face working behind his beard. "He's dead. He was there."

I started to scream. I've never screamed that way before or since. I was screaming for Denny and then crying, and at the same time trying to remember what each of these people knew. "Didn't you realize he was into drugs?" Pekko was saying to me.

I sensed Olivia trembling with distress near me as I sobbed. "He shot up in your store?" I heard Philip say.

"Apparently. He died of an overdose."

Somebody came and held me. It was Charlotte, and then I realized that they were all there. One of the men must have been hugging Charlotte and me, and maybe the girls, and the other man was hugging everybody. Sometimes when I think about this scene I wonder who was who, exactly, in the clutch of people. Well, we were all together in the dark, with food on plates at our feet. I wanted all of them to know the truth, and while I cried I made up my mind to tell everything, but I didn't. One by one, they went back to their places on the grass or on the bedspread, back into the dark, and someone said, "Eat, Daisy," as someone always will. Eating my dinner in silence that night, swallowing with difficulty, I thought about Denny and me, about what I couldn't have changed, and what might have been different. I looked at my own mind, but not too hard, something like the way I glanced at the taped, full cartons not yet unpacked in my new apartment, months after I'd moved. I rested a glass on those boxes now and then, but I no longer tried to remember what was in them.

THE WEEK DAD PICKED

IT WAS SUMMER and still twilight, though it was way past eight. Angry at traffic lights, angry at the idiots who drive cars these days, hot but not yet free to loosen his tie, Cameron Corey drove from his law office though the crowded streets of New Haven with a manila folder in his briefcase. He'd had to wait in the office until now, after he finished everything else and after his secretary went home. He was supposed to arrive with the folder at nine, but he would be a little early on purpose.

Cameron had been handling certain funds, seeing to certain deposits and withdrawals, for a firm called Gil's Cleaning Service. Now and then sums of money had to be handed on, but for no reason at all he was asked to carry out these transfers personally, after regular business hours. He disliked the man to whom he had to give what he had brought, and he thought this man, the man who had told him to arrive at nine, had a wrong notion of Cameron. Cameron was practical; he had simply learned to take what business came his way.

Money was delivered to Cameron by a courier. A young man named Dennis Ring, more or less presentable, with a lot of dark hair falling into his eyes, would show up, grinning, carrying a navy-blue Lands' End canvas attaché case. "I'm not late," he would say cheerfully as he entered the office, though he was never expected at any particular time.

The cleaning service was run by a man named Gil who sounded black on the phone. Cameron had never met him. Dennis Ring was one of several young men who cleaned offices and houses for Gil, and once a week Ring showed up without the navy-blue attaché case and cleaned Cameron's office gratis. Apparently it was part of the deal.

While Dennis emptied the trash and dusted, he talked over his shoulder to Cameron or to the secretary, Marie. He said his younger brother wanted to be a lawyer. "These are not attractive wastebaskets," he said once. "A law firm like this should have classy wastebaskets. Maybe stainless steel." Cameron had stared at his large brown battered metal wastebasket, which he did not remember acquiring.

Cameron was always uneasy when he received a phone call and had to bring money to an apartment in Crown Towers that had the name Hansen on the mailbox. Hansen—if that's who it was—was gray and old-fashioned. His hands shook. Cameron felt stagy and ridiculous as he was buzzed in, carrying his leather briefcase, which contained nothing but a typed sheet of numbers and a thick, sealed business envelope with a number typed on the outside, both clipped to the ordinary manila folder.

"Thanks very much," said Hansen as Cameron entered on this hot evening in August, although Cameron had not yet handed him the folder. Cameron advanced past Hansen as far as the back of a chair. He had to rest his briefcase on something to open it, and after looking in vain for a table the first time he had come, he compromised with this broad chair back upholstered in big pink roses. He unlocked his briefcase while Hansen watched with a smile, as if he thought it was childish to lock a briefcase. Cameron took out the folder.

But now Hansen grunted, raising one hand just a little: a languid traffic cop's "stop" gesture. Cameron jerked the folder close to his chest, and snapped the briefcase shut with his other hand.

Hansen said, "Uh—you know Dennis Ring?"

"I know him." Cameron swayed back on his heels slightly. He held the folder against his body.

"A year or two ago," Hansen said, with a slight professional lowering of the voice, "he spent some time in—well, in a rehabilitation facility."

"I don't know much about him," said Cameron, though he wasn't surprised.

"I thought you might have observed something recently," said Hansen.

Cameron said nothing. Finally he outlasted Hansen, though he wasn't sure he hadn't been outlasted himself. Hansen reached for the folder.

Cameron drove home. It was past nine, now, and he had had no dinner. He tried to remember what there was in his house to microwave. He would have stopped for takeout, but he wanted to get home to his dog, Fairleigh, who had been cooped up alone since morning. Fairleigh had his long snout at the door when Cameron turned the key. He was a big, black, silky, skinny dog rescued from the pound three years before by Cameron's airhead youngest brother, who worked there. Fairleigh sniffed and then licked Cameron's fingers and placed his sad face under Cameron's hand. Cameron stroked the dog's head and then held the front door open, leaning on it while he looked at his mail, and Fairleigh went out into the front yard and pissed without hurrying on several bushes. Then he led the way to the back of the dark house to be fed.

Cameron's answering machine was blinking, and as he opened the refrigerator, he pressed the play button. The message was from his brother John, the middle brother. Cameron was the oldest, and sometimes he thought the others meant him to look after things forever—just as, decades ago, when the three of them were first allowed to go to Whalley Avenue on their own to buy Popsicles, Cameron had carried the money and decided when it was safe to cross. "I can't reach Dad," John now said, on the machine, with a sigh. When he called with that message, sometimes he meant that the phone just rang and rang, and sometimes that there was a constant busy signal. Their father often forgot to hang up the phone after using it.

John lived a few exits away, in Wallingford, while Cameron, like their father, still lived in New Haven. When their father couldn't be reached, Cameron was supposed to drop everything and drive over to his house. He *did* invariably drop everything and drive to the two-family house on Ellsworth Avenue where he and his brothers had grown up. He would ring the doorbell and nothing would happen, because Dad was either asleep or watching TV. He was too deaf to hear the bell with the television on.

Cameron would circle the house, but it was impossible to see in, because his father insisted on keeping the windows closed and the curtains drawn, even in summer. Finally he would knock on a window, feeling foolish: a grown man—often as not in a jacket and tie—doing what a kid might do. Eventually the curtain would be moved aside and his father's tiny white face would appear—terrified, each time. Then Cameron would go around to the front door and his father would open it. "What's wrong now, Cameron?" he'd say. "What's wrong?"

Cameron scanned the contents of the refrigerator, took out a can of dog food, and closed the door. He spooned some dog food into Fairleigh's bowl, added dry food, and watched the dog eat. Then he patted his thigh, which was the signal for Fairleigh to follow him, and together they got into the car.

At his father's house, Cameron left Fairleigh in the car and rang the bell; then he did his usual parade around the building. When a knock on a window didn't produce the moving curtain and the scared face, he rapped not just on one window but on all the windows. There was a light in the living room, but he didn't hear the TV. He waited in the dark, hearing the sounds of televisions, stereos, and talk from up and down the block, where everyone but his father had opened the windows. It wasn't an air-conditioning block.

Cameron was angry with his father. It was nonsensical to keep the windows closed, nonsensical not to give any of them a key. His father always said Cameron shouldn't bother looking for him. If he had a problem he'd call them. Once Cameron had shouted at him, "How are you going to call if you're lying there dead?"

"Then I won't need to call," his father said.

Maybe his father was in the bathroom. Cameron waited the amount of time it might take for an old man who was always somewhat constipated to move his bowels, knocked again, waited again, and knocked again. He went up on the front porch and thought about breaking in. He didn't want to break a window. There were three doors between the street and his father's apartment. The first two weren't much, but the apartment door had been replaced not long ago by John, who was a contractor. "I can see daylight through Dad's door," he had said to Cameron. Of course that wasn't true, but now Mr. Corey had a fancy door with a heavy-duty lock and a deadbolt. Cameron circled his father's house once again, pushing through rhododendron bushes, and he imagined Hansen watching him with amusement. At last Cameron gave up. He drove to the Dunkin' Donuts on Whalley Avenue, had ham and cheese on a croissant, and telephoned John to say Dad wasn't home.

"Where would he be? He has to be home," said John.

"How should I know? There's no law he has to stay home."

"He doesn't go anyplace at night."

"If you weren't so quick to put in that door, we could have a look."

"I'm sorry I bothered you," John said. He had a wife and a baby, and he thought Cameron had unlimited time because all he had was a dog. Cameron got off the phone and drove home, giving Fairleigh the last bite of his sandwich.

WHEN CAMERON ARRIVED at his office in the morning, Dennis was vacuuming the carpet in the foyer. "You're here early," said Cameron, and then recalled that it was what Dennis usually said of himself. Dennis had always come in the evening, while Cameron was pulling things together and the phone was quiet. "How did you get in?" Cameron asked him.

"The man downstairs let me in."

Cameron was surprised that the man downstairs had a key. Maybe Marie had given him one. He turned on the air-conditioner and sat down, but he was restless and felt observed, so he got up and went across the street to a coffee shop. When he returned with a container of coffee, Dennis was vacuuming in the waiting room. Before this arrangement had begun, the office was cleaned much less often. Marie had the number of a firm, and when she thought it was time she'd call, and two black women would appear, late in the afternoon. Cameron's office had been part of a house, and the bathroom had a tub but no shower. It irritated him that the two women scrubbed the tub each time, though no one ever used it. He would pass the open door and see them at it. At least Dennis Ring had the brains not to scrub the tub.

"Do you ever eat frozen yogurt?" Dennis said to Cameron, passing behind him with the vacuum cleaner while Cameron sat at his desk and took the lid off the cup of coffee.

214

"Frozen yogurt?" said Cameron. "This is coffee."

"I can see that," said Dennis.

The phone rang and Cameron took it because Marie was just coming in. He drank his coffee while he talked to another lawyer, who wanted him to agree to the postponement of a hearing. Cameron did not agree immediately because he wanted the other man to think he had done a great deal of preparation and was eager to present it. When he hung up, Dennis was back. Now he vacuumed in front of Cameron's desk. He spoke but Cameron couldn't hear him over the noise of the machine. "What's that?" said Cameron. He didn't like being interrupted so much.

Dennis turned off the vacuum cleaner. "What?"

"I asked what you said."

"Oh. I said I waited to vacuum until you were off the phone."

"I don't think this is the best time of day for you to clean this office," said Cameron. He would have thought a dope addict would sleep late. Ring's hair was wet.

"I almost forgot to ask you about frozen yogurt," Dennis said, when he was finally done vacuuming. He was thorough, moving the machine back and forth several times over the same spot.

"What about it?"

"Do you eat it, man? Do you ever eat it?"

"I don't think so," said Cameron. "Look, why do you ask me so many questions? What the hell are you on?"

"There," said Dennis. "That's just what I thought. You have a cup of coffee, but you don't eat frozen yogurt."

"I don't think the one has anything to do with the other."

"Maybe not," said Dennis. "This is what I've been trying to explain to my friend Pekko. Frozen yogurt was a fad, and it was a fad for what is called a small demographic group. Men do not eat frozen yogurt."

Cameron grunted.

"Except me. I think it's very good," Dennis said. "But I tell him he has to diversify. Coffee. Muffins. Everyone eats that."

"Probably his place is a franchise," Cameron said, irritated with himself for being drawn into the conversation.

"So what?"

"There may be restrictions on what he can sell. Where is this store?"

"Oh, you know—downtown. He knows you."

"He does? Who is this we're talking about?"

"My friend Pekko Roberts, who owns the yogurt store."

At that point the phone rang again, and Cameron stared at Dennis until Dennis took the hint and wheeled the vacuum cleaner out. Marie picked it up, then buzzed him from the next room. "It's John," she called.

"John," said Cameron, picking up the receiver.

"I broke in last night," said his brother. "Listen, Dad's in the hospital. He was in there. I *told* you he was in there."

"Cut the crap and tell me what's wrong with him, will you?" Cameron said. His heart seemed to move across the inside of his chest.

"Cam, it was pathetic. He'd wet himself. . . . Well. Look, he has a broken hip, and he may have had a heart attack. He lay there for hours. He heard you."

"He heard me? Why didn't he yell?"

"He says he did yell."

"John, obviously he didn't yell. You think I'd have driven home if he yelled?" His voice was rising, and Marie came to stand in the doorway. Occasionally she was his mistress, and at the office she occasionally behaved as if she had a right to opinions about what he did. Cameron swung his arm, pointing in the general direction of the hospital. He was standing, and he started to carry the receiver toward the doorway, though he'd have to backtrack, once he got off the phone, to hang it up and retrieve his jacket, which was on the back of his chair. "Let me get off the phone, John. He's at Saint Rafe's?"

"They aren't making any predictions," said John, and Cameron hung up the phone, reached for his jacket, and hurried down the corridor that led to the back stairs and the parking lot. "My dad's in the hospital," he said to Marie as she backed out of his way.

"What is it?" she said. She knew his dad. Cameron didn't stop. As he passed the bathroom, he saw that the door was open and Dennis was kneeling at the bathtub, cleaning it. "What the hell are you doing that for?" he said, without pausing or waiting for an answer. Halfway down the stairs he understood why Dennis's hair was wet. He had come in very early. He had broken in. He had taken a bath.

Cameron thought that a sick man shouldn't have to be surrounded by everyone he knew choking off the goddamned air, but in Dad's hospital room were not only John and Eugene, Cameron's youngest brother, but John's wife, Barbara, who had to be paying a sitter. At least Eugene hadn't seen fit to invite his male lover. Everyone looked at Cameron when he walked in, as if he'd come late on purpose, as if he hadn't been tramping through the bushes on his dad's behalf at ten o'clock the night before.

He walked past them to the bed. "How are you, Dad?" His father had a tube in his nose. He was hooked up to an IV. "The doctor was in a little while ago," John said. "They would operate on his hip, but they're not sure he's stable enough."

"What do you mean, stable enough?" Cameron said. "You mean his heart?"

"I don't know."

"Why didn't you yell when you heard me?" Cameron said.

"I yelled for hours," said his father.

Cameron was startled to hear him speak. "You yelled for hours, you should have yelled at the right minute. You yell when there's someone who can do some good."

"I was faint by then," said his father.

"Cam, forget it," said Eugene. "We know you tried."

"Cut it out, will you?" Cameron said. "If he'd yelled, I'd have broken a window. It's as simple as that."

"Forget it," Eugene said again. He was a thin, redheaded man in blue jeans. Maybe it was his day off. He leaned back against the windowsill as if to make clear that he wasn't telling anybody what to do next. No, Cameron was supposed to do that, and damn him if he got it wrong.

"Cameron," said his father. "I need to ask you. You are a lawyer, there are things you can do."

"I already did your will, Dad, remember?"

"Dad," Eugene said, "you're going to be *fine*."

"No, no, I remember you made me a will, son. Now I need you to find out for me . . ." He lay back and closed his eyes.

"Find out what?"

"He was talking about this before," John said. He was sitting in the chair next to the bed, and Barbara was sitting on the arm. "He wants you to look up his old doctor. He thinks the new doctor doesn't have the right records. I think he thinks it will all be different if we get the records."

"A legal matter," said the father. "A doctor is not allowed to give the records to just anybody."

"I'm sure he sent them to the new doctor," Cameron said. "When you started with the new doctor, he would have phoned for the records."

"I don't think so," said Mr. Corey. "Do me a favor, son, I know I can trust you, call my old doctor."

"Dad, I don't even remember his name. I think he's dead."

"His name was Enright. Dr. Enright."

"I think he died. This is pointless."

"You could look him up in the phone book," said Eugene.

Cameron turned quickly. "Look, I understand how to use the phone book!"

"He's just—"

"All right, all right!" said Cameron.

"Underneath is what counts," said his father. "All my boys, underneath, are fine persons."

The nurse pulled the curtain around Mr. Corey's bed. It was time for procedures Cameron didn't want to hear about. They all left. Eugene said he'd get a cup of coffee and go back, but he urged Cameron to return to his office. "You're in business for yourself," he said in the corridor, one hand on Cameron's elbow. "I can take a personal day. You don't have that option."

Cameron shook off his brother's hand and hurried back through corridor after corridor to the garage, and then up to his car on the highest level. He'd driven it around and around, from floor to floor, coming up, and now he had to go slowly down again. He had to pay for parking, and it took him so long that they were charging him mostly for the craziness of their own design, their own complicated way of helping, or not helping.

IT WAS A busy day for Cameron, with papers to be filed. He stopped at the hospital again before he went home that night. Finally he spoke to a doctor, who said they were waiting to see. "Believe me, if I knew what was going to happen, I'd tell you," the doctor said more than once, which annoyed Cameron.

Eugene had spent the whole afternoon in his father's room. "He sleeps a lot," he said.

"Does he make sense?"

"He's sometimes confused."

The next day Cameron thought he'd run over to the hospital after a hasty lunch, but just as he was about to leave his office, he heard someone come up the stairs and ask Marie if Mr. Corey was free. Cameron went to the doorway of the waiting room, where Marie's desk was. A large man with a white beard sat on a straight chair, his hands in his lap and his big knees apart, waiting. He stood up when he saw Cameron and stuck out his hand. "Pekko Roberts." Roberts stood still, not in a hurry, like a settler deciding where to sink the foundation of his house.

Marie was watching. "You wanted to talk to me?" Cam said. Ordinarily he'd have brought a visitor into his office, but now Pekko Roberts was backing up and sitting down again, and Cameron sat down, too, uncomfortable in his own waiting room.

"Well, I'll go to lunch if that's okay, Cam," Marie said; she took her pocketbook out of the bottom drawer and left.

Roberts didn't say anything until the sound of Marie's footsteps receded down the stairs. Then he reached his hands into his pockets, which was difficult, sitting down, but brought them out again empty. "Well, you've probably guessed," he said. "I came about Denny."

"Dennis Ring."

"Dennis Ring. I've known him a long time."

"I employ him to clean this office," Cameron said. "I'd say he does a pretty fair job, on the whole, though I can't seem to influence his timing, which has no rhyme or reason that I can see."

There was a long pause. "Well, I don't like him," Pekko said at last, with a short laugh.

"He says you're his friend. Don't you have the yogurt franchise?"

"I *am* his friend. Yes, I have a yogurt franchise."

"How the hell are you his friend if you don't like him?"

"I do like him. I shouldn't say that. But he has no limits. There is nothing he won't do if he feels like it. Women, whatever."

"I wouldn't describe him as a ladies' man."

"Well, neither would I!" Pekko said. He laughed and his beard jumped. Pekko turned and looked out the window and seemed to watch the passing people and cars. "All right, here it is," he said after a while. "This may be totally paranoid. But once I start telling myself, yeah, but what if you're right, what if something happens and you didn't—"

"I don't know what you're talking about," said Cameron.

"I'm worried he's going to get killed." When he said "killed" his voice became higher, a little squeaky, as if it were almost funny to speak such a word without exaggeration. He paused. "I mean, get killed by particular people we could do something about. A kid like Denny"—Pekko had recovered himself—"a kid like Denny, he could get killed a million crazy ways you and I would never think of, which is his business. But he talks and talks and I realize people are too aware of him. I want you to tell them to forget him."

"Look, he cleans my office," Cameron said.

"I know what else he does in connection with you," Pekko said.

Cameron felt rising anger. "What did he tell you?" His instant reaction was that Denny deserved to die; he wasn't reliable, he wasn't the least bit reliable. "This is a very minor situation," he said quickly.

"He told me something I more or less knew. He told me he carried money to you from Gil Matthews and that crowd, and you're the person who transfers it to that bartender, the man with the New York connection."

Cameron hadn't known Hansen was a bartender, nor that he had a New York connection. He hadn't known what happened to the money once he left Hansen's apartment with his empty briefcase.

"What makes you such an expert?" Cameron said.

"I know everything," Pekko said. "I was born here, in Fair Haven—on East Pearl Street."

"*I* was born here, and I don't know everything in the goddamn town. Just because you're born here—"

"Denny Ring used to hang around my old shop. I had a bicycle shop. Denny was stealing from me before he was stealing from anybody." Pekko laughed again, supporting himself with his hands on the chairs on either side of him. "Then he held up the Wawa and went to prison—four, five years ago. He was maybe eighteen. He was in the can, he was out, he was at school. He started cleaning for Gil; I said to him, 'This you don't need, kid.' "

"Is he on drugs?" Cameron asked, despite himself. He had made up his mind to say nothing.

"Well, your contact certainly wants you to think he is—you and others. I suppose the idea is that if he dies of an overdose, a lot of people will know he was a user."

"How's he going to die of an overdose if he isn't on drugs?"

Pekko shrugged.

"Look," said Cameron. "My father is sick. I've already given you a lot of time."

"He's never willing to do something the simple way," Pekko said. For a moment Cameron thought Pekko meant Cameron's old father—and it was true of him, too—but then he understood that of course Pekko was still speaking of Dennis Ring. "So, naturally, eventually the folks in charge get mad."

"So this adds up to murder?"

"What do I know? I'd just like you to go to your contact and ask him to fire Denny," Pekko said. "Just to forget Denny. I will undertake to make sure that nobody ever learns anything Denny knows, or whatever they're worried about. I will personally guarantee it."

"How would you keep him quiet? He's never quiet."

"Beats me," said Pekko, smiling at Cameron as if they were suddenly friends. "I'll hide him in my cellar. I'll stuff him in the

trunk of my car and move to Montana with him. I'll kill him myself!
But what's wrong with your dad? I knew him years ago—not well.
He was in roofing, yes?"

Cameron couldn't get rid of Pekko and he was rushed all day.
He ate hastily and gave himself a cramp. He stayed too short a time
in his father's room, and even so he was late for an appointment.
His father seemed weaker. Most of the time Cameron was there, the
old man slept. This time John's wife was spending the day with
him. "I don't know why they don't do more for him," she said. Mr.
Corey looked so frail and small, Cameron thought it wouldn't be
possible to touch him without harming him, but when his sister-
in-law spoke he was overcome with anxiety. Then his father woke
up. "Cameron," he said, and Cameron, who had just been leaving,
came over to the bed.

"I can't stay, Dad," he said.

"Did you call Dr. Enright?" his father said.

"I called him," Cameron said. "He sent over the records."

"Is he sure?" said his father. "Ask him to double check."

"Right," said Cameron. He hurried back to his office and immediately called the hospital room, but Barbara said there had been
no change, and of course it had been only a few minutes. Cameron
was short with people all afternoon. At one point he looked up and
Dennis Ring was in the doorway, the navy-blue canvas attaché case
hanging from his shoulder. "I'm early," Dennis said.

"Just leave what you've brought," Cameron said.

"I wanted to wash the bathroom floor while I'm here," Dennis
said.

"It can wait."

"You're not mad at me?" said Dennis.

"No," said Cameron dryly, and soon Dennis left.

Cameron called the hospital room again. "The doctor was here,"
Barbara said. "He doesn't think surgery would be appropriate."

Cameron got off the phone and walked across the hall to Marie's desk. "They're not doing anything for him," he said. He was speaking loudly.

"Maybe they can't."

"I don't know." He stood there. "Do you know Pekko Roberts?"

"I've seen him around."

"I don't know why Dad had to pick this week to die," Cameron said.

"Maybe he'll get better," said Marie. "Do you want me to take those papers to the courthouse?"

Cameron had forgotten the papers. She was trying to be subtle. "When I want you to carry papers, I'll tell you," he said. He brought them over himself, parking illegally and hurrying inside, then rushing out again just in time to save his car from being towed.

It was a hot day, about four in the afternoon. Cameron hadn't realized how hot it was. He had only a small air-conditioner in the office, but it made a difference. The air-conditioner in the car was broken, but even so, it was a relief to be out of the office. He hadn't told Marie where he was going, but he drove to a pet supply store where he bought two large sacks of the expensive dry dog food Fairleigh ate.

On the way, and on the way back, he thought about Dennis. He didn't know how many times Dennis had taken a bath in his office, or why he might have done that. Cameron had been jealous, to his surprise, when Pekko joked that Dennis stole from him before he stole from anyone else. Dennis had not needed to get the key from the man downstairs. He would know just how to break in, through a window on the porch roof or up the back stairs. He was a young thief, a clever young thief. Dennis would have been able to slip into Cameron's father's house, the other night, with no trouble, in no time—when Cameron couldn't get in at all. Maybe Dennis would have saved Cameron's father.

Cameron drove to the apartment building where Hansen lived and parked where he always parked, though it was a different time of day. He didn't know what he'd say to Hansen if he found him. Cameron didn't think Hansen would be glad to see him unsummoned, and it pleased Cameron—and scared him—to think of displeasing Hansen. But when he pressed the buzzer, nothing happened. He went back to his office but he didn't get much done. Marie left and he sat in his chair, doing nothing, sweating in the afternoon sun—his office faced west—despite the air conditioning. Finally he left, and had a sandwich at Clark's Pizza. Then he drove to the hospital. When he asked for the pass to his father's room, he learned that there had been a change. Mr. Corey had had a stroke, and had been moved into Intensive Care. Only two visitors were allowed, and John and Barbara were in the room. Cameron had to wait in a waiting room, where he found Eugene, and then he was allowed to see his father for only a few minutes. Mr. Corey was asleep, full of tubes, breathing harshly. Cameron left the hospital, barely exchanging a word with John and Barbara, or with Eugene, who was pacing restlessly, unwilling to leave. Once again, Cameron got his car out of the garage. Once again he drove to Hansen's apartment building.

This time a voice answered when he pressed the bell, and Cameron identified himself and was buzzed in. He went upstairs. The apartment seemed different. It was lit differently, more darkly at the door and more brightly inside, so Cameron walked without hesitating through the area where he usually stood, past the chair with the broad back on which he always laid his briefcase, and into the living room. A television set was on.

Hansen seemed to be alone. "Excuse me just one moment," he said. He didn't ask Cameron to sit down. Cameron couldn't help looking at the television while Hansen walked out of the room. On the screen, a hitchhiker stood with his thumb out at the side of a road while cars passed. It was dark and wet, and the camera made the most of the gleaming roadway and the glaring headlights. A car pulled to a stop, but when the door opened, a passenger sprang out. The car spun off, while the man threw an arm over the shoulders of the hitchhiker.

Hansen came in and turned off the set. He gestured to a chair and Cameron sat. Hansen sat in the other chair. He'd brought a glass bowl of cherries. He put it on a table between them and leaned over to take a cherry by the stem. He looked expectantly at Cameron, raising his eyebrows while he ate the cherry.

"I've got a problem with your courier," Cameron said. "Ring. He comes at all hours. He breaks into my office. For God's sake, he takes a bath in my office. He's not reliable."

"I already know that," said Hansen.

"You want me to keep working with you," Cameron said, "you have to fire him."

Hansen took another cherry. Cameron didn't know what he had done with the stone from the other one. There was no dish for pits. After a long silence Cameron leaned forward and took a few cherries. He was immediately sorry because then he had to eat them, and he didn't know what to do with the stones. He had taken more cherries than Hansen had. He put his hand in front of his mouth and spit the cherrystones into his hand and held them. Soon he had a handful of stones and stems. They were sticky, and he would have liked to get rid of them and wash his hands. The cherries were large and sweet and meaty. They made him a little sick.

"The boy has imagination," said Hansen with a shrug.

"He has too much imagination."

Hansen said, "Do you know Ring is living in Pekko Roberts' store?"

"Pekko Roberts?"

"Yes, Pekko Roberts."

"Does Roberts know?" said Cameron.

"Of course he knows," Hansen said. "Every night, Ring breaks in, Roberts doesn't notice? This way, it's not as if Roberts *said* he could live in the store. What a place to live. Toilet, at least, but no shower."

"What difference does it make whether Roberts notices?" said Cameron.

"Oh, I suppose it doesn't make much difference," Hansen said, sitting back and glancing at the dark television screen. "It just catches my eye. If something happened—I don't know what—well, Roberts wouldn't have a clue. Nobody could ask him anything. For example, say someone gets so impatient with Ring and his craziness that he wants to do away with him. All this person has to do is break into Roberts' store some night. The alarm is already deactivated because Ring has broken in earlier and turned it off. Now our intruder gives Ring some kind of overdose by means of some persuasive stratagem. Ring is found in the morning. Burglary, committed by a druggie who shot up on the premises and had a bad accident."

Cameron sat back. He wanted to leave. "Why did you tell me that?" he said.

"Why not?" said Hansen.

"Well, I don't know—I could tell somebody, I could do something."

Hansen shrugged, then stood and led him to the door. "I'm sorry. I have a commitment." And Cameron was out in the hall, his left hand still filled with cherry pits. He dropped them on the elevator floor, though Hansen would see them and laugh at him.

Cameron knew he should go back to the hospital, but he hadn't been home; he hadn't fed Fairleigh. He drove to his house, trying to keep his sticky palm away from the steering wheel. Fairleigh was waiting as usual near the front door, and as usual he licked Cameron's hand. Cameron gave him his other hand, too, the sticky one. Then he held the door so Fairleigh could go outside. As he stood watching the dog, the phone rang. He didn't move toward it. He didn't want to hurry the dog, or close the door with the dog outside. He looked in the direction of the kitchen. He heard the machine pick up, and the sound of his own voice giving his phone number on the tape. Then came the beep and he heard the voice of his brother Eugene. "Cam, I wish you were there," the voice said wearily. "I don't want to say this on the machine, but I don't know what else to do. Daddy's gone, Cam. Look, I'll call you again when I get home. I'm sorry, Cam. I'm sorry." There was silence, and then the beeping of the machine as it reset itself.

Fairleigh came back into the house. Cameron knelt beside him, there in the front hall, and put his hands on the dog's head and back. Fairleigh sniffed Cameron's face and neck. Cameron closed his eyes and felt Fairleigh's soft breath pass over his face. Kneeling made Cameron remember going to mass. He thought of a priest saying, "Peace be with you." His father would have a Catholic funeral, though nobody in the family had been in a church in years. Cameron did not quite cry, though his eyes stung. He let go of the dog's fur but stroked his sides. He wouldn't tell anyone what Hansen had said. He wouldn't take his brothers in his arms. Going to Hansen was the bravest act of his life, except maybe adopting Fairleigh. If those weren't enough—well, Cameron was who he was. He stood and brushed off his knees and went to the phone, followed by his dog, about to mourn his father in his own way, mostly by blaming people.

SEBASTIAN SQUIRREL

WHEN IDA AND I decided to get married we didn't know how to go about it, but my boss, John Corey, said, "The lawyer with the downstairs toilet is a judge now. Judges marry people." At first I didn't understand, because I didn't call her the Lawyer with the Downstairs Toilet, even though John and I had built her a half bath next to her kitchen. I called her the First Breast-feeding Lady. When John, who is my sister Barbara's husband, hired me to help in his business—carpentry and renovations—the judge's was the first house we worked on together. She had a new baby then, and she breast-fed him all day long. I loved it. This is not just Lustful Tom sneaking looks at a breast. I had reverence for those breasts: reverence as a sexual man, yes, but also as a new adult, a new member of what I considered a club whose members were all the grown-ups, and whose task was to see to all the children. I couldn't get over it that women made milk and babies sucked it out.

Ida thought it was a fine idea to be married by "one of Tom's beautifully installed toilets," as she put it. I felt shy, because the Breast-feeding Lady had been so important in my imagination that it was hard to think of her as a particular person with her blouse buttoned. By this time, though, the baby would be a little kid and the lady would be like anybody, except that she was a judge, a completely different sort of particular person. So I called her. Ida and I had decided to be married at our favorite spot in Edgerton Park, not far from where we live: a flat grassy place near a stone fountain at the top of a hill. "Even if it rains," Ida insisted.

The judge remembered me. She said she'd be happy to marry us. "But when?" she said. "I'm having a baby."

"You already had one," I said.

"Oh, I want a pair."

The wedding was two months off, in the summer, and she said that would be fine. The baby would be a few weeks old by that time. "I know it's a girl," she said. "All right if I bring her? I nurse my babies often."

"Sure," I said. "But it could rain."

"Babies like rain."

Ida was delighted about the baby. She felt strongly that our wedding should be just one of the things we did the day we got married, and she wanted everything about it to be as ordinary as possible.

"So do I go to work and get married on my lunch hour?" I said.

"No, you can take the day off," she said. "And of course my mother and Aunt Freddie will come from Rochester, and your family will be there, and so forth. We'll go out to lunch after the ceremony. But in the morning, let's buy groceries or work in the garden." We had just moved in together, in an apartment on Orange Street, and the landlord said we could plant things.

"Once I was a bridesmaid," Ida said. "I hated it. It took three days for that woman to get married, and none of us did anything *but* get her married. The dinner the night before. The brunch the day after. I had to wear an itchy, light green, dopey dress made for skinny people." Ida is magnificently fat.

I wondered how Sally, Ida's mother, would feel about going to the supermarket with us the morning of our wedding, and sure enough, she and Ida had discussions on the phone. "Rehearsal dinner?" I heard Ida say once, with a hoot. "*Rehearsal?* Oh, give me a break." Then, "Oh, I suppose Kitty can stand up with me." Kitty was Ida's roommate before we lived together.

"My mother is so timid," Ida said when she hung up. "She lets me be rotten to her."

"That doesn't mean you have to be!" I said. Ida had told her mother she wasn't wearing any goddamn bridal gown.

"She wanted to talk about whether 'white is appropriate,' " said Ida, her voice getting whispery as she quoted her mother. "She wanted to talk about 'ecru.' "

My mother had asked me whether I was going to rent a tux. "What *are* we going to wear?" I said to Ida.

She shrugged. In the end she bought a dark pink skirt, very long and wide and terrific, and a funky white shirt with tucks and loose sleeves. Then I got interested and found a comparable white shirt, also with tucks. We'd look fine; we just wouldn't look like a wedding. We'd walk hand in hand to the park in our tucked shirts.

THE MORNING OF our wedding, I woke up in my old bed at my parents' house, much too early. It wasn't quite an ordinary day after all: we'd lent our bed to Sally and Aunt Freddie. But waking up at my parents' place felt right, like stepping backwards before jumping forward. Birds I never knew about sang for hours in the dark and then in the funny light. When it was late enough to call Ida, I did. She'd been up, too, on the sofa. We had the kind of good talk we had on the phone before we lived together. We discussed all the habitual breakfasts of our lives, and the things we never ate for breakfast. Whenever we talked like this, first we'd discuss our childhoods in detail, and I loved that. But Ida is six years older than I am; we first knew each other when she was my teacher in high

school, so my teenage years are embarrassing to talk about. Worse
are the years before we found each other again—the people we were
with by mistake, like wrong numbers on the phone. Once Ida had
an affair with a man who ate soup for breakfast.

Finally we decided that I'd come over right away and stop for
bagels, though the night before, Sally had said, "It's bad luck for
the groom to see the bride on the day of the wedding."

I didn't like the word "groom."

Ida said, "Oh, Jews don't think like that," and Sally said, "But
you're being married by a judge."

Later I saw Sally standing by herself near the window. She was
saying in a low voice, "Of *course* Jewish people think like that!" I
knew she didn't want me around in the morning because she wanted
her daughter to herself one last time, even though Ida hadn't lived
with her for years. I couldn't stay away, but I felt bad about it. We
love the ones we love and I don't know why it has to be a matter of
discussion. I don't know why I had to wait to grow up to get Ida.
I don't know why everyone can't have whom they love. Oh, I guess
I do know.

At our apartment, that morning, baskets of laundry were in the
living room and the book Ida was reading was open on the arm of
a chair, hanging down to keep her place. Tapes waited near the stereo
to be put back into their cases. I was surprised for a second that we
hadn't done anything about all this. It seemed that the day before
you got married you ought to clean your house, put the tapes away,
and finish the book you were reading. But no, it was an ordinary
day, just as we'd said, and on second thought I liked that better.

When I came in with the bagels, I heard voices in the kitchen.
"Turbulence!" Aunt Freddie was saying. She wore a red bathrobe.
She was drinking coffee and stabbing the table with her finger. She
is not Ida's mother's sister, but her father's sister—he died years

ago—and she's big like Ida, but with white hair. Sally is little and keeps her hands close to her body.

Ida was drinking coffee too. "Aunt Freddie says we need wildness in our lives," she said. "Maybe getting married is too easy."

"I don't care," I said.

"When I was thirty," said Aunt Freddie, "I thought I might marry a man in my office."

"I never knew that!" said Ida. "I never knew you even considered getting married."

"Oh, yes," said Aunt Freddie. "I picked him out, and I waited for him to think of marrying me. He worked down the hall. One morning I decided I ought to check several times a day with the receptionist, to see if I had messages. I'd have had to walk past him each time. Then I saw what I was up to. The messages could wait! I asked to work on a different floor, and I got fat on purpose. From then on I spent every vacation in the kind of foreign country you can't go to without awful shots. In between I thought about my next vacation." She reached into the bag for a bagel.

"But why?" I said. I liked the thought of a woman walking past a man, hoping. I didn't think anyone had ever walked past me that way.

Aunt Freddie stood, as if an answer should be made from a standing position, or maybe she just wanted to cut the bagel standing up. "I am a lover of time and chance," she said.

"Time?" I said.

"Time will talk to you," she said, "but not if everything has already been decided."

"What does time say?" said Ida, like a little girl at story hour.

"It says, 'Now.'" Freddie whispered the last word. She raised a finger, urging us to listen, and I thought maybe time had just spoken, but it was the sound of the shower. "Sally's up," she said.

"I wish I'd thought all this through sooner," said Ida.

"But we love each other," I said.

"Of course there's that, too," said Aunt Freddie. "Where are the rings?"

"Don't you want a bagel, Tom?" Ida said just then, and Aunt Freddie found that extremely funny, as if we were going to use bagels for rings, so Ida put a bagel on her finger and marched up and down the kitchen, singing, "Here comes the bride, All dressed in white, Here comes the fella, All dressed in yella. . . ." Ida was wearing a long white T-shirt she liked to sleep in—she really *was* dressed in white—and she looked great. Her hair is thick and blond and hangs over her back and shoulders. But then she stopped and said, "But where *are* the rings?"

"Didn't you put them into your bag?" I said.

"I took them out," said Ida. "Weren't they here on the counter?"

Sometimes when things were put onto the counter, they'd fall into a drawer just below it, and Ida and I started removing wooden spoons, spatulas, and the eggbeater from that drawer. When Sally came in, we hadn't found the rings but we had stopped to eat bagels. Sally said, "I hope you don't mind that I took a shower." She was wearing a fuzzy pink robe and a towel around her head.

"Mother," said Ida, "you know that's the kind of remark I don't like."

"I don't see why," said Sally. "For all I know, you don't have much hot water and you were planning to take a shower yourself."

"I'm not *planning* a shower."

"You're going to get married all sweaty?"

"I didn't say that," said Ida. "But I don't sit down and make plans. I'll take a shower when I feel like it."

Sally looked as if she were trying to figure out how never to make Ida mad again as long as she lived. She didn't eat anything until Ida poured orange juice and coffee for her and cut a bagel in half.

"I can't think where else to look," Ida said, eating the last of her own bagel and standing up.

"You still can't find them?" said Aunt Freddie.

"Find what?" said Sally.

"Oh, the rings," Ida said. "I've lost the rings, but it's just as well. I don't think I want to get married. Getting married is *nothing* but making plans. Planning to sleep with the same guy all your life, planning to live where he lives . . ."

"We do love each other," I said. I didn't think maybe we weren't getting married. I wanted to get married, I'd wanted it all along, and I figured it would happen.

"See," said Ida. "I've lost the rings. Unconsciously, I don't want to get married."

"You don't want to get married?" Sally said now.

"She doesn't mean it," I said.

"Of course I mean it!" said Ida.

Now Sally pushed her chair back and stopped eating. "Do you want me to call people and tell them not to come?" she asked. We'd invited about twenty people to the ceremony in the park.

"What people?" said Ida, who was emptying all the drawers, even though things accidentally fell into only one.

"The guests. Don't you and Tom want to be alone so you can discuss this? Shouldn't Freddie and I go to a motel?"

"Oh, Sally. They're getting married!" Freddie said.

Ida swept dish towels and potholders back into drawers. "I can't *think*!" she said.

I put my hand on Sally's hand. "Don't worry," I said. "We're getting married." We finally found the rings in Ida's big floppy turquoise bag, where things often disappeared for long periods. She had never taken them out, and had carried them everywhere for a week, which proved she wanted to marry me.

IDA AND I had planned to walk to the park—we did plan that much—but Sally and Aunt Freddie decided to drive, because Sally was wearing tricky shoes. "It looks like rain," she said. "And, Ida, are you sure it's legal to have weddings in the park?"

Ida interrupted herself while giving directions to Aunt Freddie, who was going to drive my car. "I reserved the spot," she said to her mother.

"How do you reserve a spot in a park?"

"I called the city," Ida said. "They said sure, go ahead, they love weddings. I suppose they were just relieved it wasn't a mugging we wanted to hold in the park."

"I guess that's so," said Sally.

All of a sudden I couldn't help mussing my small future mother-in-law's hair. "Why did you do that, Tom?" she said, stepping back and looking up at me. She was wearing a blue dress that looked big on her. She has short gray hair that hangs down on either side of her face. She looked even smaller than usual.

"I like you," I said, and she stared at me and blushed, but then she looked happy.

WHEN IDA AND I—both in our splendid shirts, Ida in her dark pink skirt—reached the pretty place at the top of the hill in the park, holding hands, a fine rain was in the air; Sally was standing in the grass in her high heels with one hand on Freddie's arm, looking frightened; the judge was coming over the hill from the opposite direction in a gray suit, a baby strapped to her chest, and accompanied by a man pushing a stroller with a little boy in it;

while several teenage kids wearing face paint and furry tails and leotards danced and stopped, danced and stopped on the green sloping lawn. For a second I thought they were a kind of wedding present, like people in gorilla suits who bring balloons.

"We're not quite ready," said a wild-haired woman I didn't know, coming toward us. Then she said, "We figured on kids. Do you mind sitting on the grass?"

The judge's little boy climbed out of his stroller. "How come you have a tail?" he asked one of the passing teenagers.

"I'm a raccoon," she said. "Did you come to see the play?"

"I came to get married," said the little boy.

The wild-haired woman said, "We can't start for about half an hour."

Then Ida said, "We're not here to see a play. We're having a wedding."

"Is that part of the festival?" said the woman. "Wasn't there a play in New York that was somebody's wedding?"

"No," said Ida. "I'm getting married. This is my husband."

I didn't like "groom" but I loved "husband." I stepped forward and introduced myself to the woman, whose name was Marta Lowenstein. Eventually it became clear that the friendly office at the city that said we could get married on top of this hill had also arranged for Marta to put on a play there—same time, same place—with dancing and singing and a sign language interpreter.

"The characters are animals actually found in New Haven's parks," Marta Lowenstein said. "We've been touring the parks all summer." Ida looked interested and Marta kept talking. "But I saw precisely *one* poster. I should have done the publicity myself." She was disappointed that we weren't audience. For a while she thought that the judge and her family, at least, were audience, but we had to tell her that they, too, were present for our sake.

The rain stopped. Members of the cast kept arriving. Some of them knew Ida from school. When they found out why we were there, they said they wanted to attend Ms. Feldman's wedding. Ida grinned and hugged them.

"We definitely had this place reserved," Sally said.

"What difference does it make?" Ida said. "Maybe the play is good." Musicians arrived and began practicing—three teenagers with a flute, violin, and drum. "This is wonderful!" Ida said to Marta.

"I'm glad *somebody* appreciates it," said Marta. "I've worked my tail off, and at the last park only three people showed up."

"Oh, did you have a tail, too?" I said, but nobody noticed except Aunt Freddie, who laughed her deep laugh at me.

The judge seemed to think it was her responsibility to sort everything out. She stepped forward, the baby's little legs and feet dangling from the blue cloth carrier on her chest. The baby's head came just to the top of it. Now she was making little occasional peeps, and when she peeped, the judge danced back and forth to get her back to sleep. "This is complicated," she explained to Ida and Marta and me. "If I nurse Jane now, she'll cry afterward, but if I get her to sleep a little longer, she won't. I don't know why, but it always happens." While the judge danced, she and Marta decided that they'd hold the play first and then the wedding.

"But do we have time for all this?" said the judge's husband.

"Sure," said the judge. "It's nice for Harry." Harry was the little boy.

By now our guests were arriving. Ida explained to each of them what was going on. My boss, John, arrived with my sister and *their* baby, Carolee, who looked big compared to Jane, the judge's baby. They came up the hill looking happy, with my parents behind them. John clapped me hard on the back and gave me an envelope, which I put into my pocket. His brothers arrived—one of them is gay and his boyfriend came, too—and I received more envelopes. John was my best man and I gave him the rings to hold. Marta Lowenstein greeted one of John's brothers, whom she knew from someplace.

Now Kitty, Ida's maid of honor, came along with her boyfriend. She thought what was happening was terribly funny. She tried to cheer up Sally.

The flutist shyly came up to me and Ida and offered to play at our wedding, and when we accepted, the musicians went off to practice "Here Comes the Bride." And at last an audience for the play—intending to see the play—showed up: a woman with two little kids. They were speaking a foreign language, maybe Korean. By now some of the raccoons and so forth were giving out programs, and everybody sat down on the part of the hill that felt like the audience. Ida and I held hands. The actors withdrew.

"I keep worrying about that baby," said Sally, who was sitting next to us. The judge's baby had gone back to sleep, still tied to her mother's chest. The judge and her family were just behind us.

"What's wrong with the baby?" said Ida.

"I'm sure that baby is going to suffocate," Sally said. "It's not safe for them to hang off their mothers like that."

The judge's husband was standing closer to Sally than she must have realized, looking for the best spot for his little boy, and I saw him get upset. He was tall, and he kept looking around, in eyeglasses that seemed to glint more than other people's glasses, as if the light were different up where he was. Now he turned to us. "Look, I'm not some sort of idiot!" he said.

Sally turned around. "Well, you don't *look* like an idiot," she said.

"Well, good," he said sarcastically. "Because I'm not. That baby is not suffocating, because I'm her father!"

"Oh, good," said Sally, but the judge's husband, enraged, put his hands on her shoulders and actually shook her. "I'm making a point!" he said.

"Yes?" said Sally, looking up at him. With her short, straight gray hair, she looked like an elderly child being shaken by this big man. We were all so surprised that nobody did anything.

Then he stopped and took his hands off Sally and backed away. "Sorry," he said. "Sorry! Tired of old ladies telling me—"

"Ida!" said Sally. "He assaulted me!"

"Did you assault this woman?" said the judge, who'd been fussing with Harry.

But the play was starting. Pretty young women in tails were running toward us from a grove a short distance away, and the flute and violin and drum were playing. The sign language interpreter stood by herself on the other side of the stage area, looking expectant. As the first song was beginning, I heard sounds and turned around, and the judge's husband, sitting right behind Sally, was trying to give her some money. Maybe he was afraid she'd sue him. "No, really, I owe you something," he said. "I shouldn't have—"

"Shhh!" Ida said.

"Take your daughter to lunch on me. Take her out for a drink," he whispered loudly. He persisted until he'd stuffed a bill into the pocket of Sally's dress. She kept moving away from him, as if he were one of those dogs who thinks he's going to bite you and suddenly decides he'd rather lick you all over.

The play was called *Sebastian Squirrel,* and it was about a crafty, wicked, alluring squirrel, played by a talented actor, a black girl with something sad about her. She had a clear, unsettling voice, and she sang a strange song over and over while the flute played in the background—something like "Who I am, where I'm from. . . . if only you knew . . . if only you knew. . . ."

The play began with two chipmunks on their way to do their laundry. They were funny, dragging an enormous bag of laundry, arguing and clowning around. Along came the squirrel, and he lured one of the chipmunks away from the other. He had a doll that he'd stolen, and he danced with the doll while the lost, frightened boy chipmunk danced behind him, imitating just what he did. Then Sebastian Squirrel sang about money, and how much he wanted the chipmunk's money. The audience was supposed to shout and warn the chipmunk, while the chipmunk kept misunderstanding what was being said, turning around and looking for the squirrel in the wrong place. We were a fine audience, and we shouted and shouted—in vain, of course. Finally the chipmunk leaned over, looking for the squirrel near the ground, and the squirrel sneaked up behind him and snatched an enormous ten-dollar bill from his pocket.

It was a nice play, and nobody was impatient for it to end. The squirrel led the lost chipmunk back and forth, while the chipmunk sang about his girlfriend, who was off to the side pretending to wash clothes on a rock all this time. In the end a chorus of animals plotted revenge on the squirrel, and even caught him, but when they tried to inject him with a huge make-believe needle and put him to sleep, he ran away, singing that same strange song, "If only you knew . . . if only you knew. . . ." It was the kind of song that made you think you'd heard it before but had forgotten, although of course you hadn't.

When it was over we clapped hard. We claimed that the girl who played the squirrel would be famous, and we said we'd remember her name. Then the audience wandered around as if it were intermission, including the woman with the two little kids speaking Korean, and the sign language interpreter, who had gestured away throughout the performance.

We couldn't have our wedding for a while because Jane was now awake, and the judge was breast-feeding her. She sat contentedly under a tree nursing her daughter, her suit jacket tossed over the baby, while I watched out of the corner of my eye. I could hear Jane making squeaky noises as she sucked. When she was done with one breast, the judge rearranged the jacket and nursed her on the other side, and then she buttoned herself back up, handed the baby to her husband, and put on her jacket. He tied the sling, with the baby in it, to his own chest, but the baby cried.

It had started to rain again, just a light mist. At last the judge took Jane and held her against her shoulder with one hand—she was that tiny—while she carried a book in the other hand, and she walked to what had just been the center of the stage. The audience settled down again, the sign language interpreter got ready—without even asking us—and the three musicians began to play "Here Comes the Bride." John came to stand with me, biting his lips and smiling. Kitty walked toward us from the grove, carrying flowers, grinning in all directions, and then came Ida and her mother, who was giving her away. Sally was walking briskly despite her high heels, and she and Ida were clutching each other's hands. Everybody glistened from the rain. And then we promised to love each other all our lives, and we put on the rings and kissed and it stopped raining. Everybody talked and hugged, and after a while we all separated and went where we were supposed to go. Ida and Marta ran back to exchange phone numbers. They liked each other. Then we went to a restaurant with our guests. As we drove away in my car, with Sally and Aunt Freddie in the back seat, we passed the judge and her husband walking home. He was wearing the baby and she was pushing the stroller. Everybody waved. That reminded Sally of the money he'd stuck into her pocket. He'd given her a twenty. "He said I should buy you lunch, Ida, but we're having lunch with all those people," she said.

"Oh, we'll find something good to do with it."

We had lunch and dancing and a good time all afternoon. I kept fiddling with my ring. In the evening Ida and I left on our honeymoon. We were driving to a bed-and-breakfast in Massachusetts that night, and traveling north next day, while Sally and Aunt Freddie were going to spend one more night in our house and fly back to Rochester in the morning. It was cool and I'd changed out of my wedding shirt and into a regular shirt and my denim jacket. Just before we left, Sally pulled me over and said, "I feel bad about the money that man gave me, Tom. I guess I shouldn't have said the baby was suffocating."

"But what if she *were* suffocating?" I said. "He had no right—"

"She wasn't suffocating," she said. "I think I'd like to donate the money to charity. Do you and Ida have a favorite charity you'd like to give it to?"

"Sure," I said, and stuffed the twenty-dollar bill into the pocket of my denim jacket.

Ida and I took our suitcases and hugged Sally and Aunt Freddie and we got into the car. John's brother Eugene and his boyfriend, Albert, had sneaked out of our lunch and written "Just Married" on my car, and Ida loved that. We drove off while Sally and Aunt Freddie stood in the doorway waving, but as soon as we drove around the corner, Ida said, "I forgot the snack."

"What snack?"

"Milk and cookies," said Ida. "I was too excited to eat all day. I'm going to need milk and cookies before we go to sleep. I got a quart of milk and a package of cookies all ready."

"Do you want to go back?" I said.

"No, we'd just have to have more ceremonies of leave-taking and enthusiasm," said Ida.

So we stopped at the Store 24 downtown, just in case there wasn't going to be any milk between us and the bed-and-breakfast in Massachusetts. Ida sat in the car, and I got out to buy a quart of milk and a package of chocolate chunk cookies. Outside the store was a thin old man with a cane, begging for money. One lens of his glasses was covered with Scotch tape. He held out his paper coffee cup and I said, "In a minute," because I had to think. In the store I found milk and cookies, and I waited on line while other people paid. Then I paid and went out, and I gave the old man the judge's husband's twenty-dollar bill and got back in the car to be married to my good wife Ida.